Charles James Lever

A Day's Ride

A Life's Romance - Vol. II.

Charles James Lever

A Day's Ride
A Life's Romance - Vol. II.

ISBN/EAN: 9783744676908

Printed in Europe, USA, Canada, Australia, Japan

Cover: Foto ©Andreas Hilbeck / pixelio.de

More available books at **www.hansebooks.com**

A DAY'S RIDE:

A LIFE'S ROMANCE.

BY

CHARLES LEVER,

AUTHOR OF "CHARLES O'MALLEY," "HARRY LORREQUER,
ETC., ETC.

IN TWO VOLUMES.

VOL. II.

Second Edition.

LONDON:

CHAPMAN AND HALL, 193, PICCADILLY.

1863.

A DAY'S RIDE: A LIFE'S ROMANCE.

CHAPTER I.

My reader is sufficiently acquainted with me by this time to know that there is one quality in me on which he can always count with safety—my candour! There may be braver men and more ingenious men, there may be, I will not dispute it, persons more gifted with oratorical powers, better linguists, better mathematicians, and with higher acquirements in art; but I take my stand upon candour, and say, there never lived the man, ancient or modern, who presented a more open and undisguised section of himself than I have done, am doing, and hope to do to the end. And what, I would ask you, is the reason why we have hitherto made so little progress in that greatest of all sciences—the knowledge of human nature? Is it not because we are always engaged in speculating on what goes on in the hearts of others, guessing, as it were, what people are doing next door, instead of honestly recording what takes place in our own house?

You think this same candour is a small quality. Well, show me one thoroughly honest autobiography. Of all the men who have written their own memoirs, it is fair to presume that some may have lacked personal courage; some been deficient in truthfulness; some forgetful of early friendships, and so on. Yet where will you find me one, I only ask one, who declares, "I was a coward. I never could speak truth. I was by nature ungrateful?"

Now, it would be exactly through such confessions as these our knowledge of humanity would be advanced. The ship that makes her voyage without the loss of a spar or a rope, teaches little; but there is a whole world of information in the log of the vessel with a great hole in her, all her masts carried away, the captain invariably drunk, and the crew mutinous. Then, we hear of energy and daring and ready-wittedness, marvellous resource, and indomitable perseverance. Then, we come to estimate a variety of qualities that are only evoked by danger. Just as some gallant skipper might say, "I saw that we couldn't weather the point, and so I dropped anchor in thirty fathoms, and determined to trust all to my cables;" or, "I perceived that we were settling down, so I crowded all sail on, resolved to beach her." In the same spirit, I would like to read in some personal memoir, "Knowing that I could not rely on my courage; feeling that if pressed hard, I should certainly have told a lie ———" Oh, if we only could get honesty like this! If some great statesman, some grand foreground figure of his age would sit down to give his trials as they really occurred, we should learn more of life from one such volume than we glean from all the mock memoirs we have been reading for centuries!

It is the special pleading of these records that makes them so valueless; the writer always is bent on making out his case. It is the eternal representation of that spectacle said to be so pleasing to the gods—the good man struggling with adversity. But what we want to see is the weak man, the frail man, the man who has to fight adversity with an old rusty musket and a flint lock, instead of an Enfield rifle, loading at the breech!

I'd not give a rush to see Blondin cross the Falls of Niagara on a tight-rope; but I'd cross the Atlantic to see, say the Lord Mayor, or the Master of the Rolls try it.

Now, much-respected reader, do not for a moment suppose that I have, even in my most vainglorious of raptures, ever imagined that I was here in these records supplying the void I have pointed out. Remember, that I have expressly told you, such confessions, to be valuable, ought to come from a great man. Painful as the avowal is, I am not a great man! Elements of greatness I have in me, it is true; but there are wants, deficiencies, small little details, many of them—rivets and bolts, as it were—without which the machinery can't work; and I know this, and I feel it.

This digression has all grown out of my unwillingness to mention what mention I must—that I passed my night at the little inn on the table where we supped. I had not courage to assert the right to my bed in the count's room, and so I wrapped myself in my cloak, and with my carpet-bag for a pillow, tried to sleep. It was no use—the most elastic spring-mattress and a down cushion would have failed that night to lull me. I was outraged beyond endurance: *she* had slighted, *he* had insulted me! Such a provocation as he gave me could have but one expiation. He could not, by any pretext, refuse me satisfaction. But was I as ready to ask it? Was it so very certain that I would insist upon this reparation? He was certain to wound, he might kill me! I believe I cried over that thought. To be cut off in the bud of one's youth, in the very spring-time of one's enjoyment—I could not say of one's utility—to go down unnoticed to the grave, never appreciated, never understood, with vulgar and mistaken judgments upon one's character and motives! I thought my heart would burst with the affliction of such a picture, and I said, "No, Potts, live—live and reply to such would-be slanderers by the exercise of the qualities of your great nature." Numberless beautiful little episodes came

thronging to my memory of good men, men whose
personal gallantry had won them a world-wide renown,
refusing to fight a duel. "We are to storm the citadel
to-morrow, colonel," said one; "let us see which of us
will be first up the breach." How I loved that fellow for
his speech, and I tortured my mind how, as there was no
citadel to be carried by assault, I could apply its wisdom
to my own case. What if I were to say, "Count, the
world is before us—a world full of trials and troubles.
With the common fortune of humanity, we are certain
each of us to have our share. What if we meet on this
spot, say ten years hence, and see who has best acquitted
himself in the conflict?" I wonder what he would say.
The Germans are a strange, imaginative, dreamy sort of
folk. Is it not likely that he would be struck by a
notion so undeniably original? Is it not probable that
he would seize my hand with rapture, and say, "Ja! I
agree"? Still it is possible that he might not; he
might be one of those vulgar matter-of-fact creatures
who will regard nothing through the tinted glass of
fancy; he might ridicule the project, and tell it at
breakfast as a joke. I felt almost smothered as this
notion crossed me.

I next bethought me of the privileges of my rank.
Could I, as an R.H., accept the vulgar hazards of a
personal encounter? Would not such conduct be deroga-
tory in one to whom great destinies might one day be

committed? Not that I lent myself, be it remarked, to the delusion of being a prince; but that I felt, if the line of conduct would be objectionable to men in my rank and condition, it inevitably followed that it must be bad. What I could neither do as the descendant of St. Louis, or the son of Peter Potts, must needs be wrong. These were the grievous meditations of that long, long night; and, though I arose from the hard table, weary, and with aching bones, I blessed the pinkish-grey light that ushered in the day. I had scarcely completed a very rapid toilet, when François came with a message from Mrs. Keats, "hoping I had rested well, and begging to know at what hour it was my pleasure to continue the journey." There was an evident astonishment in the fellow's face at the embassy with which he was charged; and though he delivered the message with reasonable propriety, there was a certain something in his look that said, "What delusion is this you have thrown around the old lady?"

"Say that I am ready, François; that I am even impatient to be off, and the sooner we start the better."

This I uttered with all my heart; for I was eager to get away before the odious German should be stirring, and could not subdue my anxiety to avoid meeting him again. There was every reason to expect that we should get off unnoticed, and I hastened out myself to order the horses and stimulate the postilions to greater activity. This was no labour of love, I promise you! The sluggardly inertness of that people passes all belief; entreaties, objurgations, curses, even bribes could not move them. They never admitted such a possibility as haste, and stumped about in their wooden shoes or iron-bound boots, searching for articles of horse-gear under bundles of hay or stacks of firewood, as though it was the very first time in their lives that post-horses had ever been required in that locality. "Make a great people out of such materials as these!" muttered I; "what rubbish to imagine it! How, with such intolerable apathy, are they to be moved? Where everything proceeds at the same regulated slowness, how can justice ever overtake crime? When can truth come up with falsehood? Whichever starts first here, must inevitably win. To urge the creatures on by example, I assisted with my own hands to put on the harness; not, I will own, with much advantage to speed, for I put the collar on upside down, and, in revenge for the indignity, the beast planted one of his feet upon me, and almost drove the cock of his shoe through my instep. Almost mad with pain and passion, I limped away into the garden, and sat down in a damp summer-house. A sleepless night, a lazy ostler, and a bruised foot, are, after all, not stunning calamities; but there are moments when our jarred nerves jangle at the slightest touch, and even the most trivial inconveniences grow to the size of afflictions.

"We began to fear you were lost, sir," said François, breaking in upon my gloomy reverie, I cannot say how long after. "The horses have been at the door this half-hour, and all the house searching after you."

I did not deign a reply, but followed him, as he led me by a short path to the house. Mrs. Keats and Miss Herbert had taken their places inside the carriage, and, to my ineffable disgust, there was the German chatting with them at the door, and actually presenting a bouquet the landlord had just culled for her. Unable to confront the fellow with that contemptuous indifference which I knew with a little time and preparation I could summon to my aid, I scaled up to my leathern attic and let down the blinds.

"Do you mean," said I, through a small slit in my curtain—"do you mean to sit smoking there all day? Will you never drive on?" And now, with a crash of bolts and a jarring of cordage, like what announces the launch of a small ship, the heavy conveniency lurched, surged, and, after two or three convulsive bounds, lumbered along, and we started on our day's journey. As we bumped along, I remembered that I had never wished the ladies a "good morning," nor addressed them in any way; so completely had my selfish preoccupation immersed me in my own annoyances, that I actually

forgot the commonest attentions of every-day life. I was
pained by this rudeness on my part, and waited with
impatience for our first change of horses to repair my
omission. Before, however, we had gone a couple of
miles, the little window at my back was opened, and I
heard the old lady's voice, asking if I had ever chanced
upon a more comfortable country inn, or with better
beds?

"Not bad—not bad," said I, peevishly. "I had such a
mass of letters to write that I got little sleep. In fact, I
scarcely could say I took any rest."

While the old lady expressed her regretful condolences
at this, I saw that Miss Herbert pinched her lips together
as if to avoid a laugh, and the bitter thought crossed me,
"She knows it all!"

"I am easily put out, besides," said I. "That is, at
certain times I am easily irritated, and a vulgar German
fellow who supped with us last night so ruffled my
temper, that I assure you he continued to go through
my head till morning."

"Oh, don't call him vulgar!" broke in Miss Herbert;
"surely there could be nothing more quiet or unpretending
than his manners."

"If I were to hunt for an epithet for a month,"
retorted I, "a more suitable one would never occur to me.
The fellow was evidently an actor of some kind—perhaps
a rope-dancer."

She burst in with an exclamation, but at the same time Mrs. Keats interposed, and though her words were perfectly inaudible to me, I had no difficulty in gathering their import, and saw that "the young person" was undergoing a pretty smart lecture for her presumption in daring to differ in opinion with my royal highness. I suppose it was very ignoble of me, but I was delighted at it. I was right glad that the old woman administered that sharp castigation, and I burned even with impatience to throw in a shell myself and increase the discomfiture. Mrs. Keats finished her gallop at last, and I took up the running.

"You were fortunate, madem," said I, "in the indisposition that confined you to your room, and which rescued you from the underbred presumption of this man's manners. I have travelled much, I have mixed largely, I may say with every rank and condition, and in every country of Europe, so that I am not pronouncing the opinion of one totally inadequate to form a judgment ——"

"Certainly not, sir. Listen to that, young lady," muttered she, in a sort of under growl.

"In fact," resumed I, "it is one of my especial amusements to observe and note the forms of civilisation implied by mere conventional habits. If, from circumstances not necessary to particularise, certain advantages have favoured this pursuit ——"

When I had reached thus far in my very pompous preface, the clatter of a horse coming up at full speed arrested my attention, and at the very moment the German himself, the identical subject of our talk, dashed up to the carriage window, and with a few polite words handed in a small volume to Miss Herbert, which it seems he had promised to give her, but could not accomplish before, in consequence of the abrupt haste of our departure. The explanation did not occupy an entire minute, and he was gone and out of sight at once. And now the little window was closed, and I could distinctly hear that Mrs. Keats was engaged in one of those salutary exercises by which age communicates its experiences to youth. I wished I could have opened a little chink to listen to it, but I could not do so undetected, so I had to console myself by imagining all the shrewd and disagreeable remarks she must have made. Morals has its rhubarb as well as medicine, wholesome, doubtless, when down, but marvellously nauseous and very hard to swallow, and I felt that the young person was getting a full dose; indeed, I could catch two very significant words, which came and came again in the allocution, and the very utterance of which added to their sharpness: "levity," "encouragement." There they were again!

"Lay it on, old lady," muttered I; "your precepts are sound; never was there a case more meet for their

application. Never mind a little pain either—one must
touch the quick to make the cautery effectual. She
will be all the better for the lesson, and 'she has well-
earned it!"

Oh, Potts! Potts! was this not very hard-hearted and
ungenerous? Why should the sorrow of that young
creature have been a pleasure to you? Is it possible
that the mean sentiment of revenge has had any share in
this? Are you angry with her that she liked that man's
conversation and turned to *him* in preference to *you?*
You surely cannot be actuated by a motive so base as
this? Is it for herself, for her own advantage, her
preservation, that you are thinking all this time? Of
course it is. And there now, I think I hear her sob.
Yes, she is crying; the old lady has really come to the
quick, and I believe is not going to stop there.

"Well," thought I, "old ladies are an excellent
invention; none of these cutting severities could be
done but for them. And they have a patient persistence
in this surgery quite wonderful, for when they have
flayed the patient all over, they sprinkle on salt as
carefully as a pastrycook frosting a plum-cake."

At last, I did begin to wish it was over. She surely
must have addressed herself to every phase of the
question in an hour and a half, and yet I could hear
her still grinding, grinding on, as though the efficacy of
her precepts, like a homœopathic remedy, were to be

increased by trituration.   Fortunately, we had to halt
for fresh horses, and so I got down to chat with them at
the carriage door, and interrupt the lecture.   Little was
I prepared for the reddened eyes and quivering lips of
that poor girl, as she drank off the glass of water she
begged me to fetch her, but still less for the few words
she contrived to whisper in my ear, as I took the glass
from her hands.

"I hope you have made me miserable enough *now*."

And with this the window was banged to, and away
we went.

CHAPTER II.

I WAS so hurt by the last words of Miss Herbert to me, that I maintained throughout the entire day what I meant to be a "dignified reserve," but what I half suspect bore stronger resemblance to a deep sulk. My station had its privileges, and I resolved to take the benefit of them. I dined alone. Yes, on that day I did fall back upon the eminence of my condition, and proudly intimated that I desired solitude. I was delighted to see the dismay this declaration caused. Old Mrs. Keats was speechless with terror. I was looking at her through a chink in the door when Miss Herbert gave my message, and I thought she would have fainted.

"What were his precise words? Give them to me exactly as he uttered them," said she, tremulously, "for there are persons whose intimations are half commands."

"I can scarcely repeat them, madam," said the other, "but their purport was, that we were not to expect him at dinner, that he had ordered it to be served in his own room, and at his own hour."

"And this is very probably all your doing," said the old lady, with indignation. "Unaccustomed to any levity of behaviour, brought up in a rank where familiarities are never practised, he has been shocked by your conduct with that stranger. Yes, Miss Herbert, I say shocked, because, however harmless in intention, such freedoms are utterly unknown in—in certain circles."

"I am sure, madam," replied she, with a certain amount of spirit, "that you are labouring under a very grave misapprehension. There was no familiarity, no freedom. We talked as I imagine people usually talk when they sit at the same table. Mr. —— I scarcely know his name ——"

"Nor is it necessary," said the old woman, tartly; "though, if you had, probably this unfortunate incident might not have occurred. Sit down there, however, and write a few lines in my name, hoping that his indisposition may be very slight, and begging to know if he desire to remain here to-morrow and take some repose."

I waited till I saw Miss Herbert open her writing-desk, and then I hastened off to my room to reflect over my answer to her note. Now that the suggestion was made to me, I was pleased with the notion of passing an entire day where we were. The place was Schaffhausen—the famous fall of the Rhine—not very much as a cataract, but picturesque withal; pleasant chestnut woods to ramble about and a nice old inn in a wild old wilder-ness of a garden that sloped down to the very river.

Strange perversity is it not! but how naturally one likes everything to have some feature or other out of keeping with its intrinsic purport. An inn like an old château, a chief justice that could ride a steeple-chase, a bishop that sings Moore's melodies, have an immense attraction for me. They seem all, as it were, to say, "Don't fancy life is a mere four-roomed house with a door in the middle. Don't imagine that all is humdrum, and routine, and regular. Notwithstanding his wig and stern black eyebrows, there is a touch of romance in that old chancellor's heart that you couldn't beat out of it with his great mace; and his grace the primate there has not forgotten what made the poetry of his life in days before he ever dreamed of charges or triennial visitations."

By these reflections I mean to convey that I am very fond of an inn that does not look like an inn, but resembles a faded old country-house, or a deserted convent, or a disabled mill. This Schaffhausen Gasthaus looked like all three. It was the sort of place one might come to in a long vacation, to live simply and to go early to bed, take monotony as a tonic, and fancying unbroken quiet to be better than quinine.

"Ah!" thought I, "if it had not been for that confounded German, what a paradise might not this have been to me! Down there in that garden, with the din of the waterfall around us, walking under the old cherry-trees, brushing our way through tangled sweet-briers, and arbutus, and laburnum, what delicious nonsense might I not have poured into her ear. Ay! and not unwillingly had she heard it. That something within that never deceives, that little crimson heart within the rose of conscience tells me that she liked me, that she was attracted by what, if it were not for shame, I would call the irresistible attractions of my nature; and now this creature of braten and beetroot has spoiled all, jarred the instrument and unstrung the chords that might have yielded me such sweet music."

In thinking over the inadequacy of all human institutions, I have often been struck by the fact that while the law gives the weak man a certain measure of protection against the superior physical strength of the powerful ruffian in the street, it affords none against the assaults of the intellectual bully at a dinner party. *He* may maltreat you at his pleasure, batter you with his arguments, kick you with inferences, and knock you down with conclusions, and no help for it all!

"Ah, here comes François with the note." I wrote one line in pencil for answer: "I am sensibly touched by your consideration, and will pass to-morrow here." I signed this with a P., which might mean Prince, Potts, or Pottinger. My reply despatched, I began to think how I could improve the opportunity. "I will bring her to book," thought I; "I will have an explanation." I always loved that sort of thing—there is an almost certainty of emotion; now emotion begets tears; tears, tenderness; tenderness, consolation; and when you reach consolation, you are, so to say, a tenant in possession; your title may be disputable, your lease invalid, still you are there, on the property, and it will take time at least to turn you out. "After all," thought I, "that rude German has but troubled the water for a moment, the pure well of her affections will by this time have regained its calm still surface, and I shall see my image there as before."

My meditations were interrupted, perhaps not unpleasantly. It was the waiter with my dinner. I am not unsocial—I am eminently the reverse—I may say, like most men who feel themselves conversationally gifted, I like company, I see that my gifts have in such gatherings their natural ascendancy—and yet, with all this, I have always felt that to dine splendidly, all alone, was a very grand thing. Mind, I don't say it is pleasant, or jolly, or social; but simply that it is grand to see all that table equipage of crystal and silver spread out for *you* alone; to know that the business of that gorgeous candelabrum is to light *you;* that the two decorous men in black—archdeacons they might be, from the quiet dignity of their manners—are there to wait upon *you;*

that the whole sacrifice, from the caviare to the cheese, was a hecatomb to *your* greatness. I repeat, these are all grand and imposing considerations, and there have been times when I have enjoyed these *Lucullus cum Lucullo* festivals more than convivial assemblages. This day was one of these: I lingered over my dinner in delightful dalliance. I partook of nearly every dish, but, with a supreme refinement, ate little of any, as though to imply, "I am accustomed to a very different *cuisine* from this; it is not thus that I fare habitually." And yet I was blandly forgiving, accepting even such humble efforts to please as if they had been successes. The Cliquot was good, and I drank no other wine, though various flasks with tempting titles stood around me.

Dinner over and coffee served, I asked the waiter what resources the place possessed in the way of amusement. He looked blank and even distressed at my question: he had all his life imagined that the Falls sufficed for everything; he had seen the tide of travel halt there to view them for years. Since he was a boy, he had never ceased to witness the yearly recurring round of tourists who came to see, and sketch, and scribble about them, and so he faintly muttered out a remonstrance,

"Monsieur has not yet visited the Falls."

"The Falls! why I see them from this, and if I open the window I am stunned with their uproar."

I was really sorry at the pain my hasty speech gave

him, for he looked suddenly faint and ill, and after a moment gasped out,

"But monsieur is surely not going away without a visit to the cataract? the guide-books give two hours as the very shortest time to see it effectually."

"I only gave ten minutes to Niagara, my good friend," said I, "and would not have spared even that, but that I wanted to hold a sprained ankle under the fall."

He staggered, and had to hold a chair to support himself."

"There is, besides, the Laufen Schloss ——"

"As to castles," broke I in, "I have no need to leave my own to see all that mediæval architecture can boast. No, no," sighed I out, "if I am to have new sensations, they must come through some other channel than sight. Have you no theatre?"

"No, sir. None."

"No concert-rooms, no music garden?"

"None, sir."

"Not even a circus?" said I, peevishly.

"There was, sir, but it was not attended. The strangers all come to see the Falls."

"Confound the Falls! And what became of the circus?"

"Well, they made a bad business of it; got into debt on all sides, for oil, and forage, and printing placards, and so on, and then they beat a sudden retreat one night, and slipped off, all· but two, and indeed they were about the best of the company; but somehow they lost their way in the forest, and instead of coming up with their companions, found themselves at daybreak at the outside of the town."

"And these two unlucky ones, what were they?"

"One was the chief clown, sir, a German, and the other was a little girl, a Moor they call her; but the cleverest creature to ride or throw somersaults through hoops of the whole of them."

"And how do they live now?"

"Very hardly, I believe, sir; and but for Tintefleck— that's what they call her—they might starve; but she goes about with her guitar through the cafés of an evening, and as she has a sweet voice, she picks up a few batzen. But the maire, I hear, won't permit this any longer, and says that as they have no passport or papers of any kind, they must be sent over the frontier as vagabonds."

"Let that maire be brought before *me*," said I, with a haughty indignation. "Let me tell him in a few brief words what I think of his heartless cruelty——But no, I was forgetting—I am here incog. Be careful, my good man, that you do not mention what I have so inadvertently dropped; remember that I am nobody here; I am Number Five and nothing more. Send the unfortunate creatures, however, here, and let me interrogate them. They can be easily found, I suppose?"

"In a moment, sir.   They were in the Platz just when I served the pheasant."

"What name does the man bear?"

"I never heard a name for him.   Amongst the company he was called Vaterchen, as he was the oldest of them all; and indeed they seemed all very fond of him."

"Let Vaterchen and Tintefleck, then, come hither. And bring fresh glasses, waiter."

And L spoke as might an Eastern despot giving his orders for a "nautch;" and then, waving my hand, motioned the messenger away.

CHAPTER III.

HAD Fortune decreed that I should be rich, I believe I would have been the most popular of men. There is such a natural kindness of disposition in me, blended with the most refined sense of discrimination. I love humanity in the aggregate, and, at the same time, with a rare delicacy of sentiment, I can follow through all the tortuous windings of the heart, and actually sympathise in emotions that I never experienced. No rank is too exalted, no lot too humble, for the exercise of my benevolence. I have sat in my arm-chair with a beating, throbbing heart, as I imagined the troubles of a king, and I have drunk my Bordeaux with tears of gratitude as I fancied myself a peasant with only water to slake his thirst. To a man of highly-organised temperament, the privations themselves are not necessary to eliminate the feeling they would suggest. Coarser natures would require starvation to produce the sense of hunger, naked-ness to cause that of cold, and so on; the gifted can be in rags, while enclosed in a wadded dressing-gown; they

can go supperless to bed after a meal of oysters and
toasted cheese; they can, if they will, be fatally wounded
as they sit over their wine, or cast away after shipwreck
with their feet on the fender. Great privileges all these;
happy is he who has them, happy are they amidst whom
he tries to spread the blessings of his inheritance!

Amid the many admirable traits which I recognise in
myself—and of which I speak not boastfully, but gratefully, being accidents of my nature as far removed from
my own agency as the colour of my eyes or the shape of
my nose—of these, I say, I know of none more striking
than such as fit me to be a patron. I am graceful as a
lover, touching as a friend, but I am really great as a
protector.

Revelling in such sentiments as these, I stood at my
window, looking at the effect of moonlight on the Falls.
It seemed to me as though in the grand spectacle before
my eyes I beheld a sort of illustration of my own nature,
wherein generous emotions could come gushing, foaming,
and falling, and yet the source be never exhausted, the
flood ever at full. I ought parenthetically to observe,
that the champagne was excellent, and that I had drunk
the third glass of the second bottle to the health of the
Widow Cliquot herself. Thus standing and musing, I
was startled by a noise behind me, and, turning round, I
saw one of the smallest of men in a little red Greek
jacket and short yellow breeches, carefully engaged in

spreading a small piece of carpet on the floor, a strip like a very diminutive hearth-rug. This done, he gave a little wild exclamation of "Ho!" and cut a somersault in the air, alighting on the flat of his back, which he announced by a like cry of "Ha!" He was up again, however, in an instant, and repeated the performance three times. He was about, as I judged by the arrangement of certain chairs, to proceed to other exercises equally diverting, when I stopped him by asking who he was.

"Your excellency," said he, drawing himself up to his full height of, say four feet, "I am Vaterchen!"

Every one knows what provoking things are certain chance resemblances, how disturbing to the right current of thought, how subverting to the free exercise of reason. Now, this creature before me, in his deeply indented temples, high narrow forehead, aquiline nose, and resolute chin, was marvellously like a certain great field-marshal with whose features, notwithstanding the portraits of him, we are all familiar. It was not of the least use to me that I knew he was not the illustrious general, but simply a mountebank. There were the stern traits, haughty and defiant, and do what I would, the thought of the great man would clash with the capers of the little one. Owing to this impression, it was impossible for me to address him without a certain sense of deference and respect.

"Will you not be seated?" said I, offering him a chair, and taking one myself. He accepted with all the quiet ease of good breeding, and smiled courteously as I filled a glass and passed it towards him.

I pressed my hand across my eyes for a few moments while I reflected, and I muttered to myself:

"Oh, Potts, if instead of a tumbler this had really been the hero, what an evening might this be! Lives there that man in Europe so capable of feeling in all its intensity the glorious privilege of such a meeting? Who, like you, would listen to the wisdom distilling from those lips? Who would treasure up every trait of voice, accent, and manner, remembering, not alone every anecdote, but every expression? Who, like you, could have gracefully led the conversation so as to range over the whole wide ocean of that great life, taking in battles, and sieges, and stormings, and congresses, and scenes of all that is most varied and exciting in existence? Would not the record of one such night, drawn by you, have been worth all the cold compilations and bleak biographies that ever were written? You would have presented him as he sat there in front of you." I opened my eyes to paint from the model, and there was the little dog, with his legs straight up on each side of his head and forming a sort of gothic arch over his face. The wretch had done the feat to amuse me, and I almost fainted with horror as I saw it.

"Sit down, sir," said I, in a voice of stern command. " You little know the misery you have caused me."

I refilled his glass and closed my eyes once more. In my old pharmaceutical experiences I had often made bread pills, and remembered well how, almost invariably, they had been deemed successful. What relief from pain to the agonised sufferer had they not given! What slumber to the sleepless! What appetite, what vigour, what excitement! Why should not the same treatment apply to morals as to medicine? Why, with faith to aid one, cannot he induce every wished-for mood of mind and thought? The lay figure to support the drapery suffices for the artist, the Venus herself is in his brain. Now, if that little fellow there would neither cut capers nor speak, I ask no more of him. Let him sit firmly as he does now, staring me boldly in the face that way.

"Yes," said I, lay your hand on the arm of your chair so, and let the other be clenched thus." And so I placed him. "Never utter a word, but nod to me at rare intervals."

He has since acknowledged that he believed me to be deranged, but as I seemed a harmless case, and he could rely on his activity for escape, he made no objection to my directions. The less, too, that he enjoyed his wine immensely, and was at liberty to drink as he pleased.

"Now," thought I, "one glance, only one, to see that he poses properly."

All right, nothing could be better. His face was turned slightly to one side, giving what the painters call action to the head, and he was perfect. I now resigned myself to the working of the spell, and already I felt its influence over me. Where and with what was I to begin? Numberless questions thronged to my mind. I wanted to know a thousand disputed things, and fully as many that were only disputed by myself. I felt that as such another opportunity would assuredly never present itself twice in my life, that the really great use of the occasion would be to make every inquiry subsidiary to my own case, to make all my investigations what the Germans would call "Potts - wise." My intensest anxiety was then to ascertain if, like myself, his grace started in life with very grand aspirations.

"Did you feel, for instance, when playing practical jokes on the maids of honour in Dublin, some sixty odd years ago, that you were only in sportive vein throwing off so much light ballast to make room for the weightier material that was to steady you in the storm-tossed sea before you? Have you experienced the almost necessity of these little expansions of eccentricity as I have? Was there always in your heart, as a young man, as there is now in mine, a profound contempt for the opinions of your contemporaries? Did you continually find yourself repeating, 'Respice finem! Mark where I shall be yet?'" There was another investigation which touched me still more closely, but it was long before I could approach it. I saw all the difficulty and delicacy of the inquiry, but with that same recklessness of consequences which would make me catch at a queen by the back hair if I was drowning, I clutched at this discovery now, and, although trembling at my boldness, asked: "Was your grace ever afraid? I know the impertinence of the question, but if you only guessed how it concerns me, you'd forgive it. Nature has made me many things, but not courageous. Nothing on earth could induce me to risk life; the more I reason about it the greater grows my repugnance. Now, I would like to hear, is this what anatomists call congenital? Am I likely to grow out of it? Shall I ever be a dare-devil, intrepid, fire-eating sort of creature? How will the change come over me? Shall I feel it coming? Will it come from within, or through external agencies? and when it has arrived, what shall I become? Am I destined to drive the Zouaves into the sea by a bayonet charge of the North Cork Rifles, or shall I only be great in council, and take weekly trips in the *Fairy* to Cowes? I'd like to know this, and begin a course of preparation for my position, as I once knew of a militia captain who hardened himself for a campaign by sleeping every night with his head on the window-stool."

As I opened my eyes I saw the stern features in front of me. I thought the words, "I was never afraid, sir!"

rang through my brain till they filled every ventricle with
their din.

"Not at Assaye?"

"No, sir."

"Not at the Douro?"

"No, sir."

"Not at Torres Vedras?"

"I tell you again, no, sir!"

Whether I uttered this last with any uncommon degree
of vehemence or not, I so frightened Vaterchen that he
cut a somersault clean over the chair, and stood grinning
at me through the rails at the back of it. I motioned to
him to be reseated, while, passing my hand across my
brow, I waved away the bright illusions that beset me,
and, with a heavy sigh, re-entered the dull world of reality.

"You are a clown," said I, meditatively. "What is a
clown?"

He did not answer me in words, but, placing his hands
on his knees, stared at me steadfastly, and then, having
fixed my attention, his face performed a series of the
most fearful contortions I ever beheld. With one
horrible spasm he made his mouth appear to stretch
from ear to ear; with another, his nose wagged from
side to side; with a third, his eyebrows went up and
down alternately, giving the different sides of his face
two directly antagonistic expressions. I was shocked and,
horrified, and called to him to desist.

"And yet," thought I, "there are natures who can delight in these, and see in them matter for mirth and laughter!

"Old man," said I, gravely, "has it ever occurred to you, that in this horrible commixture of expression, wherein grief wars with joy and sadness with levity, you are like one who, with a noble instrument before him, should, instead of sweet sounds of harmony, produce wild, unearthly discords, the jangling bursts of fiend-like voices?"

"The Tintefleck can play indifferently well, your excellency," said he, humbly. "I never had any skill that way myself."

Oh, what a *crassa natura* was here! What a triple wall of dulness surrounds such dark intelligences!

"And where is the Tintefleck? Why is she not here?" asked I, anxious to remove the discussion to a ground of more equality.

"She is without, your excellency. She did not dare to present herself till your excellency had desired, and is waiting in the corridor."

"Let her come in," said I, grandly; and I drew my chair to a distant corner of the room so as to give them a wider area to appear in, while I could, at the same time, assume that attitude of splendid ease and graceful protection I have seen a prince accomplish on the stage at the moment the ballet is about to begin. The door opened, and Vaterchen entered, leading Tintefleck by the hand.

CHAPTER IV.

I WAS quite right—Tinteflcck's *entrée* was quite dramatic.
She tripped into the room with a short step, nor arrested
her run till she came close to me, when, with a deep
curtsey, she bent down very low, and then, with a single
spring backward, retreated almost to the door again.
She was very pretty—dark enough to be a Moor, but
with a rich brilliancy of skin never seen amongst that
race, for she was a Calabrian; and as she stood there
with her arms crossed before her, and one leg firmly
advanced, and with the foot—a very pretty foot—well
planted, she was like—all the Italian peasants one has
seen in the National Gallery for years back. There was
the same look, half defiant, half shy; the same elevation
of sentiment in the brow, and the same coarseness of the
mouth; plenty of energy, enough and to spare of daring;
but no timidity, no gentleness.

"What is she saying?" asked I of the old man, as I
overheard a whisper pass between them. "Tell me what
she has just said to you."

"It is nothing, your excellency—she is a fool."

"That she may be, but I insist on hearing what it was she said."

He seemed embarrassed and ashamed, and instead of replying to me, turned to address some words of reproach to the girl.

"I am waiting for your answer," said I, peremptorily.

"It is the saucy way she has gotten, your excellency, all from over flattery; and now that she sees there is no audience here, none but your excellency, she is impatient to be off again. She'll never do anything for us on the night of a thin house."

"Is this the truth, Tintefleck?" asked I.

With a wild volubility, of which I could not gather a word, but every accent of which indicated passion, if not anger, she poured out something to the other, and then turned as if to leave the room. He interposed quickly, and spoke to her, at first angrily, but at last in a soothing and entreating tone, which seemed gradually to calm her.

"There is more in this than you have told, Vaterchen," said I. "Let me know at once why she is impatient to get away."

"I would leave it to herself to tell your excellency," said he, with much confusion, "but that you could not understand her mountain dialect. The fact is," added he, after a great struggle with himself—"the fact is, she is

offended at your calling her 'Tinteflcck.' She is satisfied
to be so named amongst ourselves, where we all have
similar nicknames; but that you, a great personage,
high, and rich, and titled, should do so, wounds her
deeply. Had you said ——"

Here he whispered me in my ear, and, almost inadvertently, I repeated after him, "Catinka."

"Si, si, Catinka," said she, while her eyes sparkled
with an expression of wildest delight, and at the same
instant she bounded forward and kissed my hand twice
over.

I was glad to have made my peace, and placing a
chair for her at the table, I filled out a glass of wine and
presented it. She only shook her head in dissent, and
pushed it away.

"She has odd ways in everything," said the old man;
"she never eats but bread and water. It is her notion,
that if she were to taste other food, she'd lose her gift of
fortune-telling."

"So, then, she reads destiny, too?" said I, in
astonishment.

Before I could inquire further, she swept her hands
across the strings of her guitar, and broke out into a
little peasant song. It was very monotonous, but
pleasing. Of course, I knew nothing of the words nor
the meaning, but it seemed as though one thought kept
ever and anon recurring in the melody, and would con-

tinue to rise to the surface, like the air bubbles in a well. Satisfied, apparently, by the evidences of my approval, she had no sooner finished than she began another. This was somewhat more pretentious, and, from what I could gather, represented a parting scene between a lover and his mistress. There was, at least, a certain action in the song which intimated this. The fervent earnestness of the lover, his entreaties, his prayers, and at last his threatenings, were all given with effect, and there was actually good acting in the stolid defiance she opposed to all; she rejected his vows, refused his pledges, scorned his menaces; but when he had gone and left her, when she saw herself alone and desolate, then came out a gush of the most passionate sorrow, all the pent-up misery of a heart that seemed to burst with its weight of agony.

If I was in a measure entranced while she was singing, such was the tension of my nerves as I listened, that I was heartily glad when it was over. As for her, she seemed so overcome by the emotion she had parodied, that she bent her head down, covered her face with her hands, and sobbed twice or thrice convulsively.

I turned towards Vaterchen to ask him some question, I forget what, but the little fellow had made such good use of the decanter beside him, while the music went on, that his cheeks were a bright crimson, and his little round eyes shone like coals of fire.

"This young creature should never have fallen amongst

such as you!" said I, indignantly; "she has feeling and
tenderness—the powers of expression she wields all
evidence a great and gifted nature. She has, so to say,
noble qualities."

"Noble, indeed!" croaked out the little wretch, with a
voice hoarse from the strong Burgundy.

"She might, with proper culture, adorn a very
different sphere," said I, angrily. "Many have climbed
the ladder of life with humbler pretensions."

"Ay, and stand on one leg on top of it, playing the
tambourine all the time," hiccupped he in reply.

I did not fancy the way he carried out my figure, but
went on with my reflections:

"Some, but they are few, achieve greatness at a
bound ——"

"That's what she does," broke he in. "Twelve hoops
and a drum behind them, at one spring—she comes
through like a flying-fish."

I don't know what angry rejoinder was on my lips to
this speech, when there came a tap at my door. I arose
at once and opened it. It was François, with a polite
message from Mrs. Keats, to say how happy it would
make her "if I felt well enough to join her and Miss
Herbert at tea." For a second or two I knew not what
to reply. That I was "well enough," François was sure
to report, and in my flushed condition I was, perhaps, the
picture of an exaggerated state of convalescence; so,

after a moment's hesitation, I muttered out a blundering excuse, on the plea of having a couple of friends with me, "who had chanced to be just passing through the town on their way to Italy."

I did not think François had time to report my answer, when I heard him again at the door. It was, with his mistress's compliments, to say, she "would be charmed if I would induce my friends to accompany me."

I had to hold my hand on my side with laughter as I heard this message, so absurd was the proposition, and so ridiculous seemed the notion of it. This, I say, was the first impression made upon my mind; and then, almost as suddenly, there came another and very different one. "What is the mission you have embraced, Potts?" asked I of myself. "If it have a but or an object, is it not to overthrow the mean and unjust prejudices, the miserable class distinctions, that separate the rich from the poor, the great from the humble, the gifted from the ignorant? Have you ever proposed to yourself a nobler conquest than over that vulgar tyranny by which prosperity lords it over humble fortune? Have you imagined a higher triumph than to make the man of purple and fine linen feel happy in the companionship of him in smock-frock and high-lows? Could you ask for a happier occasion to open the campaign than this? Mrs. Keats is an admirable representative of her class; she has all the rigid prejudices of her condition; her sympathies may

rise, but they never fall; she can feel for the sorrows of
the well-born, she has no concern for vulgar afflictions.
How admirable the opportunity to show her that grace,
and genius, and beauty are of all ranks! And Miss
Herbert, too, what a test it will be of *her!* If she really
have greatness of soul, if there be in her nature a spirit
that rises above petty conventionalities and miserable
ceremonials, she will take this young creature to her
heart like a sister. I think I see them with arms
entwined—two lovely flowers on one stalk—the dark
crimson rose and the pale hyacinth! Oh, Potts! this
would be a nobler victory to achieve than to rend
battalions with grape, or ride down squadrons with the
crash of cavalry.—"I will come, François," said I. "Tell
Mrs. Keats that she may expect us immediately." I took
especial care in my dialogue to keep this prying fellow
outside the room, and to interpose in every attempt that
he made to obtain a peep within. In this I perfectly
succeeded, and dismissed him, without his being able to
report any one circumstance about my two travelling
friends.

My next task was to inform them of my intentions on
their behalf; nor was this so easy as might be imagined,
for Vaterchen had indulged very freely with the wine,
and all the mountains of Calabria lay between myself
and Tintefleck. With a great exercise of ingenuity, and
more of patience, I did at last succeed in making known

to the old fellow that a lady of the highest station and
her friend were curious to see them. He only caught my
meaning after some time, b t when he had surmounted
the difficulty, as though to show me how thoroughly he
understood the request, and how nicely he appreciated its
object, he began a series of face contortions of the most
dreadful kind, being a sort of programme of what he
intended to exhibit to the distinguished company.   I
repressed this firmly, severely.   I explained that an artist
in all the relations of private life should be ever the
gentleman; that the habits of the stage were no more
necessary to carry into the world than the costume.   I
dilated upon the fact that John Kemble had been deemed
fitting company by the First Gentleman of Europe; and
that if his manner could have exposed him to a criticism,
it was in, perhaps, a slight tendency to an over-reserve, a
cold and almost stern dignity.   I'm not sure Vaterchen
followed me completely, nor understood the anecdotes I
introduced about Edmund Kean and Lord Byron, but I
now addressed myself pictorially to Tintefleck—pictorially, I say, for words were hopeless.   I signified that a
très grande dame was about to receive her.   I arose, with
my skirts expanded in both hands, made a reverent
curtsey, throwing my head well back, and looking every
inch a duchess.   But alas for my powers of representation!
she burst into a hearty laugh, and had at last to lay her
head on Vaterchen's shoulder out of pure exhaustion.

"Explain to her what I have told you, sir, and do not
sit grinning at me there, like a baboon," said I, in a
severe voice.

I cannot say how he acquitted himself, but I could
gather that a very lively altercation ensued, and it
seemed to me as though she resolutely refused to subject
herself to any further ordeals of what academicians call
a "private view." No; she was ready for the ring and
the sawdust, and the drolleries of the men with chalk on
their faces, but she would not accept high life on any
terms.   By degrees, and by arguments of his own
ingenious devising, however, he did succeed, and at last
she arose with a bound, and cried out "Eccomi!"

"Remember," said I to Vaterchen, as we left the room,
"I am doing that which few would have the courage to
dare. It will depend upon the dignity of your conduct,
the grace of your manners, the well-bred ease of your
address, to make me feel proud of my intrepidity, or, sad
and painful possibility, retire covered with ineffable
shame and discomfiture.   Do you comprehend me?"

"Perfectly," said he, standing erect, and giving even
in his attitude a sort of bail bond for future dignity.
"Lead on!"

This was more familiar than he had been yet; but I
ascribed it to the tension of nerves strung to a high
purpose, and rendering him thus inaccessible to other
thoughts than of the enterprise before him.

As I neared the door of Mrs. Keats' apartment, I hesitated as to how I should enter. Ought I to precede my friends, and present them as they followed? Or would it seem more easy and more assured if I were to give my arm to Tintefleck, leaving Vaterchen to bring up the rear? After much deliberation, this appeared to be the better course, seeming to take for granted that, although some peculiarities of costume might ask for explanation later on, I was about to present a very eligible and charming addition to the company.

I am scarcely able to say whether I was or was not reassured by the mode in which she accepted the offer of my arm. At first, the proposition appeared unintelligible, and she looked at me with one of those wide-eyed stares, as though to say, " What new gymnastic is this? What *tour de force*, of which I never heard before?" and then, with a sort of jerk, she threw my arm up in the air and made a pirouette under it, of some half-dozen whirls.

Half reprovingly, I shook my head, and offered her my hand. This she understood at once. She recognised such a mode of approach as legitimate and proper, and with an artistic shake of her drapery with the other hand, and a confident smile, she signified she was ready to go " on."

I was once on a time thrown over a horse's head into a slate quarry, a very considerable drop it was, and nearly fatal; on another occasion, I was carried in a small boat over the fall of a salmon wear, and hurried along in the flood for almost three hundred yards; each of these was a situation of excitement and peril, and with considerable confusion as the consequence; and yet I could deliberately recount you every passing phrase of my terror, from my first fright down to my complete unconsciousness, with such small traits as would guarantee truthfulness; while, of the scene upon which I now adventured, I preserve nothing beyond the vaguest and most unconnected memory.

I remember my advance into the middle of the room. I have a recollection of a large silver tea-urn, and beyond it a lady in a turban; another in long ringlets there was. The urn made a noise like a small steamer, and there was a confusion of voices—about what, I cannot tell—that increased the uproar, and we were all standing up and all talking together; and there was what seemed an angry discussion, and then the large turban and the ringlets swept haughtily past me. The turban said, "This is too much, sir!" and ringlets added, "Far too much, sir!" and as they reached the door, there was Vaterchen on his head, with a branch of candles between his feet to light them out, and Tintefleck, screaming with laughter, threw herself into an arm-chair, and clapped a most riotous applause.

I stood a moment almost transfixed, then dashed out of the room, hurried up-stairs to my chamber, bolted the door, drew a great clothes-press against it for further security, and then threw myself upon my bed in one of those paroxysms of mad confusion, in which a man cannot say whether he is on the verge of inevitable ruin, or has just been rescued from a dreadful fate. I would not, if even I could, recount all that I suffered that night. There was not a scene of open shame and disgrace that I did not picture to myself as incurring. I was every-where in the stocks or the pillory. I wore a wooden placard on my breast, inscribed, "Potts, the Impostor." I was running at top speed before hooting and yelling crowds. I was standing with a circle of protecting policemen amidst a mob eager to tear me to pieces. I was sitting on a hard stool while my hair was being cropped à la Pentonville, and a grey suit lay ready for me when it was done. But enough of such a dreary record. I believe I cried myself to sleep at last, and so soundly, too, that it was very late in the afternoon ere I awoke. It was the sight of the barricade I had erected at my door gave me a clue to the past, and again I buried my face in my hands, and wept bitterly.

CHAPTER V.

I COULD not hear the loud and repeated knockings which were made at my door, as at first waiters, and then the landlord himself, endeavoured to gain admittance. At length, a ladder was placed at the window, and a courageous individual, duly armed, appeared at my casement and summoned me to surrender. With what unspeakable relief did I learn that it was not to apprehend or arrest me that all these measures were taken; they were simply the promptings of a graceful benevolence, a sort of rumoured intimation having got about, that I had taken prussic acid, or was being done to death by charcoal. Imagine a prisoner in a condemned cell suddenly awakened, and hearing that the crowd around him consisted not of the ordinary, the sheriff, Mr. Calcraft and Co., but a deputation of respectable citizens come to offer the representation of their borough or a piece of plate, and then you can have a mild conception of the pleasant revulsion of my feelings. I thanked my public in a short but appropriate address. I assured them, although there was a popular prejudice about doing this sort of thing in November in England, that it was deemed quite unreasonable at other times, and that really in these days of domestic arsenic and conjugal strychnine, nothing but an unreasonable impatience would make a man self-destructive—suicide arguing that as a man was really so utterly valueless, it was worth nobody's while to get rid of him. My explanation over, I ordered breakfast.

"Why not dinner?" said the waiter. "It is close on four o'clock."

"No," said I; "the ladies will expect me at dinner."

"The ladies are near Constance by this, or else the roads are worse than we thought them."

"Near Constance! Do you mean to say they have gone?"

"Yes, sir, at daybreak; or, indeed, I might say before daybreak."

"Gone! actually gone!" was all that I could utter.

"They never went to bed last night, sir; the old lady was taken very ill after tea, and all the house running here and there for doctors and remedies, and the young lady, though she bore up so well, they tell me she fainted when she was alone in her own room. In fact, it was a piece of confusion and trouble until they started, and we may say, none of us had a moment's peace till we saw them off."

"And how came it that I was never called?"

"I believe, sir, but I'm not sure, the landlord tried to awake you. At all events, he has a note for you now, for I saw the old lady place it in his hand."

"Fetch it at once," said I; and when he left the room I threw some water over my face, and tried to rally all my faculties to meet the occasion.

When the waiter reappeared with the note, I bade him leave it on the table; I could not venture to read it while he was in the room. At length he went away, and I opened it. These were the contents:

"SIR,—When a person of your rank abuses the privilege of his station, it is supposed that he means to rebuke. Although innocent of any cause for your displeasure, I have preferred to withdraw myself from your notice than incur the chance of so severe a reprimand a second time.

"I am, sir, with unfeigned sorrow and humility, your most devoted follower and servant,

"MARTHA KEATS.

"To the —— de ——."

This was the whole of it; not a great deal as correspondence, but matter enough for much thought and much misery. After a long and painful review of my conduct, one startling fact stood prominently forward, which was, that I had done something which, had it been the act of a royal prince, would yet have been unpardonable, but which, if known to emanate from one such as myself, would have been a downright outrage.

I went into the whole case, as a man who detests figures might have gone into a long and complicated account; and just as he would skip small sums, and pay little heed to fractions, I aimed at arriving at some grand solid balance for or against myself.

I felt, that if asked to produce my books, they might run this wise: Potts, on the credit side, a philanthropist, self-denying, generous, and trustful ; one eager to do good, thinking no evil of his neighbour, hopeful of everybody, anxious to establish that brotherhood amongst men which, however varied the station, could and ought to subsist, and which needs but the connecting link of one sympathetic existence to establish. On the other side, Potts, I grieve to say, appeared that which Ferdinand Mendez Pinto was said to be.

When I had rallied a bit from the stunning effect of this disagreeable "total," I began to wish that I had somebody to argue the matter out with me. The way I would put my case would be thus: "Has not—from the time of Quintus Curtius down to the late Mr. Sadleir, of banking celebrity—the sacrifice of one man for the benefit of his fellows, been recognised as the noblest exposition of heroism? Now, although it is much to give up life for the advantage of others, it is far more to surrender

one's identity, to abandon that grand capital Ego! which
gives a man his self-esteem and suggests his self-
preservation.   And who, I would ask, does this so
thoroughly as the man who everlastingly palms himself
upon the world for that which he is not?   According to
the greatest happiness principle, this man may be a real
boon to humanity.   He feeds this one with hope, the
other with flattery; he bestows courage on the weak,
confidence on the wavering.   The rich man can give of his
abundance, but it is out of his very poverty this poor fellow
has to bestow all.   Like the spider, he has to weave his
web from his own vitals, and like the same spider he
may be swept away by some pretentious affectation of
propriety."

While I thus argued, the waiter came in to serve
dinner.   It looked all appetising and nice; but I could
not touch a morsel.   I was sick at heart; Kate Herbert's
last look as she quitted the room was ever before me.
Those dark grey eyes—which you stupid folk will go on
calling blue—have a sort of reproachful power in them
very remarkable.   They don't flash out in anger like black
eyes, or sparkle in fierceness like hazel; but they emit a
sort of steady, fixed, concentrated light, that seems to
imply that they have looked thoroughly into you, and
come back very sad and very sorry for the inquiry.   I
thought of the happy days I had passed beside her; I
recalled her low and gentle voice, her sweet, half sad

smile, and her playful laugh, and I said, "Have I lost all these for ever, and how? What stupid folly possessed me last evening? How could I have been so idiotic as not to see that I was committing the rankest of all enormities? How should I, in my insignificance, dare to assail the barriers and defences which civilisation has established, and guards amongst its best prerogatives? Was this old buffoon, was this piece of tawdry fringe and spangles a fitting company for that fair and gentle girl? How artistically false, too, was the position I had taken. Interweaving into my ideal life these coarse realities, was the same sort of outrage as shocks one in some of the Venetian churches, where a lovely Madonna, the work of a great hand, may be seen bedizened and disfigured with precious stones over her drapery. In this was I violating the whole poetry of my existence. These figures were as much out of keeping as would be a couple of Ostade's Boors in a grand Scripture piece by Domenichino.

"And yet, Potts," thought I, "they were *really* living creatures. They had hearts for joy and sorrow and hope and the rest of it. They were pilgrims travelling the self-same road as you were. They were not illusions, but flesh and blood folk, that would shiver when cold, and die of hunger if starved. Were they not then, as such, of more account than all your mere imaginings? would not the least of their daily miseries outweigh a whole bushel of fancied sorrow? and is it not a poor selfishness on

your part, when you deem some airy conception of your
brain of more account than that poor old man and that
dark-eyed girl. Last of all, are they not, in all their
ragged finery, more 'really true men' than you yourself,
Potts, living in a maze of delusions?   They only act
when the sawdust is raked and the lamps are lighted;
but you are *en scène* from dawn to dark, and only lay
down one motley to don another. Is not this wretched?
Is it not ignoble?   In all these changes of character, how
much of the real man will be left behind?   Will there be
one morsel of honest flesh, when all the lacquer of paint
is washed off?   And was it—oh, was it for this you first
adventured out on the wide ocean of life?"

I passed the evening and a great part of the night in
such self-accusings, and then I addressed myself to action.
I bethought me of my future, and with whom and where
and how it might be passed. The bag of money entrusted
to me by the minister to pay the charges of the road was
hanging where I had placed it—on the curtain-holder.
I opened it, and found a hundred and forty gold
Napoleons, and some ten or twelve pounds in silver.
I next set to count over my own especial hoard; it was a
fraction under a thousand francs. Forty-pounds was truly
a very small sum wherewith to confront a world to which
I brought not any art, or trade, or means of livelihood; I
say forty, because I had not the shadow of a pretext for
touching the other sum, and I resolved at once to

transmit it to the owner. Now, what could be done with so humble a capital? I had heard of a great general who once pawned a valuable sword—a sword of honour it was—wherewith to buy a horse, and so mounted, he went forth over the Alps and conquered a kingdom. The story had no moral for me, for somehow I did not feel as though I were the stuff that conquers kingdoms, and yet there must surely be a vast number of men in life with about the same sort of faculties, merits, and demerits as I have. There must be a numerous Potts family in every land, well-meaning, right-intentioned, worthless creatures, who, out of a supposed willingness to do anything, always end in doing nothing. Such people, it must be inferred, live upon what are called their wits, or, in other words, trade upon the daily accidents of life, and the use to which they can turn the traits of those they meet with.

I was resolved not to descend to this; no, I had determined to say adieu .to all masquerading, and be simply Potts, the druggist's son, one who had once dreamed of great ambitions, but had taken the wrong road to them. I would from this hour be an honest, truth-speaking, simple-hearted creature. What the world might henceforth accord me of its sympathy should be tendered on honest grounds; nay, more, in the spirit of those devotees who inspire themselves with piety by privations, I resolved on a course of self-mortification, I would not rest till I had made my former self expiate all the vainglorious wantonness of the past, and pay in severe penance for every transgression I had committed. I began boldly with my reformation. I sat down and wrote thus :

" To Mr. Dycer, Stephen's-green, Dublin.

" The gentleman who took away a dun pony from your livery stables in the month of May last, and who, from certain circumstances, has not been able to restore the animal, sends herewith twenty pounds as his probable value. If Mr. D. conscientiously considers the sum insufficient, the sender will at some future time, he hopes, make good the difference."

Doubtless my esteemed reader will say, at this place, "The fellow couldn't do less; he need not vaunt himself on a common-place act of honesty, which, after all, might have been suggested by certain fears of future consequences. His indiscretion amounted to horse-stealing, and horse-stealing is a felony."

All true, every word of it, most upright of judges: I was simply doing what I ought, or rather what I ought long since to have done. But now, let me ask, is this, after all, the invariable course in life, and is there no merit in doing what one ought when every temptation points to the other direction? and lastly, is it nothing to do what a man ought, when the doing costs exactly the half of all he has in the world?

Now, if I were, instead of being Potts, a certain great writer that we all know and delight in, I would improve the occasion here by asking my reader, does he always himself do the right thing? I would say to him, perhaps with all haste to anticipate his answer, Of course you do. You never pinch your children, or kick your wife out of bed; you are a model father and a churchwarden; but I am only a poor apothecary's son, brought up in precepts of thrift and the Dublin Pharmacopœia; and I own to you, when I placed the half of my twenty-pound crisp clean bank-note inside of that letter, I felt I was figuratively cutting myself in two. But I did it "like a man," if that be a proper phrase for an act which I thought god-like. And oh, take my word for it, when a sacrifice hasn't cost you a coach-load of regrets, and a shopful of hesitations about making it, it is of little worth. There's a wide difference between the gift of a sheep from an Australian farmer, or the present of a child's pet lamb, even though the sheep be twice the size of the lamb.

I gave myself no small praise for what I had done, much figurative patting on the back, and a vast deal of that very ambiguous consolation which beggars in Catholic countries bestow in change for alms, by assurance that it will be remembered to you in Purgatory.

"Well," thought I, "the occasion isn't very far off, for my Purgatory begins to-morrow."

CHAPTER VI.

I was in a tourist locality, and easily provided myself with a light equipment for the road, resolved at once to take the footpath in life and "seek my fortune." I use these words simply as the expression of the utter uncertainty which prevailed as to whither I should go, and what do when I got there.

If there be few more joyous things in life than to start off on foot with three or four choice companions, to ramble through some fine country, rich in scenery, varied in character and interesting in story, there are few more lonely sensations than to set out by oneself, not very decided what way to take, and with very little money to take it.

One of the most grievous features of small means is, certainly, the almost exclusive occupation it gives the mind as to every, even the most trivial, incident that involves cost. Instead of dining on fish and fowl and fruit, you feel eating so many groschen and kreutzers. You are *not* drinking wine, your beverage is a solution of

copper batzen in vinegar! When you poke the fire, every
spark that flies up the chimney is a baiocco! You come
at last to suspect that the sun won't warm you for
nothing, and that the very breeze that cooled your brow
is only waiting round the corner to ask "for something
for himself."

When the rich man lives sparingly, the conscious
power of the wealth he might employ if he pleased,
sustains him. The poor fellow has no such consolation to
fall back on; the closer his coat is examined, the more
threadbare will it appear. If it were simply that he
dressed humbly and fared coarsely, it might be borne
well, but it is the hourly depreciation that poverty is
exposed to, makes its true grievance. "An ill-looking"
— this means, generally, ill-dressed — "an ill-looking
fellow had been seen about the premises at night-fall,"
says the police report. "A very suspicious character had
asked for a bed; his wardrobe was in a 'spotted handkerchief.' The waiter remembers that a fellow, much
travel-stained and weary, stopped at the door that
evening and asked if there was any cheap house of
entertainment in the village." Heaven help the poor
wayfarer if anyone has been robbed, any house broken
into, any rick set fire to, while he passed through that
locality. There is no need of a crowd of witnesses to
convict him, since every bend in his hat, every tear in his
coat, and every rent in his shoes, are evidence against him.

If I thought over these things in sorrow and humilia-tion, it was in a very proud spirit that I called to mind how, on that same morning, I deposited the bag with all the money in Messrs. Haber's bank, saw the contents duly counted over, replaced and sealed up, and then addressed to Her Majesty's Minister at Kalbbratenstadt, taking a receipt for the same. "This was only just common honesty," says the reader. Oh, if there is an absurd collocation of words, it is that! Common honesty! why, there is nothing in this world so perfectly, so totally uncommon! Never, I beseech you, undervalue the waiter who restores the ring you dropped in the coffee-room; nor hold him cheaply who gives back the umbrella you left in the cab. These seem such easy things to do, but they are not easy. Men are more or less Cornish wreckers in life, and very apt to regard the lost article as treasure-trove. I have said all this to you, amiable reader, that you may know what it cost me, on that same morning, not to be a rogue, and not to enrich myself with the goods of another.

I underwent a very long and searching self-examina-tion to ascertain why it was I had not appropriated that bag, an offence which, legally speaking, would only amount to a breach of trust. I said, "Is it that you had no need of the money, Potts? Did you feel that your own means were ample enough? Was it that your philosophy had made you regard gold as mere dross, and

then think that the load was a burden? Or, taking
higher ground, had you recalled the first teachings of
your venerable parent, that good man and careful
apothecary, who had given you your first perceptions of
right and wrong?" I fear that I was obliged to say
No, in turn, to each of these queries. I would have been
very glad to be right, proud to have been a philosopher,
overjoyed to feel myself swayed by moral motives, but I
could not palm the imposition on my conscience, and had
honestly to own that the real reason of my conduct was
—I was in love! There was the whole of it!

There was an old sultan once so impressed with an ill
notion of the sex, that whenever a tale of misfortune or
disgrace reached him, his only inquiry as to the source of
the evil was, Who was she? Now my experiences of
life have travelled in another direction, and whenever I
read of some noble piece of heroism, or some daring act
of self-devotion, I don't ask whether he got the Bath or
the Victoria Cross, if he were made a governor here, or
a vice-governor there, but who was She that prompted
this glorious deed? I'd like to know all about *her :* the
colour of her eyes, her hair; was she slender or plump,
was she fiery or gentle; was it an old attachment or an
acute attack coming after a paroxysm at first sight?

If I were the great chief of some great public
department where all my subordinates were obliged to
give heavy security for their honesty, I would neither

ask for bail bonds or sureties, but I'd say, "Have you got a wife, or a sweetheart? either will do. Let me look at her. If she be worthy an honest man's love, I am satisfied; mount your high stool and write away."

Oh, how I longed to stand aright in that dear girl's eyes, that she should see me worthy of her! Had she yielded to all my wayward notions and rambling opinions, giving way either in careless indolence or out of inability to dispute them, she had never made the deep impression on my heart. It was because she had bravely asserted her own independence, never conceding where uncon-vinced, never yielding where unvanquished, that I loved her. What a stupid reverie was that of mine when I fancied her one of those strong-minded, determined women—a thickly-shod, umbrella-carrying female, who can travel alone and pass her trunk through a custom-house. No, she was delicate, timid, and gentle; there was no over-confidence in her, nor the slightest pre-tension. Rule me? not a bit of it. Guide, direct, support, confirm, sustain me; elevate my sentiments, cheer me on my road in life, making all 'evil odious in my eyes, and the good to seem better!

I verily believe, with such a woman, an humble con-dition in life offers more chances of happiness than a state of wealth and splendour. If the best prizes of life are to be picked up around a man's fireside, moderate means, conducing as they do to a home life, would point more certainly to these than all the splendour of grand receptions. If I were, say, a village doctor, a school-master; if I were able to eke out subsistence in some occupation, whose pursuit might place me sufficiently favourably in her eyes. I don't like grocery, for instance, or even "dry goods," but something—it's no fault of mine if the English language be cramped and limited, and that I must employ the odious word "genteel," but it conveys, in a fashion, all that I aim at.

I began to think how this was to be done. I might return to my own country, go back to Dublin, and become Potts and Son—at least son! A very horrid thought, and very hard to adopt.

I might take a German degree in physic, and become an English doctor, say, at Baden, Ems, Geneva, or some other resort of my countrymen on the Continent. I might give lectures, I scarcely well knew on what, still less to whom; or I could start as Professor Potts, and instruct foreigners in Shakespeare. There were at least "three courses" open to me; and to consider them the better, I filled my pipe, and strolled off the high road into a shady copse of fine beech-trees, at the foot of one of which, and close to a clear little rivulet, I threw myself at full length, and thus, like Tityrus, enjoyed the leafy shade, making my meerschaum do duty for the shepherd's reed.

I had not been long thus, when I heard the footsteps

of some persons on the road, and shortly after, the sound discontinuing, I judged that they must have crossed into the sward beneath the wood. As I listened I detected voices, and the next moment two figures emerged from the cover and stood before me: they were Vaterchen and Tintefleck.

"Sit down," said I, pointing to each in turn to take a place at either side of me. They had, it is true, been the cause of the great calamity of my life, but in no sense was the fault theirs, and I wished to show that I was generous and open-minded. Vaterchen acceded to my repeated invitation with a courteous humility, and seated himself at a little distance off; but Tintefleck threw herself on the grass, and with such a careless "abandon," that her hair escaped from the net that held it, and fell in great wavy masses across my feet.

"Ay," thought I, as I looked at the graceful outlines of her finely-shaped figure, here is the Amaryllis come to complete the tableau; only I would wish fewer spangles, and a little more simplicity."

I saw that it was necessary to reassure Vaterchen as to my perfect sanity by some explanation as to my strange mode of travelling, and told him briefly, "that it was a caprice common enough with my countrymen to assume the knapsack, and take the road on foot; that we fancied in this wise we obtained a nearer view of life, and at least gained companionship with many from whom the accident of station might exclude us." I said this with an artful delicacy, meant to imply that I was pointing at a very great and valuable privilege of pedestrianism.

He smiled with a sad, a very sad expression on his features, and said, "But in what wise, highly honoured sir?"—he addressed me always as Hoch Ge-ehrter Herr —"could you promise to yourself advantage from such associations as these? I cannot believe you would condescend to know us simply to carry away in memory the little traits that must needs distinguish such lives as ours. I would not insult my respect for you by supposing that you come amongst us to note the absurd contrast between our real wretchedness and our mock gaiety; and yet what else is there to gain? What can the poor mountebank teach you beyond this?"

"Much," said I, with fervour, as I grasped his hand, and shook it heartily; "much, if you only gave me this one lesson that I now listen to, and I learn that a man's heart can beat as truthfully under motley as under the embroidered coat of a minister. The man who speaks as you do, can teach me much."

He gave a short but heavy sigh, and turned away his head. He arose after a few minutes, and going gently across the grass, spread his handkerchief over the head and face of the girl, who had at once fallen into a deep sleep.

"Poor thing," muttered he, "it is well she *can* sleep! She has eaten nothing to-day!"

"But, surely," said I, "there is some village or some wayside inn near this ——"

"Yes, there is the Eckstein, a little public about two miles further; but we didn't care to reach it before nightfall. It is so painful to pass many hours in a place and never call for anything; one is ill looked on, and uncomfortable from it; and as we have only what would pay for our supper and lodging, we thought we'd wear away the noon in the forest here, and arrive at the inn by close of day."

"Let me be your travelling companion for to-day," said I, "and let us push forward and have our dinner together. Yes, yes, there is far less of condescension in the offer than you suspect. I am neither great nor milor, I am one of a class like your own, Vaterchen, and what I do for you to-day some one else will as probably do for me to-morrow."

Say what I could, the old man would persist in believing that this was only another of those eccentricities for which Englishmen are famed; and though, with the tact of a native good breeding, he showed no persistence in opposition, I saw plainly enough that he was unconvinced by all my arguments.

While the girl slept, I asked him how he chanced upon the choice of his present mode of life, since there were many things in his tone and manner that struck me as strangely unlike what I should have ascribed to his order.

"It is a very short story," said he; "five minutes will tell it, otherwise I might scruple to impose on your patience. It was thus I became what you see me-"

Short as the narrative was, I must keep it for another page.

CHAPTER VII.

I GIVE the old man's story, as nearly as I can, the way he told it.

"There is a little village on the Lago di Guarda, called Caprini. My family had lived there for some generations. We had a little wine-shop, and though not a very pretentious one, it was the best in the place, and much frequented by the inhabitants. My father was in considerable repute while he lived; he was twice named Syndic of Caprini, and I myself once held that dignity. You may not know, perhaps, that the office is one filled at the choice of the townsfolk, and not nominated by the government. Still the crown has its influence in the selection, and likes well to see one of its own partisans in power, and, when a popular candidate does succeed against their will, the government officials take good care to make his birth as uncomfortable as they can. These are small questions of politics to ask you to follow, but they were our great ones; and we were as ardent and excited and eager about the choice of our little local governor as though he wielded real power in a great state.

"When I obtained the syndicate, my great ambition was to tread in the footsteps of my father, old Gustave Gamerra, who had left behind him a great name as the assertor of popular rights, and who had never bated the very least privilege that pertained to his native village. I did my best—not very discreetly, perhaps—for my own sake, but I held my head high against all imperial and royal officials, and I taught them to feel that there was at least one popular institution in the land that no exercise of tyranny could assail. I was over-zealous about all our rights. I raked up out of old archives traces of privileges that we once possessed and had never formally surrendered; I discovered concessions that had been made to us of which we had never reaped the profit; and I was, so to say, ever at war with the authorities, who were frank enough to say, that when my two years of office expired, they meant to give me some wholesome lessons about obedience.

"They were as good as their word. I had no sooner descended to a private station than I was made to feel all the severities of their displeasure. They took away my license to sell salt and tobacco, and thereby fully one half of my little income; they tried to withdraw my privilege to sell wine, but this came from the municipality, and they could not touch it. Upon information

that they had suborned, they twice visited my house to
search for seditious papers, and, finally, they made me
such a mark of their enmity that the timid of the townsfolk were afraid to be seen with me, and gradually
dropped my acquaintance. This preyed upon me most of
all. I was all my life of a social habit; I delighted to
gather my friends around me, or to go and visit them,
and to find myself, as I was growing old, growing friendless too, was a great blow.

"I was a widower, and had none but an only
daughter."

When he had reached thus far, his voice failed him,
and, after an effort or two, he could not continue, and
turned away his head and buried it in his hands. Full
ten minutes elapsed before he resumed, which he did with
a hard, firm tone, as though resolved not be conquered by
his emotion.

"The cholera was dreadfully severe all through the
Italian Tyrol; it swept from Venice to Milan, and never
missed even the mountain villages, far away up the Alps.
In our little hamlet, we lost one hundred and eighteen
souls, and my Gretchen was one of them.

"We had all grown to be very hard-hearted to each
other; misfortune was at each man's door, and he had no
heart to spare for a neighbour's grief; and yet such was
the sorrow for her, that they came, in all this suffering
and desolation, to try and comfort and keep me up, and

though it was a time when all such cares were forgotten, the young people went and laid fresh flowers over her grave every morning. Well, that was very kind of them, and made me weep heartily, and, in weeping, my heart softened, and I got to feel that God knew what was best for all of us, and that mayhap he had taken her away to spare her greater sorrow hereafter, and left me to learn that I should pray to go to her. She had only been in the earth eight days, and I was sitting alone in my solitary house, for I could not bear to open the shop, and began to think that I'd never have the courage to do so again, but would go away and try some other place and some other means of livelihood—it was while thinking thus, a sharp, loud knock came to the door, and I arose, rather angrily, to answer it.

"It was a sergeant of an infantry regiment, whose detachment was on march for Peschiera: there were troubles down there, and the government had to send off three regiments in all haste from Vienna to suppress them. The sergeant was a Bohemian, and his regiment the Kinsky. He was a rough, coarse fellow, very full of his authority, despising all villagers, and holding Italians in especial contempt. He came to order me to prepare rations and room for six soldiers, who were to arrive that evening. I answered boldly, that I would not. I had served the office of syndic in the town, and was thus for ever exempt from the 'billet,' and I led him into my

little sitting-room and showed him my 'brevet,' framed
and glazed, over the chimney. He laughed heartily at
my remonstrance, coolly turned the 'brevet' with its face
to the wall, and said,

"'If you don't want twelve of us instead of six, you'll
keep your tongue quiet, and give us a stoup of your best
wine."

"I did not wait to answer him, but seized my hat and
hurried away to the Platz Commandant. He was an old
enemy of mine, but I could not help it; his was the only
authority I could appeal to, and he was bound to do me
justice. When I reached the bureau, it was so crowded
with soldiers and townsfolk, some seeking for billets,
some insisting on their claim to be free, that I could not
get past the door, and, after an hour's waiting, I was fain
to give up the attempt, and turned back home again,
determined to make my statement in writing, which, after
all, might have been the most fitting.

"I found my doors wide open when I got there, and
my shop crowded with soldiers, who, either seated on the
counter or squatting on their knapsacks, had helped
themselves freely to my wine, even to raising the top of
an old cask, and drinking it in large cups from the barrel,
which they handed liberally to their comrades as they
passed.

"My heart was too full to care much for the loss,
though the insult pressed me sorely, and, pushing my

way through, I gained the inner room to find it crowded like the shop. All was in disorder and confusion. The old musket my father had carried for many a year, and which had hung over the chimney as an heirloom, lay smashed in fragments on the floor; some wanton fellow had run his bayonet through my 'brevet' as syndic, and hung it up in derision as a banner; and one, he was a corporal, had taken down the wreath of white roses that lay on Gretchen's coffin till it was laid in the earth, and placed it on his head. When I saw this, my senses left me; I gave a wild shriek, and dashed both my hands in his face. I tried to strangle him; I would have torn him with my teeth had they not dragged me off and dashed me on the ground, where they trampled on me and beat me, and then carried me away to prison.

'I was four days in prison before I was brought up to be examined. I did not know whether it had been four or forty, for my senses had left me and I was mad; perhaps it was the cold dark cell and the silence restored me, but I came out calm and collected. I remembered everything to the smallest incident.

"The soldiers were heard first; they agreed in everything, and their story had all the air of truth about it. They owned they had taken my wine, but said that the regiment was ready and willing to pay for it so soon as I came back, and that all the rest they had done were only the usual follies of troops on a march. I began by

claiming my exemption as a syndic, but was stopped at
once by being told that my claim had never been sub-
mitted to the authorities, and that in my outrage on the
imperial force I had forfeited all consideration on that
score. My offence was easily proven. I did not deny it,
and I was lectured for nigh an hour on the enormity of
my crime, and then sentenced to pay a fine of a thousand
zwanzigers to the emperor, and to receive four-and-twenty
blows with the stick. 'It should have been eight-and-
forty but for my age,' he said.

"On the same stool where I sat to hear my sentence
was a circus man, waiting the Platz Commandant's leave
to give some representation in the village. I knew him
from his dress, but had never spoken to him nor he to
me; just, however, as the commandant had delivered the
words of my condemnation he turned to look at me;
mayhap to see how I bore up under my misfortune.
I saw his glance, and I did my best to sustain it.
I wanted to bear myself manfully throughout, and not
to let anyone know my heart was broken, which I felt it
was. The struggle was, perhaps, more than I was able
for, and, while the tears gushed out and ran down my
cheeks, I burst out laughing, and laughed away fit after
fit, making the most terrible faces all the while; so out-
rageously droll were my convulsions, that every one around
laughed too, and there was the whole court screaming
madly with the same impulse, and unable to control it.

"'Take the fool away!' cried the commandant at last, 'and bring him to reason with a hazel rod.' And they carried me off, and I was flogged.

"It was about a week after I was down near Commachio. I don't know how I got there, but I was in rags and had no money, and the circus people came past and saw me. 'There's the old fellow that nearly killed us with his droll face,' said the chief. 'I'll give you two zwanzigers a day, my man, if you'll only give us a few grins like that every evening. Is it a bargain?'

"I laughed. I could not keep now from laughing at everything, and the bargain was made, and I was a clown from that hour. They taught me a few easy tricks to help me in my trade, but it is my face that they care for —none can see it unmoved."

He turned on me as he spoke with a fearful contortion of countenance, but, moved by his story, and full only of what I had been listening to, I turned away and shed tears.

"Yes," said he, meditatively, "many a happy heart is kindled at the fire that is consuming another. As for myself, both joy and sorrow are dead within me. I am without hope, and, stranger still, without fear."

"But you are not without benevolence," said I, as I looked towards the sleeping girl.

"She was so like Gretchen," said he; and he bent down his head and sobbed bitterly.

I would have asked him some questions about her if I dared, but I felt so rebuked by the sorrow of the old man, that my curiosity seemed almost unfeeling.

"She came amongst us a mere child," said he, "and speedily attached herself to me. I contrived to learn enough of her dialect to understand and talk to her, and at last she began to regard me as a father, and even called me such. It was a long time before I could bear this. Every time I heard the word my grief would burst out afresh; but what won't time do? I have come to like it now."

"And is she good, and gentle, and affectionate?" asked I.

"She is far too good and true-hearted to be in such company as ours. Would that some rich person—it should be a lady—kind, and gentle, and compassionate, could see her and take her away from such associates, and this life of shame, ere it be too late. If I have a sorrow left me now, it is for her."

I was silent, for though the wish only seemed fair and natu 1 enough on his part, I could not help thinking how improbable such an incident would prove.

"She would repay it all," said he. "If ever there was a nature rich in great gifts, it is hers. She can learn whatever she will, and for a word of kindness she would hold her hand in the fire for you. Hush!" whispered he, "she is stirring. What is it, darling?" said he, creeping close to her, as she lay, throwing her arms wildly open, but not removing the handkerchief from her face.

She muttered something hurriedly, and then burst into a laugh so joyous and so catching, it was impossible to refrain from joining in it.

She threw back the kerchief at once and started to her knees, gazing steadfastly, almost sternly, at me. I saw that the old man comprehended the inquiry of her glance, and as quickly whispered a few words in her ear. She listened till he had done, and then springing towards me, she caught my hand and kissed it.

I suspect he must have rebuked the ardour of her movement, for she hung her head despondingly, and turned away from us both.

"Now for the road once more," said Vaterchen, "for if we stay much longer here, we shall have the forest flies, which are always worse towards evening."

It was not without great difficulty I could prevent his carrying my knapsack for me, and even the girl herself would gladly have borne some of my load. At last, however, we set forth, Tintefleck lightening the way with a merry canzonette, that had the time of a quick step.

CHAPTER VIII.

WHAT a pleasant little dinner we had that day. It was laid out in a little summer-house of the inn-garden. All overgrown with a fine old fig-tree, through whose leaves the summer wind played deliciously, while a tiny rivulet rippled close by, and served to cool our "Achten-thaler" —an amount of luxury that made Tintefleck quite wild with laughter.

"Is it cold enough?" she asked, archly, in her peasant dialect, each time the old man laid down his glass.

As I came gradually to pick up the occasional meaning of her words—a process which her expressive pantomime greatly aided—I was struck by the marvellous acuteness of a mind so totally without culture, and I could not help asking Vaterchen why he had never attempted to instruct her.

"What can I do?" said he, despondently; "there are no books in the only language she knows, and the only language she will condescend to speak. She can understand Italian, and I have read stories for her, and sonnets too, out of Leopardi, but though she will listen in all eagerness till they are finished, no sooner over than she breaks out into some wild Calabrian song, and asks me is it not worth all the fine things I have been giving her, thrice told."

"Could you not teach her to write?"

"I tried that. I bought a slate, and I made a bargain with her that she should have a scarlet knot for her hair when she could ask me for it in written words. Well, all seemed to go on prosperously for a time; we had got through half the alphabet very successfully, till we came to the letter H. This made her laugh immediately, it was so like a scaffold we had in the circus for certain exercises; and no sooner had I marked down the letter, than she snatched the pencil from me, and drew the figure of a man on each bar of the letter. From that hour forth, as though her wayward humour had been only imprisoned, she burst forth into every imaginable absurdity at our lessons. Every ridiculous event of our daily life she drew, and with a rapidity almost incredible. I was not very apt, as you may imagine, in acquiring the few accomplishments they thought to give me, and she caricatured me under all my difficulties."

"Si, si," broke she in at this; for, with a wonderful acuteness, she could trace something of a speaker's meaning where every word was unknown to her. As she spoke she arose, and fled down the garden at top speed.

"Why has she gone? Is she displeased at your telling me all these things about her?" asked I.

"Scarcely that; she loves to be noticed. Nothing really seems to pain her so much as when she is passed over unremarked. When such an event would occur in the circus, I have seen her sob through her sleep all the night after. I half suspect now she is piqued at the little notice you have bestowed upon her. All the better if it be so."

"But here she comes again."

With the same speed she now came back to us, holding her slate over her head, and showing that she rightly interpreted what the old man had said of her.

"Now for my turn!" said Vaterchen, with a smile. "She is never weary of drawing me in every absurd and impossible posture."

"What is it to be, Tintefleck?" asked he. "How am I to figure this time?"

She shook her head without replying, and, making a sign that she was not to be questioned or interrupted, she nestled down at the foot of the fig-tree, and began to draw.

The old man now drew near me, and proceeded to give me further details of her strange temper and ways. I could mark that throughout all he said, a tone of intense anxiety and care prevailed, and that he felt her disposition was exactly that which exposed her to the greatest perils

for her future. There was a young artist who used to
follow her through all the South Tyrol, affecting to be
madly in love with her, but of whose sincerity and
honour Vaterchen professed to have great misgivings.
He gave her lessons in drawing, and, what was less to be
liked, he made several studies of herself. " The artless
way," said the old man, " she would come and repeat to
me all his raptures about her, was at first a sort of
comfort to me. I felt reassured by her confidence, and
also by the little impression his praises seemed to make,
but I saw later on that I was mistaken. She grew each
day more covetous of these flatteries, and it was no
longer laughingly, but in earnest seriousness she would
tell me that the 'Fornarina' in some gallery had not
such eyes as hers, and that some great statue that all the
world admired was far inferior to her in shape. If I had
dared to rebuke her vanity, or to ridicule her pretensions,
all my influence would have been gone for ever. She
would have left us, gone who knows whither, and been
lost, so that I had nothing for it but to seem to credit all
she said and yet hold the matter lightly, and I said beauty
has no value except when associated with rank and
station. If queens and princesses be handsome, they are
more fitted to adorn this high estate, but for humble folk
it is as great a mockery as these tinsel gems we wear in
the circus.

" 'Max says not,' said she to me one evening, after one

of my usual lectures. 'Max says, there are queens would give their coronets to have my hair, ay, or even one of the dimples in my cheek.'

"'Max is a villain,' said I, before I could control my words.

"'Max is a vero signor!' said she, haughtily, 'and not like one of us; and more, too, I'll go and tell him what you have called him.' She bounded away from me at this, and I saw her no more till nightfall.

"'What has happened to you, poor child,' said I, as I saw her lying on the floor of her room, her forehead bleeding, and her dress all draggled and torn. She would not speak to me for a long while, but by much entreating and caressing I won upon her to tell me what had befallen her. She had gone to the top of the 'Glucksberg' and thrown herself down. It was a fearful height, and only was she saved by being caught by the brambles and tangled foliage of the cliff; and all this for 'one harsh word of mine,' she said. But I knew better; the struggle was deeper in her heart than she was aware of, and Max had gone suddenly away, and we saw no more of him."

"Did she grieve after him?"

"I scarcely can say she did. She fretted, but I think it was for her own loneliness and the want of that daily flattery she had grown so fond of. She became over-bearing, and even insolent, too, with all her equals, and though for many a day she had been the spoiled child of the troop, many began to weary of her way- wardness. I don't know how all this might have turned out, when, just as suddenly, she changed and became everything that she used to be."

When the old man had got thus, 'the girl arose, and, without saying a word, laid the slate before us. Vater- chen, not very quick-sighted, could not at once understand the picture, but I caught it at once, and laughed immo- derately. She had taken the scene where I had presented Vaterchen and herself to the ladies at the tea-table, and with an intense humour, sketched all the varying emotions of the incident. The offended dignity of the old lady, the surprise and mortification of Miss Herbert, and my own unconscious pretension as I pointed to the "friends" who accompanied me, were drawn with the spirit of high caricature. Nor did she spare Vaterchen or herself; they were drawn, perhaps, with a more exaggerated satire than all the rest.

The old man no sooner comprehended the subject than he drew his hand across it, and turned to her with words of anger and reproach. I meant, of course, to interfere in her behalf, but it was needless; she fled, laughing, into the garden, and before many minutes were over we heard her merry voice, with the tinkle of a guitar to assist it.

"There it is," said Vaterchen, moodily. "What are you to do with a temperament like that?"

That was a question I was in no wise prepared to answer. Tintefleck's temperament seemed to be the very converse of my own. *I* was over eager to plan out everything in life. *She* appeared to be just as impulsively bent on risking all. *My* head was always calculating eventualities; *hers*, it struck me, never worried itself about difficulties till in the midst of them. Now, Jean Paul tells us that when a man detects any exaggerated bias in his character, instead of endeavouring, by daily watching, to correct it, he will be far more successful if he ally himself with some one of a diametrically opposite humour. If he be rash, for instance, let him seek companionship with the sluggish. If his tendency bear to over-imagination, let him frequent the society of realists. Why, therefore, should not I and Tintefleck be mutually beneficial? Take the two different kinds of wood in a bow: one will supply resistance, the other flexibility. It was a pleasant notion, and I resolved to test it.

"Vaterchen," said I, "call me to-morrow, when you get ready for the road. I will keep you company as far as Constance."

"Ah, sir," said he, with a sigh, "you will be well weary of us before half the journey is over; but you shall be obeyed."

CHAPTER IX.

NEXT morning, just as day was breaking, we set out on foot on our road to Constance. There was a pinkish-grey streak of light on the horizon, sure sign of a fine day, and the bright stars twinkled still in the clear half-sombre sky, and all was calm and noiseless—nothing to be heard but the tramp of our own feet on the hard causeway.

With the cowardly caution of one who feels the water with his foot before he springs in to swim, I was glad that I made my first experiences of companionship with these humble friends while it was yet dark and none could see us. The old leaven of snobbery was unsubdued in my heart, and, as I turned to look at poor Vaterchen and then at the tinsel finery of Catinka, I bethought me of the little consideration the world extends to such as these and their belongings. "Vagabonds all!" would say some rich banker, as he rolled by in his massive travelling-carriage, creaking with imperials and jingling with bells; "Vagabonds all!" would mutter the Jew

pedlar, as he looked down from the *banquette* of the
diligence.   How slight is the sympathy of the realist for
the poor creature whose life-labour is to please.   How
prone to regard him as useless, or, even worse, forgetting,
the while, how a wiser than he has made many things in
this beautiful world of ours that they should merely
minister to enjoyment, gladden the eye and ear, and make
our pilgrimage less weary.   Where would be the crimson
jay? where the scarlet bustard? where the gorgeous
peacock, with the nosegay on his tail? where the rose,
and the honeysuckle, and the purple foxglove, mingling
with the wild thorns in our hedgerows, if the universe
were of *their* creation, and this great globe but one big
workshop?   You never insist that the daisy and the
daffodil should be pot-herbs; and why are there not to be
wild flowers in humanity as well as in the fields?   Is it
not a great pride to you who live under a bell-glass,
nurtured and cared for, and with your name attached to
a cleft-stick at your side,—is it not a great pride to know
that you are not like one of us poor dog-roses?   Be
satisfied, then, with that glory; we only ask to live!
Shame on me for that "only!"   As if there could be
anything more delightful than life.   Life, with all its
capacities for love, and friendship, and heroism, and self-
devotion, for generous actions and noble aspirations!
Life to feel life, to know that we are in a sphere specially
constructed for the exercise of our senses and the play of

our faculties, free to choose the road we would take, and with a glorious reward if our choice be the right one!

"'Vagabonds!' Yes," thought I, "there was once on a time such a vagabond, and he strolled along from village to village, making of his flute a livelihood; a poor performer, too, he tells us he was, but he could touch the hearts of these simple villagers with his tones as he could move the hearts of thousands more learned than they with his marvellous pathos, and this vagabond was called Oliver Goldsmith." I have no words to say the ecstasy this thought gave me. Many a proud traveller doubtless swept past the poor wayfarer as he went, dusty and foot-sore, and who was, nevertheless, journeying onward to a great immortality; to be a name remembered with blessings by generations when the haughty man that scorned him was forgotten for ever. "And so now," thought I, "some splendid Russian or some Saxon Crœsus will crash by and not be conscious that the thin and weary-looking youth, with the girl's bundle on his stick and the red umbrella under his arm, that this is Potts! Ay, sir, you fancy that to be threadbare and foot-sore is to be vulgar-minded and ignoble, and you never so much as suspect that the heart inside that poor plaid waistcoat is throbbing with ambitions high as a Kaiser's, and that the brain within that battered Jim Crow is the realm of thoughts profound as Bacon's and high-soaring as Milton's."

If I make my reader a sharer in these musings of mine, it is because they occupied me for some miles of the way. Vaterchen was not talkative, and loved to smoke on uninterruptedly. I fancy that, in his way, he was as great a dreamer as myself. Catinka would have talked incessantly if any one had listened, or could understand her. As it was, she recited legends and sang songs for herself, as happy as ever a blackbird was to listen to his own melody; and though I paid no especial attention to her music, still did the sounds float through all my thoughts, bathing them with a soothing flood; just as the air we breathe is often loaded with a sweet and perfumed breath, that steals into our breath ere we know it. On the whole, we journeyed along very pleasantly, and what between the fresh morning air, the brisk exercise, and the novelty of the situation, I felt in a train of spirits that made me delighted with everything. "This, after all," thought I, "is more like the original plan I sketched out for myself. This is the true mode to see life and the world. The student of Nature never begins his studies with the more complicated organisations; he sets out with what is simplest in structure, and least intricate in function; he begins with the extreme link of the chain: so, too, I start with the investigation of those whose lives of petty cares and small ambitions must render them easy of appreciation. This poor Mollusca Vaterchen, for instance—to see is to know him; and the girl, how absurd to connect such a guileless child of nature as that, with those stereotyped notions of feminine craft and subtlety!" I then went on to imagine some future biographer of mine engaged on this portion of my life, puzzled for materials, puzzled, still more, to catch the clue to my meaning in it. "At this time," will he say, "Potts, by one of those strange caprices which often were the mainspring of his actions, resolved to lead a gipsy life. His ardent love of ·nature, his heartfelt enjoyment of scenery, and, more than even these, a certain breadth and generosity of character, disposed him to sympathise with those who have few to pity and fewer to succour them. With these wild children of the roadside he lived for months, joyfully sharing the burdens they carried, and taking his part in their privations. It was here he first met Catinka." I stopped at this sentence, and slowly repeated to myself, "'It was here he first met Catinka!' What will he have next to record?" thought I. "Is Potts now to claim sympathy as the victim of a passion that regarded not station, nor class, nor fortune; that despised the cold conventionalities of a selfish world, and asked only a heart for a heart? Is he to be remembered as the faithful believer in his own theory—Love, above all? Are we to hear of him clasping rapturously to his bosom the poor forlorn girl?" So intensely were my feelings engaged in my speculations, that, at this critical pass, I threw my arms around Catinka's neck, and kissed her. A rebuke, not very cruel, not in the least angry or peevish, brought me quickly to myself, and as Vaterchen was fortunately in front and saw nothing of what passed, I speedily made my peace. I do not know how it happened, but in that same peace-making, I had passed my arm round her waist and there it remained—an army of occupation after the treaty was signed—and we went along, side by side, very amicably—very happily.

We are often told that a small competence—the just enough to live on—is the bane of all enterprise; that men thus placed are removed from the stimulus of necessity, and yet not lifted into the higher atmosphere of ambitions. Exactly in the same way do I believe that equality is the grave of love. The passion thrives on difficulty, and requires sacrifice. You must bid defiance to mankind in your choice, or you are a mere fortune-hunter. Show the world the blushing peasant girl you have made your wife, and say, "Yes, I have had courage to do this." Or else strive for a princess—a Russian princess. Better, far better, however, the humble-hearted child of nature and the fields, the simple, trusting, confiding girl, who regarding her lover as a sort of demi-god, would, while she clung to him ——

"You press me so hard!" murmured Catinka, half rebukingly, but with a sort of pouting expression that became her marvellously.

"I was thinking of something that interested me,

dearest," said I; but I'm not sure that I made my meaning very clear to her, and yet there was a roguish look in her black eye that puzzled me greatly. I began to like her, or, if you prefer the phrase, to fall in love with her. I knew it—I felt it just the way that a man who has once had the ague never mistakes when he is going to have a return of the fever. In the same way, exactly did I recognise all the premonitory symptoms; the giddiness, the shivering, increased action of the heart —— Halt, Potts! and reflect a bit; are you describing love, or a tertian?

How will the biographer conduct himself here? Whether will he have to say, "Potts resisted manfully this fatal attachment; had he yielded to the seductions of this early passion, it is more than probable we should never have seen him this, that, and t'other, nor would the world have been enriched with—Heaven knows what;" or shall he record, "Potts loved her, loved her as only such a nature as his ever loves? He felt keenly that, in a mere worldly point of view, he must sacrifice; but it was exactly in that love and that sacrifice was born the poet, the wondrous child of song, who has given us the most glorious lyrics of our language. He had the manliness to share his fortune with this poor girl. 'It was,' he tells us himself, in one of those little touching passages in his diary, which place him immeasurably above the mock sentimentality of Jean Jacques—'it was on the road to Constance, of a bright and breezy summer morning, that I told her of my love. We were walking along, our arms around each other, as might two happy, guileless children. I was very young in what is called the world, but I had a boundless confidence in myself; my theory was, "If I be strengthened by the deep devotion of one loving heart, I have no fears of failure." Beautiful words, and worthy of all memory! And then he goes on: "I drew her gently over to a grassy bench on the roadside, and taking my purse from my pocket, poured out before her its humble contents, in all something less than twenty sovereigns, but to her eyes a very Pactolus of wealth.'"

"What if I were to try this experiment?" thought I; "what if I were, so to say, to anticipate my own biography?" The notion pleased me much. There was something novel in it, too. It was making the experiment in the *corpore vile* of accident, to see what might come of it.

"Come here, Catinka," said I, pointing to a moss-covered rock at the roadside, with a little well at its base—"come here, and let me have a drink of this nice clear water."

She assented with a smile and a nod, detaching at the same time a little cup from the flask she wore at her side, in *vivandière* fashion. "And we'll fill my flask, too," said she, showing that it was empty. With a sort of childish

glee she now knelt beside the stream, and washed the
cup. What is it, I wonder, that gives the charm to
running water, and imparts a sort of glad feeling to its
contemplation? Is it that its ceaseless flow suggests that
"for ever" which contrasts so powerfully with all short-
lived pleasures? I cannot tell, but I was still musing
over the difficulty, when, having twice offered me the cup
without my noticing it, she at last raised it to my lips.
And I drank—oh, what a draught it was! so clear, so
cold, so pure; and all the time my eyes were resting on
hers, looking, as it were, into another well, the deepest
and most unfathomable of all.

"Sit down here beside me on this stone, Catinka, and
help me to count these pieces of money; they have got
so mingled together that I scarcely know what is left
me." She seemed delighted with the project, and sat
down at once, and I, throwing myself at her feet, poured
the contents of my purse into her lap.

"Madonna mia!" was all she could utter as she beheld
the gold. Aladdin in the cave never felt a more overwhelming rapture than did she at sight of these immense
riches. "But where did it come from?" cried she,
wildly. "Have you got mines of gold and silver? Have
you got gems, too—rubies and pearls? Oh, say if there
be pearls; I love them so! And are you really a great
prince, the son of a king; and are you wandering the
world this way to seek adventures, or in search, mayhap,

of that lovely princess you are in love with?" With wildest impetuosity she asked these and a hundred other questions, for it was only now and then that I could trace her meaning, which expressive pantomime did much to explain.

I tried to convince her that what she deemed a treasure was a mere pittance, which a week or two would exhaust; that I was no prince, nor had I a kingly father; "and last of all," said I, "I am not in pursuit of a princess. But I'll tell you what I am in search of, Catinka: one trusting, faithful, loving heart; one that will so unite itself to mine, as to have no joys, or sorrows, or cares, but mine; one content to go wherever I go, live however I live, and no matter what my faults may be, or how meanly others think of me, will ever regard me with eyes of love and devotion."

I had held her hand while I uttered this, gazing up into her eyes with ecstasy, for I saw how their liquid depth appeared to move as though about to overflow, when at last she spoke, and said,

"And there are no pearls!"

"Poor child!" thought I, "she cannot understand one word I have been saying. Listen to me, Catinka," said I, with a slow utterance. "Would you give me your heart for all this treasure?"

"Si, si!" cried she, eagerly.

"And love me always—for ever?"

"Si," said she, again; but I fancied with less of energy than before.

"And when it was spent and gone, and nothing remaining of it, what would you do?"

"Send you to gather more, mio caro," said she, pressing my hand to her lips, as though in earnest of the blandishments she would bestow upon me.

Now, I cannot affect to say that all this was very reassuring. This poor simple child of the mountains showed a spirit as sordid and as calculating as though she were baptised in May Fair. It was a terrible shock to me to see this; a dire overthrow to a very fine edifice that I was just putting the roof on! "Would Kate Herbert have made me such a speech?" thought I. "Would she have declared herself so venal and so worldly?—and why not? May it not be, perhaps, simply that a mere question of good breeding, the usages of a polite world, might have made all the difference, and that she would have felt what poor Catinka felt and owned to. If this were true, the advantages were all on the side of sincerity. With honesty as the basis, what may not one build up of character? Where there is candour there are at least no disappointments. This poor simple child, untutored in the wiles of a scheming world, where all is false, unreal, and deceptive, has the courage to say that her heart can be bought. She is ready in her innocence, too, to sell it, just as the Indians sell a great territory for a few glass beads or bright buttons. And why should not I make the acquisition in the very spirit of a new settler? It was I discovered this lone island of the sea; it was I first landed on this unknown shore; why not claim a sovereignty so cheaply established." I put the question arithmetically before me: Given, a young girl, totally new to life and its seductions, deeply impressed with the value of wealth, to find the measure of venality in a well brought-up young lady, educated at Clapham, and finished at Boulogne-sur-Mer. I expressed it thus: $D—y=T+x$, or an unknown quantity.

"What strange marks are you drawing there?" cried she, as I made these figures on the slate.

"A caprice," said I, in some confusion.

"No," said she; "I know better. It was a charm. Tell truth—it was a charm."

"A charm, dearest; but for what?"

"*I* know," said she, shaking her head and laughing, with a sort of wicked drollery.

"*You* know! Impossible, child."

"Yes," she said, with great gravity, while she swept her hand across the slate and erased all the figures. "Yes, *I* know, and I'll not permit it."

"But what, in Heaven's name, is trotting through your head, Catinka? You have not the vaguest idea of what those signs meant."

"Yes," she said, even more solemnly than before. "I know it all. You mean to steal away my heart in spite of me, and you are going to do it with a charm."

"And what success shall I have, Catinka?"

"Oh, do not ask me," said she, in a tone of touching misery. "I feel it very sore here." And she pressed her hand to her side. "Ah me," sighed she, "if there were only pearls!"

The ecstasy her first few words gave me was terribly routed by this vile conclusion, and I started abruptly, and, in an angry voice, said, "Let us go on; Vaterchen will fear we are lost."

"And all this gold; what shall I do with it?" cried she.

"What you will. Throw it into the well if you like," said I, angrily; for in good sooth I was out of temper with her, and myself, and all mankind.

"Nay," said she mildly, "it is yours; but I will carry it for you if it weary you."

I might have felt rebuked by the submissive gentleness of her words; indeed, I know not how it was that they did not so move me, and I walked on in front of her, heedless of her entreaties that I should wait till she came up beside me.

When she did join me, she wanted to talk immensely. She had all manner of questions to ask about where my treasure came from; how often I went back there to

replenish it; was I quite sure that it could never, never
be exhausted, and such-like. But I was in no gracious
mood for such inquiries, and telling her that I wished
to follow my own thoughts without interruption, I
walked along in silence.

I cannot tell the weight I felt at my heart. I am
not speaking figuratively. No; it was exactly as
though a great mass of heavy metal filled my chest,
forced out my ribs, and pressed down my diaphragm;
and though I held my hands to my sides with all my
force, the pressure still remained.

"What a bitter mockery it is," thought I, "if the
only false thing in all the world should be the human
heart! There are diamonds that will resist fire, gold
that will stand the crucible; but the moment you come
to man and his affections, all is hollow and illusory!"

Why do we give the name worldliness to traits of
selfish advancement and sordid gain, when a young
creature like this, estranged from all the commerce of
mankind, who knows nothing of that bargain-and-barter
system which we call civilisation, reared and nurtured
like a young fawn in her native woods, should, as
though by a very instinct of corruption, have a heart
as venal as any hackneyed beauty of three London
seasons?

Let no man tell me now, that it is our vicious system
of female training, our false social organisation, our

spurious morality, laxity of family ties, and the rest
of it. I am firmly persuaded that a young squaw of
the Choctaws has as many anxieties about her *"parti"*
as any belle of Belgravia, even though the settle-
ments be only paid in sharks' teeth and human
toupees.

And what an absurdity is our whole code on this
subject! A man is actually expected to court, solicit,
and even worship the object that he is after all called
upon to pay for. You do not smirk at the salmon in
your fishmonger's window, or ogle the lamb at your
butcher's; you go in boldly and say, "How much the
pound?" If you sighed outside for a week, you'd get
it never the cheaper. Why not then make an honest
market of what is so saleable. What a saving of time
to know that the splendid creature yonder, with the
queenly air, can only be had at ten thousand a-year,
but that the spicy article with the black ringlets will
go for two! Instead of all the heart-burnings and
blank disappointments we see now, we should have a
practical, contented generation; and in the same spirit
that a man of moderate fortune turns away from the
seductions of turtle and whitebait, while he orders
home his mutton chop, he would avert his gaze from
beauty, and fix his affections on the dumpy woman that
can be "got a bargain."

Why did not the poet say, Venality, thy name is

Woman? It would suit the prosody about as well, and the purpose better. The Turks are our masters in all this; they are centuries—whole centuries in advance of us. How I wish some Babbage would make a calculation of the hours, weeks, years, centuries of time, are lost in what is called love-making. Time, we are told, is money, and here, at once, is the fund to pay off our national debt. Take the "time that's lost in wooing" by a nation, say of twenty-eight or thirty millions, and at the cheapest rate of labour— take the prison rate if you like—and see if I be not right. Let the population who now heave sighs, pound oyster-shells, let those who pick quarrels, pick oakum, and we need no income-tax!

"I'll not sing any more," broke in Catinka. "I don't think you have been listening to me.

"Listening to you!" said I, contemptuously, "certainly not. When I want a siren, I take a pit ticket and go to the Opera; seven-and-sixpence is the price of Circe, and dear at the money." With this rude rebuff I waved her off, and walked along once more alone.

At a sudden bend of the road we found Vaterchen seated under a tree waiting for us, and evidently not a little uneasy at our long absence.

"What is this?" said he, angrily, to Catinka. "Why have you remained so long behind?"

"We sat down to rest at a well," said she, "and then he took out a great bag of money to count, and there was so much in it, so many pieces of bright gold, that one could not help turning them over and over, and gazing at them."

"And worshipping them too, girl!" cried he, indignantly, while he turned on me a look of sorrow and reproach. I returned his stare haughtily, and he arose and drew me to one side.

"Am I, then, once more mistaken in my judgment of men? Have *you*, too, duped me?" said he, in a voice that shook with agitation. "Was it for this you offered us the solace of your companionship? Was it for this you condescended to journey with us, and deigned to be our host and entertainer?"

The appeal came at an evil moment: a vile, contemptible scepticism was at work within me. The rasp and file of Doubt were eating away at my heart, and I deemed "all men liars."

"And is it to me—Potts—you address such words as these, you consummate old humbug? What is there about me that denotes dupe or fool?"

The old man shook his head, and made a gesture to imply he had not understood me; and now I remembered that I had uttered this rude speech in English and not in German. With the memory of this fact came also the consciousness of its cruel meaning. What if I should have wronged him? What if the poor old fellow be honest and upright? What if he be really striving to keep this girl in the path of virtue? I came close to him, and fixed my eyes steadfastly on his face. He looked at me fearlessly, as an honest man might look. He never tried to turn away, nor did he make the slightest effort to evade me. He seemed to understand all the import of my scrutiny, for he said at last:

"Well, are you satisfied?"

"I am, Vaterchen," said I, "fully satisfied. Let us be friends." And I took his hand and shook it heartily.

"You think me honest?" asked he.

"I do think so."

"And I am not more honest than she is. "No," said he, resolutely, "Tintefleck is true-hearted."

"What of *me?*" cried she, coming up and leaning her arm on the old man's shoulder—"what of *me?*"

"I have said that you are honest, and would not deceive!"

"Not *you*, Vaterchen—not *you*," said she, kissing him. And then, as she turned away, she gave me a look so full of meaning, and so strange withal, that if I were to speak for an hour I could not explain it. It seemed to mean sorrow and reproach and wounded pride, with a dash of pity, and, above all and everything, defiance; ay, that was its chief character, and I believe I winced under it.

"Let us step out briskly," said Vaterchen. "Constance is a good eleven miles off yet."

"He looks tired already," said she, with a glance at me.

"I? I'm as fresh as when I started," said I. And I made an effort to appear brisk and lively, which only ended in making them laugh heartily.

CHAPTER X.

RESPECTABLE reader, there is no use in asking you if you
have ever been in the Hotel of the "Balance," at
Constance. Of course you have not. It is neither
recorded in the book of John, nor otherwise known to
fame. It is an obscure hostel, only visited by the very
humblest wayfarers, and such poor offshoots of wretchedness as are fain to sleep on a truckle-bed and sup meanly.
Vaterchen, however, spoke of it in generous terms.
There was a certain oniony soup he had tasted there
years ago whose flavour had not yet left his memory.
He had seen, besides, the most delicious schweine fleisch
hanging down from the kitchen rafters, and it had been
revealed to him in a dream that a solvent traveller
might have rashers on demand.

Poor fellow! I had not the vaguest idea of the
eloquence he possessed till he came to talk on these
matters. From modest and distrustful, he grew assured
and confident; his hesitation of speech was replaced by a
fluent utterance and a rich vocabulary; and he repeatedly

declared that though the exterior was unprepossessing, and the service generally homely, there were substantial comforts obtainable which far surpassed the resources of more pretentious houses. "You are served on pewter, it is true," said he; "but pewter is a rare material to impart relish to a savoury mess." Though we should dine in the kitchen, he gave me to understand that even in this there were advantages, and that the polite guest of the *salon* never knew what it was to taste that rich odour of the "roast," or that fragrant incense that steamed up from the luscious stew, and which were to cookery what bouquet was to wine.

"I will not say that, honoured sir," continued he, "to you, in the mixed company which frequent such humble hearths there would be matter of interest or amusement; but, to a man like myself, these chance companionships are delightful. Here all are stragglers, all adventurers. Not a man that deposits his pack in the corner and draws in his chair to the circle but is a wanderer and a pilgrim of one sort or other." He drew me an amusing picture of one of these groups, wherein, even without telling his story, each gave such insight into his life and travels as to present a sort of drama.

Whether it was that my companion had drawn too freely on his imagination, or that we had fallen on an unfortunate moment, I cannot say, but, though we found the company at the "Balance" numerous and varied, there

was none of the sociality I looked for, still less of that
generous warmth and good greeting which he assured
me was the courtesy of such places. The men were
chiefly carriers, with their mule-teams and heavy wagons,
bound for the Bavarian Tyrol. There was a sprinkling
of Jew pedlars, on their way to the Vorarlberg; a
deserter from the Austrian army, trying to get back to
Hesse Cassel; and an Italian image carrier, with a green
parrot and a well-filled purse, going back to finish his
days at Lucca.

Now none of these were elements of a very exalted or
exclusive rank; they were each and all of them taken
from the very base of the social pyramid; and yet, would
it be believed that they regarded our entrance amongst
them as an act of rare impudence!

A more polished company might have been satisfied
with averted heads or cold looks; these were less
equivocal. One called out to the landlord to know if he
expected any gipsies; another, affecting to treat us as
solicitors for their patronage, said he had no "batzen" to
bestow on buffoonery; a third suggested we should get up
our theatricals under the cart-shed outside, and beat the
drum when we were ready; and the deserter, a poor weak-
looking, mangy wretch, with a ragged fatigue-jacket and
broken boots, put his arm round Catinka's waist, to draw
her on his knee, for the which she dealt him such a slap
on the face as fairly sent him on the floor, in which

ignoble position Vaterchen kicked him again and again.
In an instant all were upon us. Carters, pedlars, and
image man assailed us furiously. I suppose I beat
somebody; I know that several beat *me*. The impression left upon me when all was over was of a sort
of human kaleidoscope, where the people turned every
way without ceasing. Now we seemed all on our feet,
now on our heads, now on the floor, now in the air,
Vaterchen flying about like a demon, while Tintefleck
stood in a · corner, with a gleaming stiletto in her
hand, saying something in Calabrian, which sounded
like an invitation to come and be killed.

The police came at last; and, after a noisy scene of
accusation and denial, the weight of evidence went
against us, and we were marched off to prison, poor old
Vaterchen crying like a child for all the disgrace and
misery he had brought on his benefactor: and while he
kissed my hand, swearing that a whole life's devotion
would not be enough to recompense me for what he had
been the means of inflicting on me, Catinka took it
more easily, her chief regret apparently being that
nobody came near enough to give her a chance with her
knife, which she assured us she wielded with a notable
skill, and could, with a jerk, send flying through a door,
like a javelin, at full six paces' distance; nor, indeed, was
it without considerable persuasion she could be induced to
restore it to its sheath, which truth obliges me to own

was inside her garter. Our prison, an old tower adjoining the lake, had been once the dungeon of John Huss, and the torture chamber, as it was still called, continued to be used for mild transgressors, such as we were. A small bribe induced the gaoler's wife to take poor Tintefleck for the night into her own quarters, and Vaterchen and I were sole possessors of the gloomy old hall, which opened by a balcony, railed like a sort of cage, over the lake.

If the torture chamber had been denuded of its flesh pincers and thumb screws, and the other ingenious devices of human cruelty, I am bound to own that its traditions as a place of suffering had not died out, as the fleas left nothing to be desired on the score of misery. Whether it was that they had been pinched by a long fast, or that we were more tender, cutaneously, than the aborigines, I know not, but I can safely aver that I never passed such a night, and sincerely trust that I may never pass such another. Though the air from the lake was cold and chilly, we preferred to crouch on the balcony to remaining within the walls, but even here our persecutors followed us.

Vaterchen slept through it all; an occasional convulsive jerk would show, at times, when one of the enemy had chanced upon some nervous fibre; but on the whole, he bore up like one used to such martyrdom, and able to brave it. As for me, when morning broke, I looked like

a strong case of confluent small-pox, with the addition
that my heavy eyelids nearly closed over my eyes, and
my lips swelled out like a Kaffir's. How that young
minx, Catinka, laughed at me. All the old man's signs,
warnings, menaces, were in vain; she screamed aloud
with laughter, and never ceased, even as we were led
into the tribunal and before the dread presence of the
judge.

The judgment-seat was not imposing. It was a long,
low, ill-lighted chamber, with a sort of raised counter at
one end, behind which sat three elderly men, dressed like
master sweeps—that is, of the old days of climbing-boys.
The prisoners were confined in a thing like a fold, and
there leaned against one end of the same pen as ourselves a square-built, thick-set man of about eight-and-
forty, or fifty, dressed in a suit of coarse drab, and who,
notwithstanding an immense red beard and moustache, a
clear blue eye and broad brow proclaimed to be English.
He was being interrogated as we entered, but from his
total ignorance of German the examination was not
proceeding very glibly.

"You're an Englishman, ain't you?" cried he, as I
came in. "You can speak High Dutch, perhaps?"

"I can speak German well enough to be intelligible,
sir."

"All right," said he, in the same free-and-easy tone.
"Will you explain to those old beggars there that they're

making fools of themselves. Here's how it is. My passport was made out for two; for Thomas Harpar, that's me, and Sam Rigges. Now, because Sam Rigges ain't here, they tell me I can't be suffered to proceed. Ain't that stupid? Did you ever hear the like of that for downright absurdity before?"

"But where is he?"

"Well, I don't mind telling you, because you're a countryman, but I don't like blackening an Englishman to one of those confounded foreigners. Rigges has run."

"What do you mean by 'run'?"

"I mean, cut his stick; gone clean away; and what's worse, too, carried off a stout bag of dollars with him that we had for our journey."

"Whither were you going?"

"That's neither here nor there, and don't concern you in any respect. What you've to do is, explain to the old cove yonder—the fellow in the middle is the worst of them—tell him it's all right, that I'm Harpar, and that the other ain't here; or, look here, I'll tell you what's better, do you be Rigges, and it's all right."

I demurred flatly to this suggestion, but undertook to plead his cause on its true merits.

"And who are you, sir, that presume to play the advocate here?" said the judge, haughtily. "I fancied that you stood there to answer a charge against yourself."

"That matter may be very speedily disposed of, sir,"

said I, as proudly; "and you will be very fortunate if you succeed as readily in explaining your own illegal arrest of me to to the higher court of your country."

With the eloquence which we are told essentially belongs to truth, I narrated how I had witnessed, as a mere passing traveller, the outrageous insult offered to these poor wanderers as they entered the inn. With the warm enthusiasm of one inspired by a good cause, I painted the whole incident with really scarcely a touch of embellishment, reserving the only decorative portion to a description of myself, whom I mentioned as an agent of the British government, especially employed on a peculiar service, the confirmation of which I proudly established by my passport setting forth that I was a certain "Ponto, Chargé des Dépêches."

Now if there be one feature of continental life fixed and immutable, it is this, that wherever the German language be spoken, the reverence for a government functionary is supreme. If you can only show on documentary evidence that you are grandson of the man who made the broom that swept out a government office, it is enough. You are from that hour regarded as one of the younger children of Bureaucracy. You are under the protection of the state, and though you be but the smallest rivet in the machinery, there is no saying what mischief might not ensue if you were either lost or mislaid.

I saw in an instant the dread impression I had created, and I said, in a voice of careless insolence, "Go on, I beg of you; send me back to prison; chain me; perhaps you would like to torture me? The government I represent is especially slow in vindicating the rights of its injured officials. It has a European reputation for long-suffering, patience, and forbearance. Yes, Englishmen can be impaled, burned, flayed alive, disembowelled. By all means, avail yourselves of your bland privileges; have me led out instantly to the scaffold, unless you prefer to have me broken on the wheel!"

"Will nobody stop him!" cried the president, almost choking with wrath.

"Stop me; I suspect not, sir. It is upon these declarations of mine, made thus openly, that my country will found that demand for reparation which will one day cost you so dearly. Lead on, I am ready for the block." And as I said this, I untied my cravat, and appeared to prepare for the headsman.

"If he will not cease, the court shall be dissolved," called out the judge.

"Never, sir. Never, so long as I live, shall I surrender the glorious privileges of that freedom by which I assert my birthright as a Briton."

"Well, you are as impudent a chap as ever I listened to," muttered my countryman at my side.

"The prisoners are dismissed, the court is adjourned,"

said the president, rising; and amidst a very disorderly crowd, not certainly enthusiastic in our favour, we were all hurried into the street.

"Come along down here," said Mr. Harpar. "I'm in a very tidy sort of place they call the 'Golden Pig.' Come along, and bring the vagabonds, and let's have breakfast together."

I was hurt at the speech, but as my companions could not understand its coarseness, I accepted the invitation, and we followed him.

"Well, I ain't seen *your* like for many a day," said Harpar, as we went along. "If you'd have said the half of that to one of our 'Beaks,' I think I know where you'd be. But you seem to understand the fellows well. Mayhap you have lived much abroad?"

"A great deal. I am a sort of citizen of the world," said I, with a jaunty easiness.

"For a citizen of the world you appear to have strange tastes in your companionship. How did you come to foregather with these creatures?"

I tried the timeworn cant about seeing life in all its gradations—exploring the cabin as well as visiting the palace, and so on; but there was a rugged sort of incredulity in his manner that checked me, and I could not muster the glib readiness which usually stood by me on such occasions.

"You're not a man of fortune," said he, dryly, as I

finished; "one sees that plainly enough. You're a fellow that should be earning his bread somehow; and the question is—Is this the kind of life you ought to be leading? What humbug it is to talk about knowing the world and suchlike. The thing is, to know a trade, to understand some art, to be able to produce something, to manufacture something, to convert something to a useful purpose. When you've done that, the knowledge of men will come later on, never be afraid of that. It's a school that we never miss one single day of our lives. But here we are; this is the 'Pig.' Now, what will you have for breakfast? Ask the vagabonds, too, and tell them there's a wide choice here; they have everything you can mention in this little inn."

An excellent breakfast was soon spread out before us, and though my humble companions did it the most ample justice, I sat there, thoughtful and almost sad. The words of that stranger rang in my ears like a reproach and a warning. I knew how truly he had said that I was not a man of fortune, and it grieved me sorely to think how easily he saw it. In my heart of hearts, I knew it was the delusion I loved best. To appear to the world at large an eccentric man of good means, free to do what he liked and go where he would, was the highest enjoyment I had ever prepared for myself: and yet here was a coarse, common-place sort of man—at least his manners were unpolished and his tone underbred—and he saw through it all at once.

I took the first opportunity to slip away unobserved from the company, and retired to the little garden of the inn, to commune with myself and be alone. But ere I had been many minutes there, Harpar joined me. He came up smoking his cigar, with the lounging, lazy air of a man at perfect leisure, and, consequently, quite free to be as disagreeable as he pleased.

"You went off without eating your breakfast," said he, bluntly. "I saw how it was. You didn't like *my* freedom with you. You fancied that I ought to have taken all that nonsense of yours about your rank and your way of life for gospel; or, at least, that I ought to have pretended to do so. That ain't my way. I hate humbug."

It was not very easy to reply good humouredly to such a speech as this. Indeed, I saw no particular reason to treat this man's freedom with any indulgence, and drawing myself haughtily up, I prepared a very dry but caustic rejoinder.

"When I have learned two points," said I, "on which you can inform me, I may be better able to answer what you have said. The first is: By what possible right do you take to task a person that you never met in your life till now? and, secondly, What benefit on earth could it be to me to impose upon a man from whom I neither want nor expect anything?"

"Easily met, both," said he, quickly. "I'm a practical sort of fellow, who never wastes time on useless materials; that's for your first proposition. Number two: you're a dreamer, and you hate being awakened."

"Well sir," said I, stiffly, "to a gentleman so remarkable for perspicuity, and who reads character at sight, ordinary intercourse must be wearisome. Will you excuse me if I take my leave of you here?"

"Of course, make no ceremony about it; go or stay, just as you like. I never cross any man's humour."

I muttered something that sounded like a dissent to that doctrine, and he quickly added, "I mean, further than speaking my mind, that's all; nothing more. If you had been a man of fair means, and for a frolic thought it might be good fun to consort for a few days wit rapscallions of a travelling circus, all one could say was, it wasn't very good taste; but being evidently a fellow of another stamp, a young man who ought to be in his father's shop or his uncle's counting-house, following some honest craft or calling—for *you*, I say, it was downright ruin."

"Indeed!" said I, with an accent of intense scorn.

"Yes," continued he, seriously, "downright ruin. There's a poison in the lazy, good-for-nothing life of these devils, that never leaves a man's blood. I've a notion that it wouldn't hurt a man's nature so much were he to consort with housebreakers; there's at least something real about these fellows."

"You talk, doubtless, with knowledge, sir," said I, glad to say something that might offend him.

"I do," said he, seriously, and not taking the smallest account of the impertinent allusion. "I know that if a man hasn't a fixed calling, but is always turning his hand to this, that, and t'other, he will very soon cease to have any character whatsoever; he'll just become as shifty in his nature as in his business. I've seen scores of fellows wrecked on that rock, and I hadn't looked at you twice till I saw you were one of them."

"I must say, sir," said I, summoning to my aid what I felt to be a most cutting sarcasm of manner—"I must say, sir, that, considering how short has been the acquaintance which has subsisted between us, it would be extremely difficult for me to show how gratefully I feel the interest you have taken in me."

"Well, I'm not so sure of that," said he, thoughtfully.

"May I ask, then, how?"

"Are you sure, first of all, that you wish to show this gratitude you speak of?"

"Oh, sir, can you possibly doubt it?"

"I don't want to doubt it, I want to profit by it."

I made a bland bow that might mean anything, but did not speak.

"Here's the way of it," said he, boldly. "Rigges has

run off with all my loose cash, and though there's money
waiting for me at certain places, I shall find it very
difficult to reach them. I have come down here on foot
from Wildbad, and I can make my way, in the same
fashion, to Marseilles or Genoa; but then comes the
difficulty, and I shall need about ten pounds to get to
Malta. Could you lend me ten pounds?"

"Really, sir," said I, coolly, "I am amazed at the
innocence with which you can make such a demand on
the man whom you have, only a few minutes back, so
acutely depicted as an adventurer."

"It was for that very reason I thought of applying to
you. Had you been a young fellow of a certain fortune,
you'd have naturally been a stranger to the accidents
which now and then leave men penniless in out-of-the-
way places, and it is just as likely that the first thought
in your head would be, 'Oh, he's a swindler. Why
hasn't he his letters of credit or his circular notes?'
But, being exactly what I take you for, the chances are
you'll say: 'What has befallen *him* to-day may chance
to *me* to-morrow. Who can tell the day and the hour
some mishap may not overtake him? and so I'll just
help him through it.'"

"And that was your calculation?"

"That was my calculation."

"How sorry I feel to wound the marvellous gift you
seem to possess of interpreting character. I am really

shocked to think that for this time, at least, your acuteness is at fault."

"Which means that you'll not do it."

I smiled a benign assent.

He looked at me for a minute or more with a sort of
blank incredulity, and then, crossing his arms on his
breast, moved slowly down the walk without speaking.

I cannot say how I detested this man; he had offended
me in the very sorest part of all my nature; he had
wounded the nicest susceptibility I possessed; of the
pleasant fancies wherewith I loved to clothe myself he
would not leave me enough to cover my nakedness; and
yet, now that I had resented his cool impertinence, I
hated myself far more than I hated him. Dignity and
sarcasm, forsooth! What a fine opportunity to display
them, truly! The man might be rude and underbred;
he *was* rude and underbred; and was that any justifica-
tion for *my* conduct towards him? Why had I not had
the candour to say, "Here's all I possess in the world;
you see yourself that I cannot lend you ten pounds."
How I wished I had said that, and how I wished, even
more ardently still, that I had never met him, never
interchanged speech with him!

"And why is it that I am offended with him—simply
because he has discovered that I am Potts?" Now,
these reflections were all the more bitter, since it was
only twenty-four hours before that I had resolved to

throw off delusion either of myself or others; that I
would take my place in the ranks, and fight out my
battle of life, a mere soldier. For this it was that I
made companionship with Vaterchen, walking the high
road with that poor old man of motley, and actually
speculating—in a sort of artistic way—whether I should
not make love to Tintefleck! And if I were sincere in
all this, how should I feel wounded by the honest candour
of that plain-spoken fellow?   He wanted a favour at my
hands, he owned this; and yet, instead of approaching
me with flattery, he at once assails the very stronghold
of my self-esteem, and says, "No humbug, Potts; at
least, none with *me!*" He opens acquaintance with me
on that masonic principle by which the brotherhood of
Poverty is maintained throughout all lands and all
peoples, and whose great maxim is, "He who lends to
the poor man, borrows from the ragged man."

"I'll go after him at once," said I, aloud. "I'll have
more talk with him. I'm much mistaken if there's not
good stuff in that rugged nature."

When I entered the little inn, I found Vaterchen fast
asleep; he had finished off every flask on the table, and
lay breathing stentoriously, and giving a long-drawn
whistle in his snore, that smacked almost of apoplexy.
Tintefleck was singing to her guitar before a select
audience of the inn servants, and Harpar was gone!

I gave the girl a glance of rebuke and displeasure. I

aroused the old man with a kick, and imperiously demanded my bill.

"The bill has been paid by the other stranger," said the landlord; "he has settled everything, and left a 'trenkgeld' for the servants, so that you have nothing to pay."

I could have almost cried with spite as I heard these words. It would have been a rare solace to my feelings if I could have put that man down for a rogue, and then been able to say to myself how cleverly I had escaped the snares of a swindler. But to know now that he was not only honest but liberal, and to think, besides, that I had been his guest—eaten of his salt—it was more than I well could endure.

"Which way did he take?" asked I.

"Round the head of the lake for Lindau. I told him that the steamer would take him there to-morrow for a trifle, but he would not wait."

"Ah me!" sighed Vaterchen, but half awake, and with one eye still closed, "and we are going to St. Gallen."

"Who said so?" cried I, imperiously. "We are going to Lindau; at least if I be the person who gives orders here. Follow!" And as I spoke, I marched proudly on, while a slipshod, shuffling noise of feet, and a low, half-smothered sob, told me that they were coming after me.

CHAPTER XI.

MY poor companions had but a sorry time of it on that
morning. I was in a fearful temper, and made no effort
to control it. The little romance of my meeting with
these creatures was beginning to scale off, and, there
beneath, lay the vulgar metal of the natures exposed to
view. As for old Vaterchen, shuffling along in his tat-
tered shoes, half-stupid with wine and shame together, I
couldn't bear to look at him; while Tintefleck, although
at the outset abashed by my rebukeful tone and cold
manner, had now rallied, and seemed well disposed to
assert her own against all comers. Yes, there was a palpable air of defiance about her, even to the way that she
sang as she went along; every thrill and cadence seemed
to say, "I'm doing this to amuse myself; never imagine
that I care whether you are pleased or not." Indeed, she
left me no means of avoiding this conclusion, since at
every time that I turned on her a look of anger or displeasure, her reply was to sing the louder.

"And it was only yesterday," thought I, "and I dreamed

that I could be in love with this creature—dreamed that
I could replace Kate Herbert's image in my heart with
that coarse travestie of woman's gentleness. Why, I
might as well hope to make a gentleman of old Vaterchen,
and present him to the world as a man of station and
eminence."

What an insane hope was this! As well might I
shiver a fragment from a stone on the road-side, and
think to give it value by having it set as a ring. The
caprice of keeping them company for a day might be
pardonable. It was the whim of one who is, above all,
a student of mankind. But why continue the companionship? A little more of such intimacy, and who is to say
what I may not imbibe of their habits and their natures;
and Potts, the man of sentiment, the child of impulse,
romance, and poetry, become a slave of the "Ring"—a
saltimbanque! Now, though I could implicitly rely upon
the rigidity of my joints to prevent the possibility of my
ever displaying any feats of agility, I could yet picture
myself in a long-tailed blue coat and jack-boots walking
round and round in the sawdust circle, with four or five
other creatures of the same sort, and who have no consciousness of any function till they are made the butt of
some extempore drollery by the clown.

The creative temperament has this great disadvantage, that one cannot always build castles, but must occasionally construct hovels, and sometimes even dungeons

and gaols; and here was I now, with a large contract order for this species of edifice, and certainly I set to work with a will. The impatience of my mind communicated itself to my gait, and I walked along at a tremendous rate.

"I can scarcely keep up with you at this pace," said Tintefleck; "and see, we have left poor Vaterchen a long way behind."

I made some rude answer—I know not what—and told her to come on.

"I will not leave him," said she, coming to a halt, and standing in a composed and firm attitude before me.

"Then I will!" said I, angrily. "Farewell!" And waving my hand in a careless adieu, I walked briskly onward, not even turning a look on her as I went. I think I'm almost certain I heard a heavy sob close behind me, but I would not look round for worlds. I was in one of those moods—all weak men know them well—when a harsh or an ungracious act appears something very daring and courageous. The very pain my conduct gave myself, persuaded me that it must be heroic, just as a devotee is satisfied after a severe self-castigation.

. "Yes, Potts," said I, "you are doing the right thing here. A little more of such association as this, and you would be little better than themselves. Besides, and above all, you ought to be 'real.' Now, these are not real any more than the tinsel gems and tinfoil splendours they wear on their tunics." It broke on me, too, like a sudden light, that to be the fictitious Potts, the many-sided, many-tinted—what a German would call "der mit-viele-farben bedeckte Potts"—I ought to be immensely rich, all my changes of character requiring great resources and unlimited "properties," as stage folk call them; whereas, "der echte wahrhaftige mann Potts" might be as poor as Lazarus. Indeed, the poorer the more real, since more natural.

While I thus speculated, I caught sight of a man scaling one of the precipitous paths by which the winding road was shortened for foot-travellers; a second glance showed me that this was Harpar, who, with a heavy knapsack, was toiling along. I made a great effort to come up with him, but when I reached the high road, he was still a long distance in front of me. I could not, if there had been any one to question me, say why I wished to overtake him. It was a sort of chase suggested simply by the object in front; a rare type, if we but knew it, of one half the pursuits we follow throughout life.

As I mounted the last of these by-paths which led to the crest of the mountain, I felt certain that, with a lighter equipment, I should come up with him; but scarcely had I gained the top, than I saw him striding away vigorously on the road fully a mile away beneath me. "He shall not beat me," said I; and I increased

my speed. It was all in vain. I could not do it; and
when I drew nigh Lindau at last, very weary and foot-
sore, the sun was just sinking on the western shore of
the lake.

"Which is the best inn here?" asked I of a shop-
keeper who was lounging carelessly at his door.

"Yonder," said he, "where you see that post-carriage
turning into."

"To-night," said I, "I will be guilty of an extrava-
gance. I will treat myself to a good supper, and an
honest glass of wine." And on these hospitable thoughts
intent I unslung my knapsack, and, throwing as much
of distinction as I could into my manner, strolled into
the public room.

So busied was the household in attending to the
travellers who arrived "extra post," that none condescended to notice me, till at last, as the tumult sub-
sided, a venerable old waiter approached me, and said, in
a half friendly, half rebukeful tone, "It is at the 'Swan'
you ought to be, my friend; the next turning but two to
the left hand, and you'll see the blue lantern over the
gateway."

"I mean to remain where I am," said I, imperiously,
"and to remember your impertinence when I am about
to pay my bill. Bring me the *carte*."

I was overjoyed to see the confusion and shame of the
old fellow. He saw at once the grievous error he had

committed, and was so overwhelmed, that he could not reply. Meanwhile, with all the painstaking accuracy of a practised gourmand, I was making a careful note of what I wished for supper.

"Are you not ashamed," said I, rebukefully, "to have *ortolans* here, when you know in your heart they are swallows?"

He was so abject that he could only give a melancholy smile, as though to say, "Be merciful, and spare us!"

"Bohemian pheasant, too—come, come, this is too bad! Be frank and confess; how often has that one speckled tail done duty on a capon of your own raising?"

"Gracious Herr!" muttered he, "do not crush us altogether."

I don't think that he said this in actual words, but his terrified eyes and his shaking cheeks declared it.

"Never mind," said I, encouragingly, "it will not hurt us to make a sparing meal occasionally; with the venison steak, the fried salmon, the duck with olives, and the apricot tart, we will satisfy appetite, and persuade ourselves, if we can, that we have fared luxuriously."

"And the wine, sir?" asked he.

"Ah, there we *are* difficult. No little Baden vintage, no small wine of the Bergstrasse, can impose upon us! Liebfrauen-milch, or, if you can guarantee it, Marco-brunner will do; but, mind, no substitutes!"

He laid his hand over his heart and bowed low; and,

as he moved away, I said to myself, "What a mesmerism
there must be in real money, since, even with the mockery
of it, I have made that creature a bond slave." Brief
as was the interval in preparing my meal, it was enough
to allow me a very considerable share of reflection, and
I found that, do what I would, a certain voice within
would whisper, "Where are your fine resolutions now,
Potts? Is this the life of reality that you had promised
yourself? Are you not at the old work again? Are
you not masquerading it once more? Don't you know
well enough that all this pretension of yours is bad
money, and that the first ring of it on the counter you
will be found out?"

"This you may rely on, gracious sir," said the waiter,
as he laid a bottle on the table beside me with a careful
hand. "It is the orange seal;" and he then added, in
a whisper, "taken from the Margrave's cellar in the
revolution of '93, and every flask of it worth a province."

"We shall see—we shall see," said I, haughtily;
"serve the soup!"

If I had been Belshazzar, I believe I should have
eaten very heartily, and drunk my wine with a great
relish, notwithstanding that drawn sword. I don't know
how it is, but if I can only see the smallest bit of *terra
firma* between myself and the edge of a precipice, I feel
as though I had a whole vast prairie to range over.
For the life of me I cannot realise anything that may,

or may not, befal me remotely. "Blue are the hills far off," says the adage; and on the converse of the maxim do I aver, that faint are all dangers that are distant. An immediate peril overwhelms me; but I could look forward to a shipwreck this day fortnight with a fortitude truly heroic.

"This is a nice old half-forgotten sort of place," thought I, "a kind of vulgar Venice, water-washed, and muddy, and dreary, and do-nothing. I'll stay here for a week or so; I'll give myself up to the drowsy 'genius loci;' I'll Germanise to the top of my bent; who is to say what metaphysical melancholy, dashed with a strange diabolic humour, may not come of constantly feeding on this heavy cookery, and eternally listening to their gurgling gutturals? I may come out a Wieland or a Herder, with a sprinkling of Henri Heine! Yes," said I, "this is the true way to approach life; first of all, develop your own faculties, and then mark how in their exercise you influence your fellow-men. Above all, however, cultivate your individuality, respect this the greatest of all the unities."

"Ja, gnädiger Herr," said the old waiter, as he tried to step away from my grasp, for, without knowing it, I had laid hold of him by the wrist while I addressed to him this speech. Desirous to re-establish my character for sanity, somewhat compromised by this incident, I said:

"Have you a money-changer in these parts? If so, let me have some silver for this English gold." I put my hand in my pocket for my purse; not finding it, I tried another and another. I ransacked them all over again, patted myself, shook my coat, looked into my hat, and then, with a sudden flash of memory, I bethought me that I had left it with Catinka, and was actually without one sou in the world! I sat down, pale and almost fainting, and my arms fell powerless at my sides.

"I have lost my purse!" gasped I out, at length.

"Indeed!" said the old man, but with a tone of such palpable scorn that it actually sickened me.

"Ye," said I, with all that force which is the peculiar prerogative of truth; "and in it all the money I possessed."

"I have no doubt of it," rejoined he, in the same dry tone as before.

"You have no doubt of what, old man? Or what do you mean by the supercilious quietness with which you assent to my misfortune? Send the landlord to me."

"I will do more; I will send the police," said he, as he shuffled out of the room.

I have met scores of men on my way through life who would not have felt the slightest embarrassment in such a situation as mine, fellows so accustomed to shipwreck, that the cry of " Breakers ahead!" or "Man the boats!" would have occasioned neither excitement nor trepidation.

What stuff they are made of instead of nerves, muscles, and arteries, I cannot imagine, since, when the question is self-preservation, how can it possibly be more imminent than when not alone your animal existence is jeopardised, but the dearer and more precious life of fame and character is in peril?

For a moment I thought that though this besotted old fool of a waiter might suspect my probity, the more clear-sighted intelligence of the landlord would at once recognise my honest nature, and with the confidence of a noble conviction say, "Don't tell me that the man yonder is a knave. I read him very differently. Tell me your story, sir." And then I would tell it. It is not improbable that my speculation might have been verified had it not been that it was a landlady and not a landlord who swayed the destinies of the inn. Oh, what a wise invention of our ancestors was the Salique law! How justly they appreciated the unbridled rashness of the female nature in command! How well they understood the one-idea'd impetuosity with which they rush to wrong conclusions!

Until I listened to the Frau von Wintner, I imagined the German language somewhat weak in the matter of epithets. She undeceived me on this head, showing resources of abusive import that would have done credit to a Homeric hero. Having given me full ten minutes of a strong vocabulary, she then turned on the waiter,

scornfully asking him if, at his time of life, he ought to
have let himself be imposed upon by so palpable and
undeniable a swindler as myself? She clearly showed
that there was no extenuation of his fault, that rogue
and vagabond had been written on my face, and inscribed
in my manner; not to mention that I had followed the
well-beaten track of all my fraternity in fraud, and
ordered everything the most costly the house could command. In fact, so strenuously did she urge this point,
and so eager did she seem about enforcing a belief in her
statement, that I almost began to suspect she might
suggest an anatomical examination of me to sustain her
case. Had she been even less eloquent, the audience
would still have been with her, for it is a curious but
unquestionable fact that in all little visited localities the
stranger is ungraciously regarded and ill looked on.

Whenever I attempted to interpose a word in my
defence, I was overborne at once. Indeed, public opinion
was so decidedly against me, that I felt very happy in
thinking Lynch law was not a Teutonic institution. The
room was now filled with retainers of the inn, strangers,
town-folk, and police, and, to judge by the violence of
their gestures and the loud tones of their voices, one
would have pronounced me a criminal of the worst sort.

"But what is it that he has done? What's his
offence?" I heard a voice say from the crowd, and I
fancied his accent was that of a foreigner. A perfect

inundation of vituperative accusation, however, now poured in, and I could gather no more. The turmoil and uproar rose and fell, and fell and rose again, till at last, my patience utterly exhausted, I burst out into a very violent attack on the uncivilized habits of a people who could thus conduct themselves to a man totally unconvicted of any offence.

"Well, well, don't give way to passion; don't let temper get the better of you," said a fat, citizen-like man beside me. "The stranger there has just paid for what you have had, and all is settled."

I thought I should have fainted as I heard these words. Indeed, until that instant, I had never brought home to my own mind the utter destitution of my state; but now, there I stood, realizing to myself the condition of one of those we read of in our newspapers as having received five shillings from the poor-box, while D 490 is deputed to "make inquiries after him at his lodgings," and learn particulars of his life and habits. I could have borne being sent to prison. I could have endured any amount of severity, so long as I revolted against its injustice; but the sense of being an object of actual charity crushed me utterly, and I could nearly have cried with vexation.

By degrees the crowd thinned off, and I found myself sitting alone beside the table where I had dined, with the hateful old waiter, as though standing sentinel over me.

"Who is this person," asked I, haughtily, "who, with an indelicate generosity, has presumed to interfere with the concerns of a stranger?"

"The gracious nobleman who paid for your dinner is now eating his own at No. 8," said the old monster, with a grin.

"I will call upon him when he has dined," said I, transfixing the wretch with a look so stern, as to make rejoinder impossible; and then, throwing my plaid wrapper and my knapsack on a table near, I strolled out into the street.

Lindau is a picturesque old place, as it stands rising, as it were, out of the very waters of the Lake of Constance, and the great mountain of the Sentis, with its peak of six thousand feet high, is a fine object in the distance; while the gorge of the Upper Rhine offers many a grand effect of Alpine scenery, not the less striking when looked at with a setting sun, which made the foreground more massive and the hill-tops golden; and yet I carried that in my heart which made the whole picture as dark and dreary as Poussin's Deluge. It was all very beautiful. There, was the snow-white summit, reflected in the still water of the lake; there, the rich wood, browned with autumn, and now tinted with a golden glory, richer again; there, were the white-sailed boats, asleep on the calm surface, streaked with the variegated light of the clouds above, and it was peaceful as it was picturesque. But do what I could, I could not enjoy it, and all because I had lost my purse, just as if certain fragments of a yellow metal the more or the less, ought to obscure eyesight, lull the sense of hearing, and make a man's whole existence miserable. "And after all," thought I, "Catinka will be here this evening, or to-morrow at furthest. Vaterchen was tired, and could not come on. It was *I* who left *them;* I, in my impatience and ill humour. The old man doubtless knew nothing of the purse confided to the girl, nor is it at all needful that he should. They will certainly follow me, and why, for the mere inconvenience of an hour or two, should I persist in seeing the whole world so crape-covered and sad-looking? Surely this is not the philosophy my knowledge of life has taught me. I ought to know and feel that these daily accidents are but stones on the road one travels. They may, perchance, wound the foot or damage the shoe, but they rarely delay the journey, if the traveller be not faint-hearted and craven. I will treat the whole incident in a higher spirit. I will wait for their coming in that tranquil and assured condition of mind which is the ripe fruit of a real insight into mankind. Pitt said, after long years of experience, that there was more of good than of bad in human nature. Let it be the remark of some future biographer that Potts agreed with him."

When I got back to the inn, I was somewhat puzzled

what to do. It would have been impossible with any success to have resumed my former tone of command, and for the life of me I could not bring myself down to anything like entreaty. While I thus stood, uncertain how to act, the old waiter approached me, almost courteously, and said my room was ready for me when I wished it.

"I will first of all wait upon the traveller in No 8," said I.

"He has retired for the night," was the answer. "He seems in very delicate health, and the fatigue of the journey has overcome him."

"To-morrow will do, then," said I, easily; and not venturing upon any inquiry as to the means by which my room was at my disposal, I took my candle and mounted the stairs.

As I lay down in my bed, I resolved I would take a calm survey of my past life: what I had done, what I had failed to do, what were the guiding principles which directed me, and whither they were like to bear me. But scarcely had I administered to myself the pre-liminary oath to tell nothing but the truth, than I fell off sound asleep.

My first waking thought the next morning was to inquire if two persons had arrived in search of me—an elderly man and a young woman. I described them. None such had been seen. "They will have sought

shelter in some of the humbler inns," thought I; "I'll
up and look after them." I searched the town from end
to end; I visited the meanest halting-places of the wayfarer; I inquired at the police bureaus—at the gate—
but none had arrived who bore any resemblance to those
I asked after. I was vexed—only vexed at first—but
gradually I found myself growing distrustful. The
suspicion that the ice is not strong enough for your
weight, and then, close upon that, the shock of fear that
strikes you when the loud crash of a fracture breaks on
the ear, are mere symbols of what one suffers at the first
glimmering of a betrayal. I repelled the thought with
indignation; but certain thoughts there are which, when
turned out, stand like sturdy duns at the gate, and will
not be sent away. This was one of them. It followed
me wherever I went, importunately begging for a
hearing, and menacing me with sad consequences if I
were obdurate enough not to listen. "You are a
simpleton, Potts, a weak, foolish, erring creature! and
you select as the objects of your confidence those whose
lives of accident present exactly as the most irresistible
of all temptations to them—the Dupe! How they must
have laughed—how they must yet be laughing at you!
How that old drunken fox will chuckle over your simplicity, and the minx Tintefleck indulge herself in
caricatures of your figure and face! I wonder how much
of truth there was in that old fellow's story? Was he

ever the syndic of his village, or was the whole narrative
a mere fiction like—like ——" I covered my face with
my hands in shame as I muttered out, "like one of your
own, Potts ? "

I was very miserable, for I could no longer stand
proudly forward as the prosecutor, but was obliged to
steal ignominiously into the dock and take my place beside the other prisoners.   What became of all my honest
indignation as I bethought me, that I of all men could
never arraign the counterfeit and the sham ?

"Let them go, then," cried I, "and prosper if they can;
I will never pursue them.   I will even try and remember
what pleased and interested me in their fortunes, and, if
it may be, forget that they have carried away my little
all of wealth."

A loud tramping of post-horses, and the cracking of
whips, drew me to the window, and I saw beneath in the
court-yard, a handsome travelling britschka getting ready
for the road.   Oh how suggestive is a well-cushioned
calèche, with its many appliances of ease and luxury, its
trim imperials, its scattered litter of wrappers and guide-
books—all little episodes of those who are to journey in it!

"Who are the happy souls about to travel thus enjoy-
ably?" thought I, as I saw the waiter and the courier
discussing the most convenient spot to deposit a small
hamper with eatables for the road; and then I heard the
landlady's voice call out:

"Take up the bill to No. 8."

So, then, this was No. 8 who was fast getting ready to depart—No. 8 who had interposed in, my favour the evening before, and towards whom a night's rest and some reflection had modified my feelings and changed my sentiments very remarkably.

" Will you ask the gentleman at No. 8 if I may be permitted to speak with him ?" said I to the man who took in the bill.

" He'll scarcely see you now—he's just going off."

"Give the message as I speak it," said I; and he disappeared.

There was a long interval before he issued forth again, and when he did so he was flurried and excited. Some overcharges had to be taken off and some bad money in change to be replaced by honest coin, and it was evident that various little well-intended rogueries had not achieved their usual success.

"Go in, you'll find him there," said the waiter, insolently, as he went down to have the bill rectified.

I knocked, a full round voice cried "Come in !" and I entered.

CHAPTER XII.

"WELL, what next? have you bethought you of anything more to charge me with?" cried a large full man, whose angry look and manner showed how he resented these cheatings.

I staggered back sick and faint, for the individual before me was Crofton, my kind host of long ago in Ireland, and from whose hospitable roof I had taken such an unceremonious departure.

"Who are you?" cried he, again. "I had hoped to have paid everything and everybody. Who are you?"

Wishing to retire unrecognised, I stammered out something very unintelligibly indeed about my gratitude, and my hope for a pleasant journey to him, retreating all the while towards the door.

"It's all very well to wish the traveller a pleasant journey," said he, "but you innkeepers ought to bear in mind that no man's journey is rendered more agreeable by roguery. This house is somewhat dearer than the 'Clarendon' in London, or the 'Hôtel du Rhin' at Paris.

Now, there might be perhaps some pretext to make a man pay smartly who travels post, and has two or three servants with him, but what excuse can you make for charging some poor devil of a foot traveller, taking his humble meal in the common room, and, naturally enough, of the commonest fare, for making him pay eight florins —eight florins and some kreutzers—for his dinner? Why, our dinner here for two people was handsomely paid at six florins ahead, and yet you bring in a bill of eight florins against that poor wretch."

I saw now, that, what between the blinding effects of his indignation, and certain changes which time and the road had worked in my appearance, it was more than probable I should escape undetected, and so I affected to busy myself with some articles of his luggage that lay scattered about the room until I could manage to slip away.

"Touch nothing, my good fellow!" cried he, angrily; "send my own people here for these things. Let my courier come here—or my valet!"

This was too good an opportunity to be thrown away, and I made at once for the door, but at the same instant it was opened, and Mary Crofton stood before me. One glance showed me that I was discovered, and there I stood, speechless with shame and confusion. Rallying, however, after a moment, I whispered, "Don't betray me," and tried to pass out. Instead of minding my

entreaty, she set her back to the door, and laughingly
cried out to her brother :

"Don't you know whom we have got here ?"

"What do you mean ?" exclaimed he.

"Cannot you recognise an old friend, notwithstanding
all his efforts to cut us ?"

"Why—what—surely it can't be—it's not possible—
eh ?" And by this time he had wheeled me round to the
strong light of the window, and then, with a loud burst,
he cried out, " Potts, by all that's ragged ! Potts himself !
Why, old fellow, what could you mean by wanting to
escape us ?" and he wrung my hand with a cordial shake
that at once brought the blood back to my heart, while
his sister completed my happiness by saying :

"If you only knew all the schemes we have planned to
catch you, you would certainly not have tried to avoid us."

I made an effort to say something—anything, in short
—but not a word would come. If I was overjoyed at the
warmth of their greeting, I was no less overwhelmed
with shame; and there I stood, looking very pitiably
from one to the other, and almost wishing that I might
faint outright, and so finish my misery.

With a woman's fine tact, Mary Crofton seemed to read
the meaning of my suffering, and, whispering one word
in her brother's ear, she slipped away and left us alone
together.

"Come," said he good naturedly, as he drew his arm

inside of mine, and led me up and down the room, "tell
me all about it. How have you come here? What are
you doing?"

I have not the faintest recollection of what I said.
I know that I endeavoured to take up my story from the
day I had last seen him, but it must have proved a very
strange and bungling narrative, from the questions which
he was forced occasionally to put, in order to follow me
out.

"Well," said he, at last, "I will own to you that, after
your abrupt departure, I was sorely puzzled what to make
of you, and I might have remained longer in the same
state of doubt, when a chance visit that I made to Dublin
led me to Dycer's, and there, by a mere accident, I heard
of you—heard who you were, and where your father lived.
I went at once and called upon him, my object being to
learn if he had any tidings of you, and where you then
were. I found him no better informed than myself. He
showed me a few lines you had written on the morning
you left home, stating that you would probably be absent
some days, and might be even weeks, but that since that
date nothing had been heard of you. He seemed vexed
and displeased, but not uneasy or apprehensive about
your absence, and the same tone I observed in your
college tutor, Doctor Tobin. He said: 'Potts will come
back, sir, one of these days, and not a whit wiser than he
went. His self-esteem is to his capacity, in the redupli-

cate ratio of the inverse proportion of his ability, and he will be always a fool.' I wrote to various friends of ours travelling about the world, but none had met with you; and at last, when about to come abroad myself, I called again on your father, and found him just re-married."

" Re-married ! "

"Yes! he was lonely, he said, and wanted companion-ship, and so on; and all I could obtain from him was a note for a hundred pounds, and a promise that, if you came back within the year, you should share the business of his shop with him."

" Never! never!" said I. "Potts may be the fool they deem him, but there are instincts and promptings in his secret heart that they know nothing of. I will never go back. Go on."

"I now come to my own story. I left Ireland a day or two after and came to England, where business detained me some weeks. My uncle had died and left me his heir—not, indeed, so rich as I had expected, but very well off for a man who had passed his life on very moderate means. There were a few legacies to be paid, and one which he especially entrusted to me by a secret paper, in the hope that, by delicate and judicious manage-ment, I might be able to persuade the person in whose interest it was bequeathed to accept. It was, indeed, a task of no common difficulty, the legatee being the widow of a man who had, by my uncle's cruelty, been driven to destroy himself. It is a long story, which I cannot now enter upon; enough that I say it had been a trial of strength between two very vindictive unyielding men which should crush the other, and my uncle being the richer—and not from any other reason—conquered.

"The victory was a very barren one. It embittered every hour of his life after, and the only reparation in his power, he attempted on his death-bed, which was to settle an annuity on the family of the man he had ruined. I found out at once where they lived, and set about effecting this delicate charge. I will not linger over my failure—but it was complete. The family was in actual distress, but nothing would induce them to listen to the project of assistance; and, in fact, their indignation compelled me to retire from the attempt in despair. My sister did her utmost in the cause, but equally in vain, and we prepared to leave the place, much depressed and cast down by our failure. It was on the last evening of our stay at the inn of the little village, a townsman of the place, whom I had employed to aid my attempt by his personal influence with the family, asked to see me and speak with me in private.

"He appeared to labour under considerable agitation, and opened our interview by bespeaking my secrecy as to what he was about to communicate. It was to this purport: A friend of his own, engaged in the Baltic

trade, had just declared to him that he had seen W., the
person I allude to, alive and well, walking on the quay
at Riga, that he traced him to his lodging, but, on inquiring for him the next day, he was not to be found,
and it was then ascertained that he had left the city.
W. was, it would seem, a man easily recognised, and the
other declared that there could not be the slightest doubt
of his identity. The question was a grave one how to
act, since the assurance company with which his life was
insured were actually engaged in discussing the propriety
of some compromise by paying to the family a moiety of
the policy, and a variety of points arose out of this con-
tingency; for while it would have been a great cruelty
to have conveyed hopes to the family that might, by
possibility, not be realised, yet, on the other hand, to
have induced them to adopt a course on the hypothesis
of his death when they believed him still living, was
almost as bad.

"I thought for a long while over the matter, and with
my sister's counsel to aid me, I determined that we
should come abroad and seek out this man, trusting that,
if we found him, we could induce him to accept of the
legacy which his family rejected. We obtained every
clue we could think of to his detection. A perfect
description of him, in voice, look, and manner; a copy
of his portrait, and a specimen of his handwriting; and
then we bethought ourselves of interesting you in the

search. You were rambling about the world in that
idle and desultory way in which any sort of a pursuit
might be a boon—as often in the by-paths as on the
high roads—you might chance to hit off this discovery
in some remote spot, or, at all events, find some clue to
it. In a word, we grew to believe, that, with you to aid
us, we should get to the bottom of this mystery; and
now that by a lucky chance we have met you, our hopes
are all the stronger."

"You'll think it strange," said I, "but I already know
something of this story; the man you allude to was Sir
Samuel Whalley."

"How on earth have you guessed that?"

"I came by the knowledge on a railroad journey,
where my fellow-passengers talked over the event, and I
subsequently travelled with Sir Samuel's daughter, who
came abroad to fill the station of a companion to an
elderly lady. She called herself Miss Herbert."

"Exactly! The widow resumed her family name after
W.'s suicide—if it were a suicide."

"How singular to think that you should have chanced
upon this link of the chain. And do you know her?"

"Intimately; we were fellow-travellers for some days."

"And where is she now?"

"She is, at this moment, at a villa on the Lake of
Como, living with a Mrs. Keats, the sister of her
Majesty's Envoy at Kalbbratenstadt."

"You are marvellously accurate in this narrative, Potts," said he, laughing; "the impression made on you by this young lady can scarcely have been a transcient one."

I suppose I grew very red—I felt that I was much confused by this remark—and I turned away to conceal my emotion. Crofton was too delicate to take any advantage of my distress, and merely added:

"From having known her, you will naturally devote yourself with more ardour to serve her. May we then count upon your assistance in our project?"

"That you may," said I. "From this hour, I devote myself to it."

Crofton at once proposed that I should order my luggage to be placed on his carriage, and start off with them; but I firmly opposed this plan. First of all, I had no luggage, and had no fancy to confess as much; secondly, I resolved to give at least one day for Vaterchen's arrival—I'd have given a month rather than come down to the dreary thought of his being a knave, and Tintefleck a cheat! In fact, I felt that if I were to begin any new project in life with so slack an experience, that every step I took would be marked with distrust, and tarnished with suspicion. I therefore pretended to Crofton that I had given rendezvous to a ' friend at Lindau, and could not leave without waiting for him. I am not very sure that he believed me, but he was most careful in not dropping a word that might show incredulity; and once more we addressed ourselves to the grand project before us.

"Come in, Mary!" cried he, suddenly rising from his chair, and going to meet her. "Come in, and help us by your good counsel."

It was not possible to receive me with more kindness than she showed. Had I been some old friend who came to meet them there by appointment, her manner could not have been more courteous nor more easy; and when she learned from her brother how warmly I had associated myself in this plan, she gave me one of her pleasantest smiles, and said:

"I was not mistaken in you."

With a great map of Europe before us on the table, we proceeded to plan a future line of operations. We agreed to take certain places, each of us, and to meet at certain others, to compare notes and report progress. We scarcely permitted ourselves to feel any great confidence of success, but we all concurred in the notion that some lucky hazard might do for us more than all our best-devised schemes could accomplish; and, at last, it was settled that, while *they* took Southern Germany and the Tyrol, *I* should ramble about through Savoy and Upper Italy, and our meeting-place be in Italy. The great railway centres, where Englishmen of every class and gradation were much employed, offered the best prospect of meeting with the object of our search, and these were precisely the sort of places such a man would be certain to resort to.

Our discussion lasted so long, that the Croftons put off their journey till the following day, and we dined all together very happily, never wearied of talking over the plan before us, and each speculating as to what share of acuteness he could contribute to the common stock of investigation. It was when Crofton left the room to search for the portrait of Whalley, that Mary sat down at my side, and said:

" I have been thinking for some time over a project in which you can aid me greatly. My brother tells me that you are known to Miss Herbert. Now, I want to write to her; I want to tell her that there is one who, belonging to a family from which hers has suffered heavily, desires to expiate so far, maybe, the great wrong, and, if she will permit it, to be her friend. While I can in a letter explain what I feel on this score, I am well aware how much aid it would afford me to have the personal corroboration of one who could say, ' She who writes this is not altogether unworthy of your affection; do not reject the offer she makes you, or, at least, reflect and think over it before you refuse it.' Will you help me so far ?"

My heart bounded with delight as I first listened to her plan; it was only a moment before, that I remembered how difficult, if not impossible, it would be for me to approach Miss Herbert once more. How or in what character could I seek her? To appear before her in any feigned part would be, under the circumstances, ignoble and unworthy, and yet, was I, out of any merely personal consideration, any regard for the poor creature Potts, to forego the interests, mayhap the whole happiness, of one so immeasurably better and worthier? Would not any amount of shame and exposure to myself be a cheap price for even a small quantity of benefit bestowed on *her?* What signified it that I was poor and ragged—unknown, unrecognised—if *she* were to be the gainer? Would not, in fact, the very sacrifice of self in the affair be ennobling and elevating to me, and would I not stand better in my own esteem for this one honest act, than I had ever done after any mock success or imaginary victory?

"I think I can guess why you hesitate," cried she; "you fear that I will say something indiscreet—something that would compromise you with Miss Herbert—but you need not dread that; and, at all events, you shall read my letter."

"Far from it," said I; "my hesitation had a very different source. I was solely thinking whether, if you were aware of how I stood in my relations to Miss Herbert, you would have selected me as your advocate; and though it may pain me to make a full confession, you shall hear everything."

With this I told her all—all, from my first hour of

meeting her at the railway station, to my last parting
with her at Schaffhausen. I tried to make my narrative
as grave and common-place as might be, but, do what I
would, the figure in which I was forced to present myself
overcame all her attempts at seriousness, and she laughed
immoderately. If it had not been for this burst of merri-
ment on her part, it is more than probable I might have
brought down my history to the very moment of telling,
and narrated every detail of my journey with Vaterchen
and Tintefleck. I was, however, warned by these circumstances, and concluded in time to save myself from
this new ridicule.

"From all that you have told me here," said she, "I
only see one thing—which is, that you are deeply in love
with this young lady."

"No," said I; "I was so once—I am not so any
longer. My passion has fallen into the chronic stage,
and I feel myself her friend—only her friend.

"Well, for the purpose I have in mind, this is all the
better. I want you, as I said, to place my letter in her
hands, and, so far as possible, enforce its arguments—
that is, try and persuade her that to reject our offers on
her behalf, is to throw upon us a share of the great
wrong our uncle worked, and make us, as it were, parti-
cipators in the evil he did them. As for myself," said
she, boldly, "all the happiness that I might have derived
from ample means is dashed with remembering what

misery it has been attended with to that poor family. If
you urge that one theme forcibly, you can scarcely fail
with her."

"And what are your intentions with regard to her?"
asked I.

"They will take any shape she pleases. My brother
would either enable her to return home, and, by per-
suading her mother to accept an annuity, live happily
under her own roof; or she might—if the spirit of independence fires her—she might yet use her influence over
her mother and sister to regard our proposals more
favourably; or she might come and live with us, and
this I would prefer to all; but you must read my letter,
and more than once, too You must possess yourself of
all its details, and, if there be anything to which you
object, there will be time enough still to change
it."

"Here he is—here is the portrait of our lost sheep,"
said Crofton, now entering with a miniature in his hand.
It represented a bluff, bold, almost insolently bold man
in full civic robes, the face not improbably catching an
additional expression of vulgar pride from the fact that
the likeness was taken in that culminating hour of greatness when he first took the chair as chief magistrate of
his town.

"Not an over-pleasant sort of fellow to deal with, I
should say," remarked Crofton. "There are some stern

lines here about the corners of the eyes, and certain very suspicious-looking indentations next the mouth."

"His eye has no forgiveness in it," said his sister.

"Well, one thing is clear enough, he ought to be easily recognized; that broad forehead, and those widespread nostrils and deeply divided chin, are very striking marks to guide one. I cannot give you this," said Crofton to me, "but I'll take care to send you an accurate copy of it at the first favourable moment; meanwhile, make yourself master of its details, and try if you cannot carry the resemblance in your memory."

"Disabuse yourself, too," said she laughing, "of all this accessorial grandeur, and bear in mind that you'll not find him dressed in ermine, or surrounded with a collar and badge. Not very like his daughter, I'm sure," whispered she in my ear, as I continued to gaze steadfastly at the portrait. "Can you trace any likeness?"

"Not the very faintest; she is beautiful, said I, "and her whole expression is gentleness and delicacy."

"Well, certainly," said Crofton, shutting up the miniature, "these are not the distinguishing traits of our friend here, whom I should call a hard-natured, stern, obstinate fellow, with great self-reliance, and no great trust of others."

"I was just thinking," said I, "that were I to come up with such a man as this, what chance would my poor, frail, yielding temperament have, in influencing the rugged granite of his nature? He'd terrify me at once."

"Not when your object was a good and generous one," said Miss Crofton. "You might well enough be afraid to confront such a man as this if your aim was to over-reach and deceive him; but bear in mind the fable of the man who had the courage to take the thorn out of the lion's paw. The operation, we are told, was a painful one, and there might have been an instant in which the patient felt disposed to eat his doctor; but, with all these perils, strong in a good purpose, the surgeon persevered, and by his skill and his courage made the king of the beasts his fast friend for life. The lesson is worth re-membering."

I was still pondering over this apopthegm, when Crofton aroused me by pushing across the table a great heap of gold. "This is all yours, Potts," said he; "and remember, that as you are now my agent, travelling for the house of Crofton and Co., that you journey at my cost."

Of course I would not listen to this proposal, and, although urged by Miss Crofton with all a woman's tact and delicacy, I persisted so firmly in my refusal, that they were obliged to yield. I now had a hundred pounds all my own, and though the sum be not a very splendid one, I remember some French writer—I'm not sure it is not Jules Janin—saying, "Any man who can put his hand into his pocket and find five Napoleons there, is rich;" and he certainly supports his theory with considerable sophistry and cleverness, mainly depending on the assumption, that any of the reasonable daily necessities of life, even in a luxurious point of view, are attainable with such means. Now, although a hundred pounds would not very long supply resources for such a life, yet, as I am not a Frenchman, nor living in Paris, still less had I habits or tastes of a costly kind, I might very well eke out three months pleasantly on this sum and in these three months what might not happen? In a "hundred days" the great Napoleon crushed the whole might of the Austrian empire, and secured an emperor's daughter for his bride; and in another "hundred days" he made the tour of France, from Cannes to Rochefort, and lost an empire by the way! Wonderful things might then be compassed within three months.

"What are you saying about three months, Potts?" asked Crofton, for unwittingly I had uttered these words aloud.

"I was observing," said I, "that in three months from this day, we should arrange to meet somewhere. Where shall we say?"

"Geneva is very central; shall we name Geneva?"

"Oh, on no account. Let our rendezvous be in Italy. Let us say Rome.

"Rome be it then," cried Crofton. "Now for another

point: let us have a wager as to who first discovers the object of our search. I'll bet you twenty Napoleons, Potts, to ten—for as we are two to one, so should the wager be."

"I take you," cried I, entering into his humour, "and I feel as certain of success as if I had your money in my hand."

"Will you have another wager with *me?*" whispered Mary Crofton, as she came behind my chair. "It is, that you'll not persuade Miss Herbert to wear this ring for *my* sake."

"I'll bet my life on it," said I, taking the opal ring she drew from her finger, as she spoke; "I'm in that mood of confidence now, I feel there is nothing I could not promise."

"If so then, Potts, let me have the benefit of this fortunate interval, and ask you to promise me one thing, which is, not to change your mind more than twice a day; don't be angry with me, but hear me out. You are a good-hearted fellow, and have excellent intentions; I don't think I know one less really selfish, but at the same time you are so fickle of purpose, so undecided in action, that I'd not be the least astonished to hear, when we asked for you to-morrow at breakfast-time, that you had started for a tour in Norway, or on a voyage to the Southern Pacific."

"And is this your judgment of me also, Miss Crofton?" said I, rising from my seat.

"Oh, no, Mr. Potts. I would only suspect you of going off into the Tyrol, or the Styrian Alps, and forgetting all about us, amidst the glaciers and the cataracts."

"I wish you a good night, and a better opinion of your humble servant," said I, bowing.

"Don't go, Potts—wait a minute—come back. I have something to tell you."

I closed the door behind me, and hastened off, not, however, perfectly clear whether I was the injured man, or one who had just achieved a great outrage.

CHAPTER XIII.

I AM obliged to acknowledge that I was vain-glorious enough to accept a seat in the Crofton carriage on the morning of their departure, and accompany them for a mile or so of the way—even at the price of returning on foot—just that I might show myself to the landlady and that odious old waiter in a position of eminence, and make them do a bitter penance for the insults they had heaped on an illustrious stranger. It was a poor and paltry triumph, and over very contemptible adversaries, but I could not refuse it to myself. Crofton, too, contributed largely to the success of my little scheme, by insisting that I should take the place beside his sister, while he sat with his back to the horses; and though I refused at first, I acceded at last, with the bland compliance of a man who feels himself once more in his accustomed station.

As throughout this true history I have candidly revealed the inmost traits of my nature—well knowing the while how deteriorating such innate analogy must prove—I have ever felt that he who has small claims to interest by the events of his life, can make some compensation to the world by an honest exposure of his motives, his weaknesses, and his struggles. Now, my present confession is made in this spirit, and is not absolutely without its moral, for, as the adage tells us, "Look after the pence, and the pounds will take care of themselves;" so would I say, Guard yourself carefully against petty vices. You and I, most esteemed reader, are—I trust fervently—little likely to be arraigned on a capital charge. I hope sincerely that transportable felonies, and even misdemeanours, may not picture among the accidents of our life; such-like are the pounds that take care of themselves, but the "small pence," which require looking after, are little envies, and jealousies, and rancours, petty snobberies of display, small exhibitions of our being better than this man or greater than that; these, I repeat to you, accumulate on a man's nature just the way barnacles fasten on a ship's bottom—from mere time, and it is wonderful what damage can come of such paltry obstacles.

I very much doubt if a Roman conqueror regarded the chained captive who followed his chariot with a more supreme pride than I bestowed upon that miserable old waiter who now bowed himself to the ground before me, and when I ordered my dinner for four o'clock, and said, that probably I might have a friend to dine with me, his humiliation was complete.

"I wish I knew the secret of your staying here," said Mary Crofton, as we drove along; "why will you not tell it?"

"Perhaps it might prove indiscreet, Mary' our friend Potts may have become a *mauvais sujet* since we have seen him last?"

I wrapped myself in a mysterious silence, and only smiled.

"Lindau, of all places, to stop at!" resumed she, pettishly. "There is nothing remarkable in the scenery, no art treasures, nothing socially agreeable; what can it possibly be that detains you in such a place?"

"My dear Mary," said Crofton, "you are, without knowing it, violating a hallowed principle; you are no less than leading into temptation. Look at poor Potts there, and you will see that while he knows in his inmost heart the secret which detains him here is some passing and insignificant circumstance unworthy of mention, you have, by imparting to it a certain importance, suggested to his mind the necessity of a story; give him now but five minutes to collect himself, and I'll engage that he will 'come out' with a romantic incident that would never have seen the light but for a woman's curiosity."

"Good Heavens!" thought I, "can this be a true interpretation of my character? Am I the weak and impressionable creature this would bespeak me?" I must have blushed deeply at my own reflection, for Crofton quickly added:

"Don't get angry with me, Potts, any more than you would with a friend who'd say, 'Take care how you pass over that bridge, I know it is rotten and must give way.'"

"Let me answer you," said I, courageously, for I was acutely hurt to be thus arraigned before another. "It is more than likely that you, with your active habits and stirring notions of life, would lean very heavily on him who, neither wanting riches nor honours, would adopt some simple sort of dreamy existence, and think that the green alleys of the beech wood, or the little path beside the river, pleasanter sauntering than the gilded ante-chamber of a palace; and just as likely is it that you would take him roundly to task about wasted opportu-nities, misapplied talents, and stigmatise as inglorious indolence what might as possibly be called a contented humility. Now, I would ask you, why should one man be the measure of another? The load you could carry with ease might serve to crush me, and yet there may be some light burdens that would suit *my* strength, and in bearing which I might taste a sense of duty grateful as your own."

"I have no patience with you," began Crofton, warmly; but his sister stopped him with an imploring look, and then, turning to me, said:

"Edward fancies that every one can be as energetic

and active as himself, and occasionally forgets what you
have just so well remarked as to the relative capacities
of different people."

"I want him to do something, to be something besides
a dreamer!" burst he in, almost angrily.

"Well, then," said I, "you shall see me begin this
moment, for I will get down here and walk briskly back
to the town." I called to the postilions to pull up at the
same time, and in spite of remonstrances, entreaties—
almost beseechings from Mary Crofton—I persisted in
my resolve, and bade them farewell.

Crofton was so much hurt that he could scarcely
speak, and when he gave me his hand it was in the
coldest of manners.

"But you'll keep our rendezvous, wont you?" said
Mary; "we shall meet at Rome?"

"I really wonder, Mary, how you can force our
acquaintanceship where it is so palpably declined.
Good-by—farewell," said he to me.

"Good-by," said I, with a gulp that almost choked me;
and away drove the carriage, leaving me standing in the
train of dust it had raised. Every crack of the postboys'
whips gave me a shock as though I had felt the thong on
my own shoulders; and, at last, as sweeping round a turn
of the road the carriage disappeared from view, such was
the sense of utter desolation that came over me, that I
sat down on a stone by the wayside, overwhelmed. I do

not know if I ever felt such an utter sense of destitution
as at that moment. "What a wealth of friends must a
man possess," thought I, "who can afford to squander
them in this fashion! How could I have repelled the
counsels that kindness alone . could have prompted?
Surely Crofton must know far more of life than I did?"
From this, I went on to inquire why it was that the
world showed itself so unforgiving to idleness in men of
small fortune, since, if no burden to the community, they
ought to be as free as their richer brethren. It was a
puzzling theme, and though I revolved it long, I made
but little of it, the only solution that occurred to me was,
that the idleness of the humble man is not relieved by
the splendours and luxuries which surround a rich man's
leisure, and that the world resents the pretensions of ease
unassociated with riches. In what a profound philosophy
was it, then, that Diogenes rolled his tub about the
streets! there was a mock purpose about it that must
have flattered his fellow-citizens. I feel assured that a
great deal of the butterfly-hunting and beetle-gathering
that we see around us is done in this spirit. They are a
set of idle folk anxious to indulge their indolence without
reproach.

Thus pondering and musing, I strolled back to the
town. So still and silent was it, so free from all movement of traffic or business, that I was actually in the
very centre of it without knowing it. There were streets

without passengers, and shops without customers, and
even *cafés* without guests, and I wondered within myself
why people should thus congregate to do nothing, and I
rambled on from street to alley, and from alley to lane,
never chancing upon one who had anything in hand. At
last I gained the side of the lake, along which a little
quay ran for some distance, ending in a sort of terraced
walk, now grass-grown and neglected. There were at
least the charms of fresh air and scenery here, though
the worthy citizens seemed to hold them cheaply, and I
rambled along to the end, where, by a broad flight of
steps, the terrace communicated with the lake; a spot,
doubtless, where, once on a time, the burghers took the
water and went out a pleasuring with fat fraus and
fräuleins. I had reached the end, and was about to turn
back again, when I caught sight of a man seated on one
of the lower steps, employed in watching two little toy
ships which he had just launched. Now this seemed to
me the very climax of indolence, and I sat myself down
on the parapet to observe him. His proceedings were
indeed of the strangest, for as there was no wind to fill
the sails and his vessels lay still and becalmed, he
appeared to have bethought him of another mode to
impart interest to them. He weighted one of them with
little stones till she brought her gunwale level with the
water, and then pressing her gently with his hand he
made her sink slowly down to the bottom. I'm not

quite certain whether I laughed outright, or that some exclamation escaped me as I looked, but some noise I must unquestionably have made, for he started and turned up his head, and I saw Harpar, the Englishman whom I had met the day before at Constance.

"Well, you're not much the wiser after all," said he, gruffly, and without even saluting me.

There was in the words, and fierce expression of his face, something that made me suspect him of insanity, and I would willingly have retired without reply had he not risen and approached me.

"Eh," repeated he, with a sneer, "ain't I right? You can make nothing of it?"

"I really don't understand you!" said I. "I came down here by the merest accident, and never was more astonished than to see you."

"Oh, of course; I am well used to that sort of thing," went he on in the same tone of scoff. "I've had some experience of these kinds of accidents before; but, as I said, it's no use, you're not within one thousand miles of it, no, nor any man in Europe."

It was quite clear to me now that he *was* mad, and my only care was to get speedily rid of him.

"I'm not surprised," said I, with an assumed ease— "I'm not surprised at your having taken to so simple an amusement, for really in a place so dull as this any mode of passing the time would be welcome."

"Simple enough when you know it," said he, with a peculiar look.

"You arrived last night, I suppose?" said I, eager to get conversation into some pleasanter channel.

"Yes, I got here very late. I had the misfortune to sprain my ankle, and this detained me a long time on the way, and may keep me for a couple of days more."

I learned where he was stopping in the town, and seeing with what pain and difficulty he moved, I offered him my aid to assist him on his way.

"Well, I'll not refuse your help," said he, dryly; "but just go along yonder, about five-and-twenty or thirty yards, and I'll join you. You understand me, I suppose?"

Now, I really did not understand him, except to believe him perfectly insane, and to suggest to me the notion of profiting by his lameness to make my escape with all speed. I conclude some generous promptings opposed this course, for I obeyed his injunctions to the very letter, and waited till he came up to me. He did so very slowly, and evidently in much suffering, assisted by a stick in one hand, while he carried his two little boats in the other.

"Shall I take charge of these for you?" said I, offering to carry them.

"No, don't trouble yourself," said he, in the same rude tone, "Nobody touches these but myself."

I now gave him my arm, and we moved slowly along.

"What has become of the vagabonds? Are they here with you?" asked he, abruptly.

"I parted with them yesterday," said I, shortly, and not wishing to enter into further explanations.

"And you did wisely," rejoined he, with a serious air. "Even when these sort of creatures have nothing very bad about them, they are bad company, out of the haphazard chance way they gain a livelihood. If you reduce life to a game, you must yourself become a gambler. Now, there's one feature of that sort of existence intolerable to an honest man : it is, that to win himself, some one else must lose. Do you understand me?"

"I do, and am much struck by what you say."

"In that case," said he, with a nudge of his elbow against my side—"in that case you might as well have not come down to watch *me!*—eh?"

I protested stoutly against this mistake, but I could plainly perceive with very little success.

"Let it be, let it be," said he, with a shake of the head. "As I said before, if you saw the thing done before your eyes you'd make nothing of it. I'm not afraid of you, or all the men in Europe! There now, there's a challenge to the whole of ye! Sit down every man of ye, with the problem before ye, and see what you'll make of it."

"Ah," thought I, "this is madness. Here is a poor monomaniac led away into the land of wild thoughts and fancies by one dominating caprice; who knows whether out of the realm of this delusion he may not be a man acute and sensible."

"No, no," muttered he, half aloud; "there are, maybe, half a million of men this moment manufacturing steam-engines; but it took one head, just one head, to set them all working, and if it wasn't for old Watt, the world at this day would'nt be five miles in advance of what it was a century back. I see," added he, after a moment, "you don't take much interest in these sort of things. *Your* line of parts, is the walking gentleman, eh? Well, bear in mind it don't pay; no, sir, it don't pay! Here, this is my way; my lodging is down this lane. I'll not ask you to come further; thank you for your help, and good-by."

"Let us not part here; come up to the inn and dine with me," said I, affecting his own blunt and abrupt manner.

"Why should *I* dine with *you*?" asked he, roughly.

"I can't exactly say," stammered I, "except out of good-fellowship, just as, for instance, I accepted your invitation t'other morning to breakfast."

"Ah, yes, to be sure, so you did. Well, I'll come. We shall be all alone, I suppose?"

"Quite alone."

"All right, for I have no coat but this one," and he looked down at the coarse sleeve as he spoke, with a strange and sad smile, and then waving his hand in token of farewell, he said, "I'll join you in half an hour," and disappeared up the lane.

I have already owned that I did not like this man; he had a certain short abrupt way that repelled me at every moment. When he differed in opinion with me, he was not satisfied to record his dissent, but he must set about demolishing my conviction, and this sort of intolerance pervaded all he said. There was, too, that business-like, practical tone about him, that jars fearfully on the sensitive fibre of the idler's nature.

It was exactly in proportion as his society was distasteful to me, that I felt a species of pride in associating with him, as though to say, "I am not one of those who must be fawned on and flattered. I am of a healthier and manlier stamp; I can afford to hear my judgments arraigned, and my opinions opposed." And in this humour I ascended the stairs of the hotel, and entered the room where our table was already laid out.

To compensate, so far as they could, for the rude reception of the day before, they had given me now the "grand apartment" of the inn, which, by a long balcony, looked over the lake, and that fine mountain range that leads to the Splugen pass. A beautiful bouquet of fresh flowers ornamented the centre of the small dinner-table, tastily decked with Bohemian glass, and napkins with lace borders. I rather liked this

little display of elegance. It was a sort of ally on
my side against the utilitarian plainness of my
guest.

As I walked up and down the room, awaiting his
arrival, I could not help a sigh, and a very deep one
too, over the thought of what had been my enjoyment
that moment if my guest had been one of a different
temperament—a man willing to take me on my own
showing, and ready to accept any version I should like
to give of myself. How gracefully, how charmingly I
could have played the host to such a man! What
vigour would it have imparted to my imagination—what
brilliancy to my fancy! With what a princely grace
might I have dispensed my hospitalities, as though such
occasions were the daily habit of my life; whereas a
dinner with Harpar would be nothing more or less than
an airing with a "slave in the chariot"—a perpetual
reminder, like the face of a poor relation, that my lot
was cast in an humble sphere, and it was no use trying
to disguise it.

"What's all this for?" said Harpar's harsh voice, as
he entered the room. "Why didn't you order our
mutton-chop below stairs in the common room, and not
a banquet in this fashion? You must be well aware I
couldn't do this sort of thing by *you*. Why then have
you attempted it with *me*?"

"I have always thought it was a host's prerogative,"

said I, meekly, "to be the arbiter of his own entertainment."

"So it might where he was the arbiter of his purse, but you know well enough neither you nor I have any pretension to these costly ways, and they have this disadvantage, that they make all intercourse stilted and unnatural. If you and I had to sit down to table, dressed in court suits, with wigs and bags, ain't it likely we'd be easy and cordial together? Well, this is precisely the same.

"I am really sorry," said I, with a forced appearance of courtesy, "to have incurred so severe a lesson, but you must allow me this one transgression before I begin to profit by it." And so saying, I rang the bell and ordered dinner.

Harpar made no reply, but walked the room, with his hands deep in his pockets, humming a tune to himself as he went.

At last we sat down at table; everything was excellent and admirably served, but we ate on in silence, not a syllable exchanged between us. As the dessert appeared I tried to open conversation. I affected to seem easy and unconcerned, but the cold half stern look of my companion repelled all my attempts, and I sat very sad and much discouraged sipping my wine.

"May I order some brandy-and-water? I like it better than these French wines," asked he, abruptly; and, as I arose to ring for it, he added, "and you'll not object to my having a pipe of strong Cavendish?" And therewith he produced a leather bag and a very much smoked meerschaum, short and ungainly as his own figure. As he thrust his hand into the pouch, a small boat, about the size of a lady's thimble, rolled out from amidst the tobacco, he quickly took it and placed it in his waistcoat-pocket—the act being done with a sort of hurry that with a man of less self-possession might have perhaps evinced confusion.

"You fancy you've seen something, don't you?" said he, with a defiant laugh. "I'd wager a five-pound note, if I had one, that you think at this moment you have made a great discovery. Well, there it is, make much of it!" As he spoke, he produced the little boat and laid it down before me. I own that this speech and the act convinced me that he was insane; I was aware that intense suspectfulness is the great characteristic of madness, and everything tended to show that he was deranged.

Rather to conceal what was passing in my own mind than out of any curiosity, I took up the little toy to examine it. It was beautifully made, and finished with a most perfect neatness: the only thing I could not understand being four small holes on each side of the keel, fastened by four little plugs.

"What are these for?" asked I.

"Can't you guess?" said he, laughingly.

"No; I have never seen such before."

"Well," said he, musingly, "perhaps they *are* puzzling —I suppose they are. But mayhap, too, if I thought you'd guess the meaning, I'd not have been so ready to show it to you." And with this he replaced the boat in his pocket and smoked away. "You ain't a genius, my worthy friend, that's a fact," said he, sententiously.

"I opine that the same judgment might be passed upon a great many?" said I, testily.

"No," continued he, following on his own thoughts without heeding my remark, "*you'll* not set the Thames a-fire."

"Is that the best test of a man's ability?" asked I, sneeringly.

"You're the sort of fellow that ought to be—let us see now what you ought to be—yes, you're just the stamp of man for an apothecary."

"You are so charming in your frankness," said I, "that you almost tempt me to imitate you."

"And why not? sure we oughtn't to talk to each other like two devils in waiting. Out with what you have to say."

"I was just thinking," said I—"led to it by that speculative turn of yours—I was just thinking in what station *your* abilities would have pre-eminently distinguished you."

"Well, have you hit it?"

"I'm not quite certain," said I, trying to screw up my courage for an impertinence, "but I half suspect that in our great national works—our lines of railroad, for instance—there must be a strong infusion of men with tastes and habits resembling yours."

"You mean the navvies?" broke he in. "You're right, I was a navvy once; I turned the first spadeful of earth on the Coppleston Junction, and, seeing what a good thing might be made of it, I suggested task-work to my comrades, and we netted from four-and-six to five shillings a day, each. In eight months after, I was made an inspector: so that you see strong sinews can be good allies to a strong head and a stout will."

I do not believe that the most angry rebuke, the most sarcastic rejoinder, could have covered me with a tenth part of the shame and confusion than did these few words. I'd have given worlds, if I had them, to make a due reparation for my rudeness, but I knew not how to accomplish it. I looked in his face to read if I might hit upon some trait by which his nature could be approached; but I might as well have gazed at a line of railroad to guess the sort of town that it led to. The stern, rugged, bold countenance seemed to imply little else than daring and determination, and I could not but wonder how I had ever dared to take a liberty with one of his stamp.

"Well, said I, at last, and wishing to lead him back to his story, "and after being made inspector ——"

"You can speak German well," said he, totally inattentive to my question; "just ask one of these people when there will be any conveyance from this to Ragatz."

"Ragatz of all places!" exclaimed I.

"Yes; they tell me it's good for the rheumatics, and I have got some old shoulder pains I'd like to shake off before winter. And then this sprain too: I foresee I shall not be able to walk much for some days to come."

"Ragatz is on my road; I am about to cross the Splugen into Italy; I'll bear you company so far, if you have no objection."

"Well, it may not seem civil to say it, but I have an objection," said he, rising from the table. "When I've got weighty things on my mind I've a bad habit of talking of them to myself aloud. I can't help it, and so I keep strictly alone till my plans are all fixed and settled; after that, there's no danger of my revealing them to any one. There now, you have my reason, and you'll not dispute that it's a good one."

"You may not be too distrustful of yourself," said I, laughing, "but assuredly you are far too flattering in your estimate of *my* acuteness."

"I'll not risk it," said he, bluntly, as he sought for his hat.

"Wait a moment," said I. "You told me at Constance

that you were in want of money; at the time I was not
exactly in funds myself. Yesterday, however, I received
a remittance, and if ten or twenty pounds be of any
service, they are heartily at your disposal."

He looked at me fixedly, almost sternly, for a minute
or two, and then said,

"Is this true, or is it that you have changed your mind
about me?"

"True," said I—"strictly true."

"Will this loan—I mean it to be a loan—inconvenience you much?"

"No, no; I make you the offer freely."

"I take it, then. Let me have ten pounds; and write
down there an address where I am to remit it some day
or other, though I can't say when."

"There may be some difficulty about that," said I.
"Stay! I mean to be at Rome some time in the winter;
send it to me there."

"To what banker?"

"I have no banker, I never had a banker. There's
my name, and let the post-office be the address."

"Whichever way you're bent on going you're not on
the road to be a rich man," said Harpar, as he deposited
my gold in his leather purse; "but I hope you'll not lose
by me. Good-by." He gave me his hand, not very
warmly or cordially either, and was gone ere I well
knew it.

CHAPTER XIV.

I WENT the next morning to take leave of Harpar before
starting, but found to my astonishment that he was already
off! He had, I learned, hired a small carriage to convey
him to Bregenz, and had set out before daybreak. I do
not know why this should have annoyed me, but it did so,
and set me a thinking over the people whom Echstein, in
his "Erfährungen," says, are born to be dupes. "There
is," says he, "a race of men who are 'eingeborne Narren'
—'native numbskulls,' one might say—who muddy the
streams of true benevolence by indiscriminating acts
of kindness, and who, by always aiding the wrong-doer,
make themselves accomplices of vice." Could it be that
I was in this barren category? Harpar had told me, the
evening before, that he would not leave Lindau till his
sprain was better, and now he was off, just as if, having
no further occasion for me, he was glad to be rid of my
companionship—just as if—— I was beginning again to
start another conjecture, when I bethought me that there
is not a more deceptive formula in the whole cyclopædia

of delusion than that which opens with those same words, "just as if." Rely upon it, amiable reader, that whenever you find yourself driven to explain a motive, trace a cause, or reconcile a discrepancy, by "just as if," the chances are about seven to three you are wrong. If I was not in all the bustle of paying my bill and strapping on my knapsack, I'd convince you on this head, but as the morning is a bright, but mellow one of early autumn, and my path lies along the placid lake, waveless and still, with many a tinted tree reflected in its fair mirror, let us not think of knaves and rogues, but rather dwell on the pleasanter thought of all the good and grateful things which daily befal us in this same life of ours. I am full certain that almost all of us enter upon what is called the world in too combative a spirit. We are too fond of dragon slaying, and rather than be disappointed of our sport, we'd fall foul of a pet lamb, for want of a tiger. Call it self-delusion, credulity, what you will, it is a faith that makes life very livable, and, without it,

> We feel a light has left the world,
>   A nameless sort of treasure,
> As though one pluck'd the crimson heart
>   From out the rose of pleasure.
> I could forgive the fate that made
>   Me poor and young to-morrow,
> To have again the soul that played
>   So tenderly in sorrow,
> So buoyantly in happiness.
>   Ay, I would brook deceiving,
> And even the deceiver bless,
>   Just to go on believing!

" Still," thought I, " one ought to maintain self-respect;
one should not willingly make himself a dupe." And then
I began to wish that Vaterchen had come up, and that
Tintefleck was rushing towards me with tears in her eyes,
and my money-bag in her hands. I wanted to forget
them. I tried in a hundred ways to prevent them crossing my memory; but though there is a most artful
system of artificial "mnemonics" invented by some one,
the Lethan art has met no explorer, and no man has ever
yet found out the way to shut the door against by-gones.
I believe it is scarcely more than five miles to Bregenz
from Lindau, and yet I was almost as many hours on the
road. I sat down, perhaps, twenty times, lost in reverie;
indeed, I'm not very sure that I didn't take a sound sleep
under a spreading willow, so that, when I reached the
inn, the company was just going in to dinner at the *table
d'hôte.* Simple and unpretentious as that board was, the
company that graced it was certainly distinguished, being
no less than the Austrian field-marshal in command of
the district, and the officers of his staff. To English
notions, it seemed very strange to see a nobleman of the
highest rank, in the proudest state of Europe, seated at a
dinner-table open to all comers, at a fraction less than
one shilling a head, and where some of the government
officials of the place daily came.

It was not without a certain sense of shame that I
found myself in the long low chamber, in which about

twenty officers were assembled, whose uniforms were all glittering with stars, medals, and crosses; in fact, to a weak-minded civilian like myself, they gave the impression of a group of heroes fresh come from all the triumphant glories of a campaign. Between the staff which occupied one end of the long table and the few townsfolk who sat at the other, there intervened a sort of frontier territory uninhabited, and it was here that the waiter located me—an object of observation and remark to each. Resolving to learn how I was treated by my critics, I addressed the waiter in the very worst French, and protested my utter ignorance of German. I had promised myself much amusement from this expedient, but was doomed to a severe disappointment—the officers coolly setting me down for a servant, while the townspeople pronounced me a pedlar; and when these judgments had been recorded, instead of entering upon a psychological examination of my nature, temperament, and individuality, they never noticed me any more. I felt hurt at this, more indeed for their sakes than my own, since I bethought me of the false impression that is current of this people throughout Europe, where they have the reputation of philosophers deeply engaged in researches into character, minute anatomists of human thought and man's affections; "and yet," muttered I, "they can sit at table with one of the most remarkable of men, and be as ignorant of all about him, as the husbandman who toils at his daily labour is of the mineral treasures that lie buried down beneath him.

. "I will read them a lesson," thought I. "They shall see that in the humble guise of foot-traveller it may be the pleasure of men of rank and station to journey." The townsfolk, when the dessert made its appearance, rose to take their departure, each before he left the room making a profound obeisance to the general, and then another but less lowly act of homage to the staff, showing by this that strangers were expected to withdraw, while the military guests sat over their wine. Indeed, a very significant look from the last person who left the room conveyed to me the etiquette of the place. I was delighted at this—it was the very opportunity I longed for—and so, with a clink of my knife against my wine-glass, the substitute for a bell in use amongst humble hostels, I summoned the waiter, and asked for his list of wines. I saw that my act had created some astonishment amongst the others, but it excited nothing more, and now they had all lighted their pipes, and sat smoking away quite regardless of my presence. I had ordered a flask of Steinberger at four florins, and given most special directions that my glass should have a " roped rim," and be of a tender green tint, but not too deep to spoil the colour of the wine.

My admonitions were given aloud, and in a tone of command, but I perceived that they failed to create any impression upon my moustached neighbours. I might have ordered nectar or hypocras for all that they seemed: to care about me. I raked up in memory all the imper- tinent and insolent things Henri Heine had ever said of Austria; I bethought me how they tyrannized in the various provinces of their scattered empire, and how they were hated by Hun, Slavac, and Italian; I revelled in those slashing leading articles that used to show up the great but bankrupt bully, and I only wished I was " own correspondent " to something at home to give my im- pressions of " Austria and her military system."

Little as you think of that pale sad-looking stranger, who sits sipping his wine in solitude at the foot of the table, that he is about to transmit yourselves and your country to a remote posterity. " Ay ! " muttered I, " to be remembered when the Danube will be a choked-up rivulet, and the park of Schönbrunn a prairie for the buffalo." I am not exactly aware how or why these changes were to have occurred, but Lord Macaulay's New Zealander might have originated them.

While I thus mused and brooded, the tramp of four horses came clattering down the street, and soon after swept into the arched door-way of the inn with a rolling and thunderous sound.

"Here he comes—here he is at last!" said a young officer, who had rushed in haste to the window, and at the announcement a very palpable sentiment of satis- faction seemed to spread itself through the company,

even to the grim old field-marshal, who took his pipe
from his mouth to say:

"He is in time—he saves 'arrest!'"

As he spoke, a tall man in uniform entered the room,
and walking with military step till he came in front of
the general, said, in a loud but respectful voice:

· "I have the honour to report myself as returned to
duty."

The general replied something I could not catch, and
then shook him warmly by the hand, making room for
him to sit down next him.

" How far did your royal highness go? Not to Coire?"
said the general.

"Far beyond it, sir," said the other. "I went the
whole way to the Splugen, and if it were not for the
terror of your displeasure, I'd have crossed the mountain
and gone on to Chiavenna."

The fact that I was listening to the narrative of a
royal personage was not the only bond of fascination to
me, for somehow the tone of the speaker's voice sounded
familiarly to my ears, and I could have sworn I had
heard it before. As he was at the same side of the table
with myself, I could not see him, but while he continued
to talk, the impression grew each moment more strong
that I must have met him previously.

I could gather—it was easy enough to do so—from the
animated looks of the party, and the repeated bursts of

laughter that followed his sallies, that the newly-arrived officer was a wit and authority amongst his comrades. His elevated rank, too, may have contributed to this popularity. Must I own that he appeared in the character that to me is particularliy offensive? He was a "narrator." That vulgar adage of "two of a trade" has a far wider acceptance when applied to the operations of intellect than when addressed to the work of men's hands. To see this jealousy at its height, you must look for it amongst men of letters, artists, actors, or, better still, those social performers who are the bright spirits of dinner-parties—the charming men of society. All the animosities of political or religious hate are mild compared to the detestation this rivalry engenders; and now, though the audience was a foreign one, which I could have no pretension to amuse, I conceived the most bitter dislike for the man who had engaged their attention.

I do not know how it may be with others, but to myself there has always been this difficulty in a foreign language, that until I have accustomed myself to the tone of voice and the manner of a speaker, I can rarely follow him without occasional lapses. Now, on the present occasion, the narrator, though speaking distinctly, and with a good accent, had a very rapid utterance, and it was not till I had familiarised my ear with his manner that I could gather his words correctly. Nor was my difficulty lessened by the fact that, as he pre-

tended to be witty and epigrammatic, frequent bursts of
laughter broke from his audience and obscured his
speech. He was, as it appeared, giving an account of
a fishing excursion he had just taken to one of the small
mountain lakes near Poppenheim, and it was clear
enough he was one who always could eke an adventure
out of even the most ordinary incident of daily life.

This fishing story had really nothing in it, though he
strove to make out fifty points of interest or striking
situations out of the veriest common-place. At last,
however, I saw that, like a practised story-teller, he was
hoarding up his great incident for the finish.

"As I have told you," said he, "I engaged the entire
of the little inn for myself; there were but five rooms in
it altogether, and though I did not need more than two,
I took the rest, that I might be alone and unmolested.
Well, it was on my second evening there, as I sat
smoking my pipe at the door, and looking over my
tackle for the morrow, there came up the glen the
strange sound of wheels, and, to my astonishment, a
travelling carriage soon appeared, with four horses
driven in hand, and I saw in a moment it was a lohn-
kutcher, who had taken the wrong turning after leaving
Ragatz, and mistaken the road, for the highway ceases
about two miles above Poppenheim, and dwindles down
to a mere mule-path. Leaving my host to explain the
mistake to the travellers, I hastily re-entered the house,

just as the carriage drove up. The explanation seemed a very prolix one, for when I looked out of the window, half an hour afterwards, there were the horses still standing at the door, and the driver, with a large branch of alder, whipping away the flies from them, while the host continued to hold his place at the carriage door. At last he entered my room, and said that the travellers, two foreign ladies—he thought them Russians—had taken the wrong road, but that the elder, what between fatigue and fear, was so overcome, that she could not proceed farther, and entreated that they might be afforded any accommodation—mere shelter for the night—rather than retrace their road to Ragatz.

"Well,' said I, carelessly, 'let them have the rooms on the other side of the hall; so that they only stop for one night, the intrusion will not signify.' Not a very gracious reply, perhaps, but I did not want to be gracious. The fact was, as the old lady got out, I saw something like an elephant's leg, in a fur boot, that quite decided me on not making acquaintance with the travellers, and I was rash enough to imagine they must be both alike. Indeed, I was so resolute in maintaining my solitude undisturbed, that I told my host on no account whatever to make me any communication from the strangers, nor, on any pretext, to let me feel that they were lodged under the same roof with myself. Perhaps, if the next day had been one to follow my usual sport, I should have forgotten all about them, but it was one of such rain as made it perfectly impossible to leave the house. I doubt if I ever saw rain like it. It came down in sheets, like water splashed out of buckets, flattening the small trees to the earth, and beating down all the light foliage into the muddy soil beneath; meanwhile the air shook with the noise of the swollen torrents, and all the mountain-streams crashed and thundered away, like great cataracts. Rain can really become grand at such moments, and no more resembling a mere shower than the cry of a single brawler in the street is like the roar of a mighty multitude. It was so fine, that I determined I would go down to a little wooden bridge over the river, whence I could see the stream as it came down, tumbling and splashing, from a cleft in the mountain. I soon dressed myself in all my best waterproofs —hat, cape, boots, and all—and set out. Until I was fully embarked on my expedition, I had no notion of the severity of the storm, and it was with considerable difficulty I could make head against the wind and rain together, while the slippery ground made walking an actual labour.

"At last I reached the river, but of the bridge, the only trace was a single beam, which, deeply buried in the bank at one extremity, rose and fell in the surging flood, like the arm of a drowning swimmer. The stream had completely filled the channel, and swept along, with

fragments of timber, and even furniture, in its muddy
tide; farm produce, and implements too, came floating
by, showing what destruction had been effected higher
up the river. As I stood gazing on the current, I saw,
at a little distance from me, a man, standing motionless
beside the river, and apparently lost in thought—so at
least he seemed—for though not at all clad in a way to
resist the storm, he remained there, wet and soaked
through, totally regardless of the weather. On inquiring
at the inn, I learned that this was the lohnkutscher—the
' vetturino '—of the travellers, and who, in attempting
to ascertain if the stream were fordable, had lost one of
his best horses, and barely escaped being carried away
himself. Until that, I had forgotten all about the
strangers, whom, it now appeared, were close prisoners
like myself. While the host was yet speaking, the lohn-
kutscher came up, and in a tone of equality, that showed
me he thought I was in his own line of business, asked
if I would sell him one of my nags then in the stable.

"Not caring to disabuse him of his error regarding
my rank, I did not refuse him so flatly as I might, and
he pressed the negotiation very warmly in consequence.
At last, to get rid of him, I declared that I would not
break up my team, and retired into the house. I was
not many minutes in my room, when a courier came,
with a polite message from his mistress, to beg I would
speak with her. I went at once, and found an old lady

—she was English, as her French bespoke—very well mannered and well bred, who apologized for troubling me, but having heard from her vetturino that my horses were disengaged, and that I might, if not disposed to sell one of them, hire out the entire team, to take their carriage as far as Andeer—— By the time she got thus far, I perceived that she, too, mistook me for a lohn-kutscher. It just struck me what good fun it would be to carry on the joke. To be sure, the lady herself presented no inducement to the enterprise, and as I thus balanced the case, there came into the room one of the prettiest girls I ever saw. She never turned a look towards where I was standing, nor deigned to notice me at all, but passed out of the room as rapidly as she entered; still, I remembered that I had already seen her before, and passed a delightful evening in her company at a little inn the Black Forest."

' When the narrator had got thus far in his story, I leaned forward to catch a full view of him, and saw, to my surprise, and I own to my misery, that he was the German count we had met at the Titi-See. So overwhelming was this discovery to me, that I heard nothing for many minutes after. All of that wretched scene between us on the last evening at the inn came full to my memory, and I bethought me of lying the whole night on the hard table, fevered with rage and terror alternately. If it were not that his narrative regarded Miss

Herbert now, I would have skulked out of the room, and out of the inn, and out of the town itself, never again to come under the insolent stare of those wicked grey eyes, but in that name there was a fascination—not to say that a sense of jealousy burned at my heart like a furnace.

The turmoil of my thoughts lost me a great deal of his story, and might have lost me more, had not the hearty laughter of his comrades recalled me once again to attention.

He was describing how, as a "vetturino," he drove their carriage with his own spanking grey horses to Coire, and thence to Andeer. He had bargained, it seemed, that Miss Herbert should travel outside in the cabriolet, but she failed to keep her pledge, so that they only met at stray moments during the journey. It was in one of these she said laughingly to him,—

"'Nothing would surprise me less than to learn, some fine morning, that you were a prince in disguise, or a great count of the empire, at least. It was only the other day we were honoured with the incognito presence of a royal personage; I do not exactly know who, but Mrs. Keats could tell you. He left us abruptly at Schaff-hausen.'

"'You can't mean the creature,' said I, 'that I saw in your company at the Titi-See?'

"'The same,' said she, rather angrily.

"'Why, he is a saltimbanque; I saw him the morning

I came through Constance with some others of his troop dragged before the maire for causing a disturbance in a cabaret; one of the most consummate impostors, they told me, in Europe.' "

"An infamous falsehood, and a base liar the man who says it," cried I, springing to my legs, and standing revealed before the company in an attitude of haughty defiance. "I am the person you have dared to defame. I have never assumed to be a prince, and as little am I a rope-dancer. I am an English gentleman, travelling for his pleasure, and I hurl back every word you have said of me with contempt and defiance."

Before I had finished this insolent speech, some half-dozen swords were drawn and brandished in the air, very eager, as it seemed, to cut me to pieces, and the count himself required all the united strength of the party to save me from his hands. At last, I was pushed, hustled, and dragged out of the room to another smaller one on the same floor, and, the key being turned on me, left to my very happy reflections.

CHAPTER XV.

I HAD no writing materials, but I had just composed a
long letter to the *Times* on "the outrageous treatment
and false imprisonment of a British subject in Austria,"
when my door was opened by a thin, lank-jawed, fierce-
eyed man in uniform, who announced himself as the
Rittmeister von Mahony, of the Keyser Hussars.

"A countryman — an Irishman," said I, eagerly,
clasping his hand with warmth.

"That is to say, two generations back," replied he;
"my grandfather Terence was a lieutenant in Trenck's
Horse, but since that none of us have ever been out of
Austria."

If these tidings fell coldly on my heart just beginning
to glow with the ardour of home and country, I soon saw
that it takes more than two generations to wash out the
Irishman from a man's nature. The honest Rittmeister,
with scarcely a word of English in his vocabulary, was as
hearty a countryman as if he had never journeyed out of
the land of Bog.

"He had heard 'all about it,'" he said, by way of arresting the eloquent indignation that filled me; and he added, "And the more fool myself to notice the matter;" asking me, quaintly, if I had never heard of our native maxim that says, "One man ought never to fall upon forty"? "Well, said he, with a sigh, "what's done can't be undone; and let us see what's to come next? I see you are a gentleman, and the worse luck yours."

"What do you mean by that?" asked I.

"Just this: you'll have to fight; and if you were a 'Gemeiner'—a plebeian—you'd get off."

I turned away to the window to wipe a tear out of my eye; it had come there without my knowing it, and, as I did so, I devoted myself to the death of a hero.

"Yes," said I, "*she* is in this incident—*she* has her part in this scene of my life's drama, and I will not disgrace her presence. I will die like a man of honour rather than that her name should be disparaged."

He went on to tell me of my opponent, who was brother to a reigning sovereign, and himself a royal highness—Prince Max of Swabia. "He was not," he added, "by any means a bad fellow, though not reputed to be perfectly sane on certain topics." However, as his eccentricities were very harmless ones, merely offshoots of an exaggerated personal vanity, it was supposed that some active service, and a little more intercourse with the world, would cure him. "Not," added he, "that one can

say he has shown many signs of amendment up to this,
for he never makes an excursion of half-a-dozen days
from home, without coming back filled with the resistless
passion of some young queen or archduchess for him.
As he forgets these as fast as he imagines them, there is
usually nothing to lament on the subject. Now you are
in possession of all that you need know about *him*.
Tell me something of yourself; and first, have you
served?"

"Never."

"Was your father a soldier, or your grandfather?"

"Neither."

"Have you any connections on the mother's side in the
army?"

"I am not aware of one."

He gave a short, hasty cough, and walked the room
twice with his hands clasped at his back, and then,
coming straight in front of me, said, "And your name?
What's your name?"

"Potts! Potts!" said I, with a firm energy.

"Potztausend!" cried he, with a grim laugh; "what a
strange name!"

"I said Potts, Herr Rittmeister, and not Potztausend,"
rejoined I, haughtily.

"And I heard you," said he; "it was involuntary on
my part to add the termination. And who are the
Pottses? Are they noble?"

"Nothing of the kind—respectable middle-class folk; some in trade, some clerks in mercantile houses, some holding small government employments, one, perhaps the chief of the family, an eminent apothecary!"

As if I had uttered the most irresistible joke, at this word, he held his hands over his face and shook with laughter.

"Heilege Joseph!" cried he at last, "this is too good! The Prince Max going out with an apothecary's nephew, or, maybe, his son!"

"His son upon this occasion," said I, gravely.

He did not reply for some minutes, and then, leaning over the back of a chair, and regarding me very fixedly, he said:

"You have only to say who you are, and what your belongings, and nothing will come of this affair. In fact, what with your little knowledge of German, your imperfect comprehension of what the Prince said, and your own station in life, I'll engage to arrange everything and get you off clear!"

"In a word," said I, "I am to plead in *formâ inferioris* —isn't that it?"

"Just so," said he, puffing out a long cloud from his pipe.

"I'd rather die first!" cried I, with an energy that actually startled him.

"Well," said he, after a pause, "I think it is very

probable that will come of it; but, if it be your choice, I have nothing to say."

"Go back, Herr Rittmeister," cried I, and arrange the meeting for the very earliest moment."

"I said this with a strong purpose, for I felt if the event were to come off at once I could behave well.

"As you are resolved on this course," said he, "do not make any such confidences to others as you have made to me; nothing about those Pottses in haberdashery and dry goods, but just simply you are the high and well-born Potts of Pottsheim. Not a word more."

I bowed an assent, but so anxious was he to impress this upon me that he went over it all once more.

"As it will be for me to receive the prince's message, the choice of weapons will be yours. What are you most expert with? I mean, after the pistol?" said he, grinning.

"I am about equally skilled in all. Rapier, pistol, or sabre are all alike to me."

"Der Teufel!" cried he: "I was not counting upon this; and as the sabre is the prince's weakest arm, we'll select it."

I bowed again, and more blandly.

"There is but one thing more," said he, turning about just as he was leaving the room. "Don't forget that in this case the gross provocation came from *you*, and therefore be satisfied with self-defence, or at most a mere

flesh wound. Remember that the prince is a near connection of the royal family of England, and it would be
irreparable ruin to you were he to fall by your hand."
And with this he went out.

Now, had he gravely bound me over not to strangle the
lions in the Tower it could not have appeared more
ridiculous to me than this injunction, and if there had
been in my heart the smallest fund of humour, I could
have laughed at it; but, Heaven knows, none of my
impulses took a mirthful turn at that moment, and there
never was invented the drollery that could wring a smile
from me.

I was sitting in a sort of stupor—I know not how
long—when the door opened, and the Rittmeister's head
peered in.

"To-morrow morning at five!" cried he. "I will
fetch you half an hour before." The door closed, and he
was off.

It was now a few minutes past eight o'clock, and there
were, therefore, something short of nine hours of life left
to me. I have heard that Victor Hugo is an amiable
and kindly disposed man, and I feel assured, if he ever
could have known the tortures he would have inflicted,
he would never have designed the terrible record entitled
Le Dernier Jour d'un Condamné. I conclude it was
designed as a sort of appeal against death punishments.
I doubt much of its efficacy in altering legislation, while

I feel assured, that if ever it fall in the way of one whose hours are numbered, it must add indescribably to his misery.

When, how, or by whom my supper was served, I never knew. I can only remember that a very sleepy waiter roused me out of a half drowsy reverie about midnight, by asking if he were to remove the dishes, or let them remain till morning. I bade him leave them, and me also, and when the door was closed I sat down to my meal. It was cold and unappetising. I would have deemed it unwholesome, too, but I remembered that the poor stomach it was destined for would never be called on to digest it, and that for once I might transgress without the fear of dyspepsia. My case was precisely that of the purseless traveller, who, we are told, can sing before the robber, just as if want ever suggested melody, or that being poor was a reason for song. So with me any excess was open to me just because it was impossible!

"Still," thought I, "great criminals—and surely I am not as bad as they—eat very heartily." And so I cut the tough fowl vigorously in two, and placed half of it on my plate. I filled myself out a whole goblet of wine, and drank it off. I repeated this, and felt better. I fell to now with a will, and really made an excellent supper. There were some potted sardines that I secretly resolved to have for my breakfast, when the sudden thought flashed across me that I was never to breakfast any more.

I verily believe that I tasted in that one instant a whole lifelong of agony and bitterness.

There was in my friendless, lone condition, my youth, the mild and gentle traits of my nature, and my guileless simplicity, just that combination of circumstances which would make my fate peculiarly pathetic, and I imagined my countrymen standing beside the gravestone and muttering "Poor Potts!" till I felt my heart almost bursting with sorrow over myself.

"Cut off at three-and-twenty!" sobbed I; "in the very opening bud of his promise!"

"Misfortune is a pebble with many facets," says the Chinese adage, "and wise is he who turns it around till he find the smooth one."

"Is there such here?" thought I. "And where can it be?" With all my ingenuity I could not discover it, when at last there crossed my mind, how the event would figure in the daily papers, and be handed down to remote posterity. I imagined the combat itself described in the language almost of a lion-hunt. "Potts, who had never till that moment had a sword in his hand—Potts, though at this time severely wounded, and bleeding profusely, nothing dismayed by the ferocious attack of his opponent —Potts maintained his guard with all the coolness of a consummate swordsman." How I wished my life might be spared just to let me write the narrative of the combat. I would like, besides, to show the world how generously I could treat an adversary, with what delicacy I could respect his motives, and how nobly deal even with his injustice.

"Was that two o'clock?" said I, starting up, while the humming sound of the gone bell filled the room. "Is it possible that but three hours now stand between me and ———" I gave a shudder that made me feel as if I was standing in a fearful thorough draught, and actually looked up to see if the window were not open; but no, it was closed, the night calm, and the sky full of stars. "Oh!" exclaimed I, "if there are Pottses up amongst you yonder, I hope destiny may deal more kindly by them than down here. I trust that in those glorious regions a higher and purer intelligence prevails, and, above all things, that duelling is proclaimed the greatest of crimes." Remnant of barbarism! it is worse ten thousand times; it is the whole suit, costume, and investure of an uncivilised age. "Poor Potts!" said I; "you went out upon your life-voyage with very generous intentions towards posterity. I wonder how it will treat *you?* Will it vindicate your memory, uphold your fame, and dignify your motives? Will it be said in history, 'Amongst the memorable events of the period was the duel between the Prince Max of Swabia and an Irish gentleman named Potts?' To understand fully the circumstance of this remarkable conflict, it is necessary to premise that Potts was not what is vulgarly called

constitutionally brave; but he was more. He was ——'
Ah! there was the puzzle. How was that miserable
biographer ever to arrive at the secret of an organization
fine and subtle as mine? If I could but leave it on
record—if I could but transmit to the ages that will
come after me the invaluable key to the mystery of my
being—a few days would suffice—a week certainly would
do it—and why should I not have time given me for
this? I will certainly propose this to the Rittmeister
when he comes. There can be little doubt but he will see
the matter with my own eyes."

As if I had summoned him by enchantment, there he
stood at the door, wrapped in his great white cavalry
cloak, and looking gigantic and ominous together.

"There is no carriage-road," said he, " to the place we
are going, and I have come thus early that we may stroll
along leisurely, and enjoy the fresh air of the morning."

Until that moment I had never believed how heartless
human nature could be! To talk of enjoyment, to recal
the world and its pleasures, in any way, to one situated
like I, was a cold and scarcely credible cruelty; but the
words did me good service—they armed me with a
sardonic contempt for life and mankind—and so I
protested that I was charmed with the project, and out
we set.

My companion was not talkative; he was a quiet,
almost depressed man, who had led a very monotous

existence, with little society among his comrades; so that
he did not offer me the occasion I sought for, of saying
saucy and sneering things of the world at large. Indeed,
the first observation he made was, that we were in a locality
that ought to be interesting to Irishmen, since an ancient
shrine of St. Patrick marked the spot of the convent to
which we were approaching. No remark could have
been more ill-timed; to look back into the past, one
ought to have some vista of the future. Who can
sympathise with bygones when he is counting the
minutes that are to make him one of them?

What a bore that old Rittmeister was with his
antiquities, and how I hated him as he said, "If your
time was not so limited, I'd have taken you over to St.
Gallen to inspect the manuscripts." I felt choking as
he uttered these words. How was my time so limited?
I did not dare to ask. Was he barbarous enough to
mean that if I had another day to live, I might have
passed it pleasantly in turning over musty missals, in a
monastery?

At last we came to a halt in a little grove of pines,
and he said, "Have you any address to give me of friends
or relatives, or have you any peculiar directions on any
subject."

"You made a remark last night, Herr Rittmeister,"
said I, "which did not at the moment produce the
profound impression upon me that subsequent reflection

has enforced. You said that if his royal highness were fully aware that his antagonist was the son of a practising chemist and apothecary ——"

"That I could have put off this event; true enough, but when you refused that alternative, and insisted on satisfaction, I myself, as your countryman, gave the guarantee for your rank, which nothing will now make me retract. Understand me well—nothing will make me retract."

"You are pleased to be precipitate," said I, with an attempt to sneer; "my remark had but one object, and that was my personal disinclination to obtain a meeting under a false pretext."

"Make your mind easy on that score. It will be all precisely the same in about an hour hence."

I nearly fainted as I heard this, it seemed as though a cold stream of water ran through my spine and paralysed the very marrow inside.

"You have your choice of weapons," said he, curtly; "which are you best at."

I was going to say the "javelin," but I was ashamed, and yet should a man sacrifice life for a false modesty; while I reasoned thus, he pointed to a group of officers close to the garden wall of the convent, and said:

"They are all waiting yonder, let us hasten on."

If I had been mortally wounded, and was dragging my feeble limbs along to rest them for ever on some particular spot, I might have, probably, effected my progress as easily as I now did. The slightest inequality of ground tripped me, and I stumbled at every step.

"You are cold," said my companion, "and probably unused to early rising, taste this."

He gave me his brandy-flask, and I finished it off at a draught. Blessings be on the man who invented alcohol! all the ethics that ever were written cannot work the same miracle in a man's nature as a glass of whisky. Talk of all the wonders of chemistry, and what are they to the simple fact that two-pennyworth of cognac can convert a coward into a hero?

I was not quite sure that my antagonist had not resorted to a similar sort of aid, for he seemed as light-hearted and as jolly as though he was out for a pic-nic. There was a jauntiness, too, in the way he took out his cigar, and scraped his lucifer match on a beech-tree, that quite struck me, and I should like to have imitated it if I could.

"If it's the same to you, take the sabre, it's his weakest weapon," whispered the Rittmeister in my ear, and I agreed. And now there was a sort of commotion about the choice of the ground and the places, in which my friend seemed to stand by me most manfully. Then there followed a general measurement of swords, and a fierce comparison of weapons. I don't know how many were not thrust into my hand, one saying, "Take this,

it is well balanced in the wrist, or if you like a heavy
guard, here's your arm!"

"To *me*, it is a matter of perfect indifference," said I,
jauntily. "All weapons are alike."

"He will attack fiercely, and the moment the word is
given," whispered the Rittmeister, "so be on your guard;
keep your hilt full before you, or he'll slice off your nose
before you are aware of it."

"Be not so sure of that till you have seen my sword
play," said I, fiercely; and my heart swelled with a
fierce sentiment that must have been courage, for I
never remember to have felt the like before. I know I
was brave at that moment, for if, by one word, I could
have averted the combat, I would not have uttered it.

"To your places," cried the umpire, "and on your
guard! Are you ready?"

"Ready," re-echoed I, wildly, while I gave a mad
flourish of my weapon round my head that threw the
whole company into a roar of laughter; and, at the same
instant, two figures, screaming fearfully, rushed from
the beech copse, and, bursting their way through the
crowd, fell upon me with the most frantic embraces,
amidst the louder laughter of the others. O shame and
ineffable disgrace! O misery never to be forgotten!
It was Vaterchen who now grasped my knees, and
Tintefleck who clung round my neck and kissed me
repeatedly. From the time of the Laocoon, no one

ever struggled to free himself as I did, but all in vain —my efforts, impeded by the sword, lest I might unwillingly wound them, were all fruitless, and we rolled upon the ground inextricably commingled and struggling.

"Was I right?" cried the prince. "Was I right in calling this fellow a saltimbanque? See him now with his comrades around him, and say if I was mistaken."

"How is this?" whispered the Rittmeister. "Have you dared to deceive *me?*"

"I have deceived no one," said I, trying to rise, and I poured forth a torrent of not very coherent eloquence, as the mirth of my audience seemed to imply; but, fortunately, Vaterchen had now obtained a hearing, and was detailing in very fluent language, the nature of the relations between us. Poor old fellow, in his boundless gratitude I seemed more than human; and his praises actually shamed me to hear them. How I had first met them, he recounted in the strain of one assisted by the gods in classic times; his description made me a sort of Jove coming down on a rosy cloud to succour suffering humanity; and then came in Tintefleck with her broken words, marvellously aided by "action," as she poured forth the heap of gold upon the grass and said it was all mine!

Wonderful metal, to be sure, for enforcing conviction on the mind of man: there is a sincerity about it far more impressive than any vocal persuasion. The very clink of it implies that the real and the positive are in question, not the imaginary and the delusive. "This is all his!" cried she, pointing to the treasure with the air of one showing Aladdin's cave; and though her speech was not very intelligible, Vaterchen's "vulgate" ran underneath and explained the text.

"I hope you will forgive me. I trust you will be satisfied with my apologies, made thus openly," said the prince, in the most courteous of manners. "One who can behave with such magnanimity can scarcely be wanting in another species of generosity." And ere I could well reply, I found myself shaking hands with every one, and every one with me; nor was the least pleasurable part of this recognition the satisfaction displayed by the Rittmeister at the good issue of this event. I had great difficulty in resisting their resolution to carry me back with them to Bregenz. Innumerable were the plans and projects devised for my entertainment. Field sports, sham fights, rifle-shooting, all were displayed attractively before me; and it was clear, that if I accepted their invitations, I should be treated like the most favoured guest. But I was firm in my refusal; and, pleading a pretended necessity to be at a particular place by a particular day, I started once more, taking the road with the "vagabonds," who now seemed bound to me by an indissoluble bond; at least, so Vaterchen

assured me by the most emphatic of declarations, and
that, do with him what I might, he was my slave till
death.

"Who is ever completely happy?" says the sage;
and with too good reason is the doubt expressed. Here,
one might suppose, was a situation abounding with the
most pleasurable incidents. To have escaped a duel,
and come out with honour and credit from the issue;
to have refound not only my missing money, but to have
my suspicions relieved as to those whose honest name
was dear to me, and whose discredit would have darkened
many a bright hope of life,—these were no small successes; and yet—I shame to own it—my delight in them
was dashed by an incident so small and insignificant, that
I have scarce courage to recal it. Here it is, however.
While I was taking a kindly farewell of my military
friends, hand-shaking and protesting interminable friendships, I saw, or thought I saw, the prince, with even a
more affectionate warmth, making his adieus to Tintefleck! If he had not his arm actually round her waist,
there was certainly a white leather cavalry glove
curiously attached to her side, and one of her cheeks
was deeper coloured than the other, and her bearing
and manner seemed confused, so that she answered, when
spoken to, at cross purposes.

"How did you come by this brooch, Tintefleck? I
never saw it before."

"Oh, is it not pretty? It is a violet; and these leaves, though green, are all gold.

"Answer me, girl! who gave it thee?" said I, in the voice of Othello.

"Must I tell?" murmured she, sorrowfully.

"On the spot—confess it!"

"It was one who bade me keep it till he should bring me a prettier one."

"I do not care for what he said, or what you promised I want his name."

"And that I was never to forget him till then— never."

"Do you say this to irritate and offend me, or do you prevaricate out of shame?" said I, angrily.

"Shame!" repeated she, haughtily.

"Ay, shame or fear."

"Or fear! Fear of what, or of whom?"

"You are very daring to ask me. And now, for the last time, Tintefleck—for the last time, I say, who gave you this?"

As I said these words we had just reached the borders of a little rivulet, over which we were to cross by stepping-stones. Vaterchen was, as usual, some distance behind, and now calling to us to wait for him. She turned at his cry, and answered him, but made no reply to me.

This continued defiance of me overcame my temper

altogether, sorely pushed as it was by a stupid jealousy, and seizing her wrist with a strong grasp, I said, in a slow, measured tone, "I insist upon your answer to my question, or ——"

"Or what?"

"That we part here, and for ever."

"With all my heart. Only remember one thing," said she, in a low, whispering voice: "you left me once before—you quitted me, in a moment of temper, just as you threaten it now. Go, if you will, or if you must; but let this be our last meeting and last parting."

"It is as such I mean it—good-by!" I sprang on the stepping-stone as I spoke, and at the same instant a glittering object splashed into the stream close to me. I saw it, just as one might see the lustre of a trout's back as it rose to a fly. I don't know what demon sat where my heart ought to have been, but I pressed my hat over my eyes, and went on without turning my head.

CHAPTER XVI.

VERY conflicting and very mixed were my feelings, as I
set forth alone. I had come well, very well, out of a
trying emergency. I was neither driven to pretend I
was something other than myself, with grand surround-
ings and illustrious belongings, nor had I masqueraded
under a feigned name and a false history; but as Potts,
son of Potts the apothecary, I had carried my head high
and borne myself creditably.

"*Magna est veritas*," indeed! I am not so sure of the
"*prævalebit semper*," but assuredly where it does succeed,
the success is wonderful.

Heaven knows into what tortuous entanglements might
my passion for the "imaginative"—I liked this name for
it—have led me, had I given way to one of my usual
temptations. In more than one of my flights have I
found myself carried up into a region, and have had to
sustain an atmosphere very unsuited to my respiration,
and now, with the mere prudence of walking on the
terra firma, and treading the common highway of life,

I found I had reached my goal safely and speedily. Flowers do not assume to be shrubs, nor shrubs affect to be forest trees; the limestone and granite never pretend that they are porphyry and onyx. Nature is real, and why should man alone be untruthful and unreal? If I liked these reflections, and tried to lose myself in them, it was in the hope of shutting out others less gratifying; but, do what I would, there before me arose the image of Catinka, as she stood at the edge of the rivulet, that stream which seemed to cut me off from one portion of my life, and make the past the irrevocably gone for ever.

I am certain I was quite right in parting with that girl. Any respectable man, a father of a family, would have applauded me for severing this dangerous connection. What could come of such association except unhappiness? "Potts," would the biographer say— "Potts saw, with the unerring instinct of his quick perception, that this young creature would one day or other have laid at his feet the burnt-offering of her heart, and then, what could he have done? If Potts had been less endowed with genius, or less armed in honesty, he had not anticipated this peril, or, foreseeing, had undervalued it. But he both saw and feared it. How very differently had a libertine reasoned out this situation!" And then I thought how wicked I might have been; a monster of crime and atrocity. Every one knows the sensation of lying snugly a-bed on a stormy night, and, as the rain plashes and the wind howls, drawing more closely around him the coverlet, and the selfish satisfaction of his own comfort, heightened by all the possible hardships of others outside. In the same benevolent spirit, but not by any means so reprehensible, is it pleasant to imagine oneself a great criminal, standing in the dock, to be stared at by a horror-struck public, photographed, shaved, prison costumed, exhorted, sentenced, and then, just as the last hammer has driven the last nail into the scaffold, and the great bell has tolled out, to find that you are sitting by your wood fire, with your curtains drawn, your uncut volume beside you, and your peculiar weakness, be it tea, or sherry-cobbler, at your elbow. I constantly take a "rise" out of myself in this fashion, and rarely a week goes over that I have not either poisoned a sister or had a shot at the Queen. It is a sort of intellectual Russian bath, in which the luxury consists in the exaggerated alternative between being scalded first and rolled in the snow afterwards. It was in this figurative snow I was now disporting myself, pleasantly and refreshingly, and yet remorse, like a sturdy dun, stood at my gate, and refused to go away.

Had I, indeed, treated her harshly? had I rejected the offer of her young and innocent heart? Very puzzling and embarrassing question this, and especially to a man who had nothing of the coxcomb in his nature, none of that prompting of self-love that would suggest a vain reply. I felt that it was very natural *she* should have been struck by the attractive features of my character, but I felt this without a particle of conceit. I even experienced a sense of sorrow as I thought over it, just as a conscientious syren might have regretted that nature had endowed her with such a charming voice; and this duty—for it was a duty—discharged, I bethought me of my own future. I had a mission, which was to see Kate Herbert and give her Miss Crofton's letter. In doing so, I must needs throw off all disguises and mockeries, and be Potts, the very creature she sneered at, the man whose mere name was enough to suggest a vulgar life and a snob's nature! No matter what misery it may give, I will do it manfully. *She* may never appreciate—the world at large may never appreciate—what noble motives were hidden beneath these assumed natures, mere costumes as they were, to impart more vigour and persuasiveness to sentiments which, uttered in the undress of Potts, would have carried no convictions with them. Play Macbeth in a paletot, perform Othello in "pegtops," and see what effect you will produce! Well, my pretended station and rank were the mere gaudes and properties that gave force to my opinions. And now to relinquish these, and be the actor, in the garish light of the noonday, and a shabby-genteel coat and hat! "I will do it," muttered I, "I will

do it, but the suffering will be intense!" When the
prisoner sentenced to a long captivity is no more
addressed by his name, but simply called No. 18, or 43,
it is said that the shock seems to kill the sense of identity
within him, and that nothing more tends to that stolid air
of indifference, that hopeless inactivity of feature, so
characteristic of a prison life; in the very same way am
I affected when limited to my Potts nature, and condemned to confine myself within the narrow bounds of
that one small identity. From what Prince Max had
said at the *table d'hôte* at Bregenz, it was clear that Mrs.
Keats had already learned I was not the young prince of
the House of Orleans; but, in being disabused of one
error, she semed to have fallen into another, and it
behoved me to explain that I was not a rope-dancer or a
mountebank. "She, too, shall know me in my Potts
nature," said I; "she also shall recognise me in the
'majesty of myself.'" I was not very sure of what that
was, but found it in Hegel.

And when I have completed this task, I will throw
myself like a waif upon the waters of life. I will be
that which the moment or the event shall make me—
neither trammelled by the past nor awed by the future.
I will take the world as the drama of a day. Were men
to do this, what breadth and generosity would it impart
to them! It is in self-seeking and advancement that we
narrow our faculties and imprison our natures. A man

fancies he owns a palace and a demesne, but it is the palace that owns *him*, obliges him to maintain a certain state, live in a certain style, surrounded with certain observances, not one of which may be perhaps native to him. It is the poor man, who comes to visit and gaze on his splendours, who really enjoys them; *he* sees them without one detracting influence—not to say that in *his* heart are no corroding jealousies of some other rich man, who has a finer Claude, or a grander Rubens. Instead, besides, of owning one palace and one garden, it is the universe he owns: the vast Savannah is his race-ground; Niagara his own private cascade.

My heart bounded with these buoyant fancies, and I stepped out briskly on my road. Now that I had made this vow of poverty to myself, I felt very light-hearted and gay. So long as a man is struggling for place and pre-eminence in life, how can he be generous, how even gracious? "Thou shalt not covet thy neighbour's ox," says the commandment, but surely it must have been your neighbour's before it was yours, and if you have striven for it, it is likely that you have coveted it. Now, I will covet nothing—positively nothing—and I will see if in this noble spirit there will not be a reward proportionately ample and splendid.

My road led through that wild and somewhat dreary

valley by which the Upper Rhine descends, fed by many
an Alpine stream and torrent, to reach the fertile plains
of Germany. It was a desolate expanse of shingle, with
here and there little patches of oak scrub, or, at rare
intervals, small enclosures of tillage, though how tilled,
or for whom, it was hard to say, since not a trace of
inhabitant could be seen, far or wide. Deep fissures, the
course of many a mountain stream, cut the road at places,
and through these the foot traveller had to pass on
stepping-stones; while wheel carriages, descending into
the chaos of rocks and stones, fared even worse, and
incurred serious peril to spring and axle in the passage.
On the mountain-sides, indeed, some châlets were to be
seen, very high up, and scarcely accessible, but ever
surrounded with little tracts of greener verdure and
more varied foliage. From these heights, too, I could
hear the melodious ring of the bells worn by the cattle
—sure signs of peasant comfort. "Might not a man
find a life of simple cares and few sorrows, up yonder?"
asked I, as I gazed upward. While I continued to
look, the great floating clouds that soared on the
mountain-tops began to mass and to mingle together,
thickening and darkening at every moment, and then,
as though overweighted, slowly to descend, shutting
out châlet and shady copse and crag, as they fell, on
their way to the plain beneath. It was a grievous
change from the bright picture a few moments back, and

not the less disheartening, that the heavily charged mist
now melted into rain, that soon fell in torrents. With
not a rock nor a shrub to shelter under, I had nothing
for it but to trudge onward to the nearest village,
wherever that might be. How speedily the slightest
touch of the real will chase away the fictitious and
imaginary! No more dreams nor fancies now, as wet
and soaked I plodded on, my knapsack seeming double
its true weight, and my stick appearing to take root each
time it struck the ground. The fog, too, was so dense
that I was forced to feel my way as I went. The dull
roar of the Rhine was the only sound for a long time;
but this at length became broken by the crashing noise of
timber carried down by the torrents, and the louder din
of the torrents themselves as they came tumbling down
the mountain. I would have retraced my steps to
Bregenz, but that I knew the places I had passed
dryshod in the morning would by this time have become
impassable rivers. My situation was a dreary one, and
not without peril, since there was no saying when or
where a mountain cataract might not burst its way down
the cliffs and sweep clean across the road towards the
Rhine.

Had there been one spot to offer shelter, even the
poorest and meanest, I would gladly have taken it, and
made up my mind to await better weather; but there
was not a bank, nor even a bush, to cower under, and I

was forced to trudge on. It seemed to me at last that I
must have been walking many hours; but having no
watch, and being surrounded with impenetrable fog, I
could make no guess of the time, when at length a
louder and deeper sound appeared to fill the air, and
make the very mist vibrate with its din. The surging
sound of a great volume of water, sweeping along
through rocks and fallen trees, apprised me that I was
nearing a torrent; while the road itself, covered with
some inches of water, showed that the stream had
already risen above its embankments. There was real
danger in this; light carriages—the great lumbering
diligence itself—had been known to be carried away
by these suddenly swollen streams, and I began seriously
to fear disaster. Wading cautiously onward, I reached
what I judged to be the edge of the torrent, and felt
with my stick that the water was here borne madly
onward, and at considerable depth. Though through the
fog I could make out the opposite bank, and see that the
stream was not a wide one, I plainly perceived that the
current was far too powerful for me to breast without
assistance, and that no single passenger could attempt it
with safety. I may have stood half-an-hour thus, with
the muddy stream surging over my ankles, for I was
stunned and stupefied by the danger, when I thought I
saw through the mist two gigantic figures looming
through the fog, on the opposite bank. When and how

they had come there, I knew not, if they were indeed
there, and if these figures were not mere spectres of my
imagination. It was not till having closed my eyes, and
opening them again, beheld the same objects, that I could
fully assure myself of their reality.

CHAPTER XVII.

THE two great figures I had seen looming through the fog while standing in the stream, I at last made out to be two horsemen, who seemed in search of some safe and fordable part of the stream to cross over. Their apparent caution was a lesson by which I determined to profit, and I stood a patient observer of their proceedings. At times I could catch their voices, but without distinguishing what they said, and suddenly I heard a plunge, and saw that one had dashed boldly into the flood, and was quickly followed by the other. If the stream did not reach to their knees, as they sat, it was yet so powerful that it tested all the strength of the horses and all the skill of the riders to stem it; and as the water splashed and surged, and as the animals plunged and struggled, I scarcely knew whether they were fated to reach the bank, or be carried down in the current. As they gained about the middle of the stream, I saw that they were mounted gendarmes, heavy men, with heavy equipments, favourable enough to stem the tide, but hopelessly incapable to save themselves if over-turned. "Go back—hold in—go back! the water is far deeper here!" I cried out at the top of my voice; but either not hearing, or not heeding my warning, on they came, and, as I spoke, one plunged forward and went headlong down under the water, but, rising im-mediately, his horse struck boldly out, and, after a few struggles, gained the bank. The other, more fortunate, had headed up the stream, and reached the shore without difficulty.

With the natural prompting of a man towards those who had just overcome a great peril, I hastened to say how glad I felt at their safety, and from what intense fear their landing had rescued me; when one, a corporal, as his cuff bespoke, muttered a coarse exclamation of impatience, and something like a malediction on the service that exposed men to such hazards, and at the same instant the other dashed boldly up the bank, and with a bound placed his horse at my side, as though to cut off my retreat.

"Who are you?" cried the corporal to me, in a stern voice.

"A traveller," said I, trying to look majestic and indignant.

"So I see; and of what nation?"

"Of that nation which no man insults with impunity."

"Russia?"

"No; certainly not—England."

"Whence from last?"

"From Bregenz."

"And from Constance by Lindau?" asked he quickly, as he read from a slip of paper he had just drawn from his belt.

I assented, but not without certain misgivings, as I saw so much was known as to my movements.

"Now for your passport. Let me see it," said the corporal again. "Just so," said he, folding it up. "Travelling on foot, and marked 'suspected.'"

Though he muttered these words to his companion, I perceived that he cared very little for my having over-heard them.

"Suspected of what, or by whom?" asked I, angrily.

Instead of paying any attention to my question, the two men now conversed together in a low tone and confidentially.

"Come," said I, with an assumed boldness, "if you have quite done with that passport of mine, give it to me, and let me pursue my journey."

So eager were they in their own converse, that this speech, too, was unheeded; and now, grown rasher by impunity and impatience, I stepped stoutly forward, and attempted to take the passport from the soldier's hand.

"Sturm und Gewitter!" swore out the fellow, while he struck me sharply on the wrist, "do you mean to try force with us?" And the other drew his sabre, and flourishing it over his head, held the point of it within a few inches of my chest.

I cannot imagine whence came the courage that now filled my heart, for I know I am not naturally brave, but I felt for an instant that I could have stormed a breach; and, with an insulting laugh, I said, "Oh, of course, cut me down. I am unarmed and defenceless. It is an admirable opportunity for the display of Austrian chivalry."

"Bey'm Henker! It's very hard not to slice off his ear," said the soldier, seeming to ask leave for this act of valour.

"Get out your cords," said the corporal; "we're losing too much time here."

"Am I a prisoner, then?" asked I, in some trepidation.

"I suspect you are, and likely to be for some time to come," was the gruff answer.

"On what charge—what is alleged against me?" cried I, passionately.

"What has sent many a better-looking fellow to Spielberg," was the haughty rejoinder.

"If I *am* your prisoner," said I, haughtily—"and I warn you at once of your peril in daring to arrest a British subject travelling peacefully—You are not going to tie my hands! You are not going to treat me

as a felon?" I screamed out these words in a voice of
wildest passion, as the soldier, who had dismounted for
the purpose, was now proceeding to tie my wrists
together with a stout cord, and in a manner that
displayed very little concern for the pain he occasioned
me.

As escape was totally out of the question, I threw
myself upon the last resource of the injured. I fell back
upon eloquence. I really wish I could remember even
faintly the outline of my discourse; for though not by
any means a fluent German, the indignation that makes
men poets converted me into a great master of prose, and
I told them a vast number of curious, but not compli-
mentary, traits of the land they belonged to. I gave,
too, a rapid historical sketch of their campaigns against
the French, showing how they were always beaten, the
only novelty being whether they ran away or capitulated.
I reminded them that the victory over *me* would resound
through Europe, being the only successful achievement
of their arms for the last half-century. I expressed a
fervent hope that the corporal would be decorated with
the "Maria Theresa," and his companion obtain the
"valour medal," for what they had done. Pensions, I
hinted, were difficult in the present state of their finances,
but rank and honour certainly ought to await them. I
don't know at what exact period of my peroration it was
that I was literally "pulled up," each of the horsemen

holding a line fastened to my wrists, and giving me a drag forward that nearly carried me off my feet, and flat on my face. I stumbled, but recovered myself; and now saw that, bound as I was, with a gendarme on each side of me, it required all the activity I could muster, to keep my legs.

Another whispered conversation here took place across me, and I thought I heard the words Bregenz and Feldkirch interchanged, giving me to surmise that they were discussing to which place they should repair. My faint hope of returning to the former town was, however, soon extinguished, as the corporal, turning to me, said, " Our orders are to bring you alive to head-quarters. We'll do our best; but if, in crossing these torrents, you prefer to be drowned, it's no fault of ours."

" Do you mean by that," cried I, " that I am to be dragged through the water in this fashion ? "

" I mean that you are to come along as best you may."

" It is all worthy of you, quite worthy ! " screamed I, in a voice of wildest rage. " You reserve all your bravery for those who cannot resist you—and you are right, for they are your only successes. The Turks beat you "—here they chucked me close up, and dashed into the stream. " The Prussians beat you ! " I was now up to my waist in water. " The Swiss beat you ! " Down I went over head and ears. " The French always—

thrashed you "—down again—" at Ulm—Auster—litz—
Aspern "—nearly suffocated, I yelled out, " Wagram!"—
and down I went, never to know any further consciousness till I felt myself lying on the soaked and muddy
road, and heard a gruff voice saying, " Come along—we
don't intend to pass the night here!"

CHAPTER XVIII.

BENUMBED, bedraggled, and bewildered, I entered Feld-kirch late at night, my wrists cut with the cords, my clothes torn by frequent falls, my limbs aching with bruises, and my wet rags chafing my skin. No wonder was it that I was at once consigned from the charge of a gaoler to the care of a doctor, and ere the day broke I was in a raging fever.

I would not if I could, preserve any memory of that grievous interval. Happily for me, no clear traces remain on my mind—pangs of suffering are so mingled with little details of the locality, faces, words, ludicrous images of a wandering intellect, long hours of silent brooding, sound of church bells and such other tokens as cross the lives of busy men in the daily walk of life, all came and went within my brain, and still I lay there in fever.

In my first return of consciousness I perceived I was the sole occupant of a long arched gallery, with a number of beds arranged along each side of it. In their uniform simplicity, and the severe air of the few articles of furni-

ture, my old experiences at once recalled the hospital;
not that I arrived at this conclusion without much labour
and a considerable mental effort. It was a short journey,
to be sure, but I was walking with sprained ankles. It
was, however, a great joy and a great triumph to me to
accomplish even this much. It was the recognition to
myself that I was once more on the road to health, and
again to feel the sympathies that make a brotherhood of
this life of ours; and so happy was I with the prospect,
that when I went to sleep at night my last thought was
of the pleasure that morning would bring me. And I was
not disappointed; the next day, and the next, and several
more that followed, were all passed in a calm and tranquil enjoyment. Looking back upon this period, I have
often been disposed to imagine that when we lie in the
convalescence that follows some severe illness, with no
demands upon our bodily strength, no call made upon
our muscular energies, the very activity of digestion not
evoked, as our nourishment is of the simplest and lightest,
our brain must of necessity exercise its functions more
freely, untrammelled by passing cares or the worries incident to daily life, and that at such times our intellect has
probably a more uncontested action than at any other
period of our existence. I do not want to pursue my
theory, or endeavour to sustain it, my reader has here
enough to induce him to join his experience to my own, or
reject the notion altogether.

I lay thus, not impatiently, for above a fortnight. I
regained strength very slowly; the least effort or exertion
was sure to overcome me. But I wished for none; and
as I lay there, gazing for whole days long at a great coat
of arms over the end of the gallery, where a huge double-
headed eagle seemed to me screaming in the agony of
strangulation, but yet never to be choked outright, I
revelled in many a strange rambling as to the fate of the
land of which it was the emblem and the shield. Doubtless some remnant of my passionate assault on Austria
lingered in my brain, and gave this turn to its operations.

My nurse was one of that sisterhood whose charities
call down many a blessing on the Church that organises
their benevolences. She was what is called a "graue
Schwester;" and of a truth she seemed the incarnation of
greyness. It was not her dress alone, but her face and
hands, her noiseless gait, her undemonstrative stare, her
half-husky whisper, and her monotonous ways, had all a
sort of pervading greyness that enveloped her, just as a
cloud mist wraps a landscape. There was besides a kind
of fog-like indistinctness in her few and muttered words
that made a fitting atmosphere of drowsy uniformity for
the sick room.

Her first care, on my recovery, was to supply me with
a number of little religious books—lives of saints and
martyrs, accounts of miracles, and narratives of holy pil-
grimages—and I devoured them with all the zest of a

devotee. They seemed to supply the very excitement my
mind craved for, and the good soul little suspected how
much more she was ministering to a love for the marvellous than to a spirit of piety.   In the Flowers of St.
Francis, for instance, I found an adventure seeker after
my own heart. To be sure, his search was after sinners in
need of a helping hand to rescue them, but as his contests
with Satan were described as stand-up encounters, with
very hard knocks on each side, they were just as exciting
combats to read of, as any I had ever perused in stories
of chivalry.

Mistaking my zest for these readings for something far
more praiseworthy, "the grey sister" enjoined me very
seriously to turn from the evil advisers I had formerly
consorted with, and frequent the society of better-minded
and wiser men.   Out of these counsels, dark and dim at
first, but gradually growing clearer, I learned that I was
regarded as a member of some terrible secret society,
banded together for the direst and blackest of objects;
the subversion of thrones, overthrow of dynasties, and
assassination of sovereigns being all labours of love to us.
She had a full catalogue of my colleagues from Sand, who
killed Kotzebue, to Orsini, and seemed thoroughly persuaded that I was a very advanced member of the order.
It was only after a long time, and with great address on
my part, that I obtained these revelations from her, and
she owned that nothing but witnessing how the holy

studies had influenced me would ever have induced her
to make these avowals. As my convalescence progressed,
and I was able to sit up for an hour or so in the day, she
told me that I might very soon expect a visit from the
Staats Procurator, a kind of district attorney-general, to
examine me. So little able was I to carry my mind back
to the bygone events of my life, that I heard this as a sort
of vague hope that the inquiry would strike out some clue
by which I could connect myself with the past, for I was
sorely puzzled to learn what and who I had been before I
came there. Was I a prosecutor or was I a prisoner?
Never was a knotty point more patiently investigated,
but, alas! most hopelessly. The intense interest of the
inquiry, however, served totally to withdraw me from my
previous readings, and " the grey sister" was shocked to
see the mark in my book remain for days long unchanged.
She took courage at length to address me on the subject,
and even went so far as to ask if Satan himself had not
taken occasional opportunity of her absence to come and
sit beside my bed? I eagerly caught at the suggestion,
and said it was as she suspected : that he never gave me
a moment's peace, now torturing me with menaces, now
asking for explanations, how this could be reconciled with
that, and why such a thing should not have prevented
such another?

Instead of expressing any astonishment at my confession, she appeared to regard it as one of the most ordinary

incidents, and referred me to my books, and especially to
St. Francis, to see that these were usual and every-day
snares in use.   She went further, and in her zeal actually
showed a sort of contempt for the Evil One in his intellectual capacity that startled me; showing how St. Jude
always got the better of him, and that he was a mere
child when opposed by the craft of St. Anthony of Pavia.

"It is the truth," said she, "always conquers him.
Whenever, by any chance, he can catch you concealing or
evading, trying to make out reasons that are inconsistent,
or affecting intentions that you had not, then he is your
master."

There was such an air of matter of fact about all she
said, that when—our first conversation on this theme over
—she left the room, a cold sweat broke over me at the
thought that my next visitor would be the "Lebendige
Satan" himself.

It had come to this, that I had furnished my own mind
with such a subject of terror that I could not endure to be
alone, and lay there trembling at every noise, and shrink-
ing at every shadow that crossed the floor.   Many and
many times, as the dupe of my own deceivings, did I find
myself talking aloud in self-defence, averring that I
wanted to be good, and honest, and faithful, and that
whenever I lapsed from the right path, it was in moments
of erring reason, sure to be followed after by sincere
repentance.

It was after an access of this kind, "the grey sister" found me one morning, bathed in cold perspiration, my eyes fixed, my lips livid, and my fingers fast knotted together.

"I see," said she, " he has given you a severe turn of it to-day. What was the temptation?"

For a long while I refused to answer; I was weak as well as irritable, and I desired peace, but she persisted, and pressed hard to know what subject we had been discussing together.

"I'll tell you, then," said I, fiercely, for a sudden thought, prompted perhaps by a sense of anger, flashed across me: "he has just told me that you are his sister."

She screamed out wildly, and rushing to the end of the gallery, threw herself at the foot of a little altar.

Satisfied with my vengeance, I lay back and said no more. I may have dropped into a half-slumber afterwards, for I remember nothing till, just as evening began to fall, one of the servants came up and placed a table and two chairs beside my bed, with writing materials and a large book, and shortly after two men dressed in black, and with square black caps on their heads, took their places at the table, and conversed together in low whispers.

Resolving to treat them with a show of complete indifference, I turned away and pretended to go asleep.

"The Herr Staats Procurator Schlässel has come to

read the act of accusation," said the shorter man, who
seemed a subordinate; "take care that you pay proper
respect to the law and the authorities."

"Let him read away," said I, with a wave of my hand,
"I will listen."

In a low, sing-song, dreary tone, he began to recite
the titles and dignities of the Emperor. I listened for
a while, but as he got down to the Banat and Herze-
govine, sleep overcame me, and I dozed away, waking up
to hear him detailing what seemed his own greatness,
how he was "Ober" this, and "Unter" that, till I fairly
lost myself in the maze of his description. Judging
from the monotonous, business-like persistence of his
manner, that he had a long road before him, I wrapped
myself comfortably in the bed-clothes, closed my eyes,
and soon slept.

There were two candles burning on the table when I
next opened my eyes, and my friend the procurator was
reading away as before. I tried to interest myself for a
second or two; I rubbed my eyes, and endeavoured to be
wakeful; but I could not, and was fast settling down
into my former state, when certain words struck on my
ear and aroused me:

"'The well-born Herr von Rigges further denounces
the prisoner Harpar——'"

"Read that again," cried I, aloud, "for I cannot
clearly follow what you say."

"'The well-born Herr von Rigges,'" repeated he, "'further denounces the prisoner Harpar as one of a sect banded together for the darkest purposes of revolution!'"

"Forgive my importunity, Herr Procurator," said I, in my most insinuating tone, "but in compassion for the weakness of faculties sorely tried by fever, will you tell me who is Rigges?"

"Who is Rigges? Is that your question?" said he, slowly.

"Yes, sir; that was my question."

He turned over several pages of his voluminous report, and proceeded to search for the passage he wanted.

"Here it is," said he, at last; and he read out: "'The so-called Rigges, being a well-born and not-the-less-from-a-mercantile-object-engaging pursuit highly-placed and much-honoured subject of her Majesty the Queen of England, of the age of forty-two years and eight months, unmarried, and professing the Protestant religion.' Is that sufficient?"

"Quite so; and now, will you, with equal urbanity, inform me who is Harpar?"

"Who is Harpar? Who is Harpar? You surely do not ask me that?"

"I do; such is my question."

"I must confess that you surprise me. You ask me for information about yourself!"

"Oh, indeed! So that I am Harpar?"

"You can, of course, deny it. We are in a measure prepared for that. The proofs of your identity will be, however, forthcoming; not to add, that it will be difficult to disprove the offence."

"Ha, the offence! I'm really curious about that. What is the offence with which I am charged?"

"What I have been reading these two hours. What I have recited with all the clearness, brevity, and per-spicuity that characterize our imperial and royal legisla-tion, making our code at once the envy and admiration of all Europe."

"I'm sure of that. But what have I done?"

"With what for a dulness-charged and much-be-clouded intellect are you afflicted," cried he, "not to have followed the greatly-by-circumstances-corroborated and in-various-ways-by-proofs-brought-home narrative that I have already read out?"

"I have not heard one word of it!"

"What a deplorable and all-the-more-therefore-hope-less intelligence is yours! I will begin it once more." And with a heavy sigh he turned over the first pages of his manuscript.

"Nay, Herr Procurator," interposed I, hastily. "I have the less claim to exact this sacrifice on your part, that even when you have rendered it, it will be all fruit-less and unprofitable. I am just recovering from a severe illness. I am, as you have very acutely remarked, a man of very narrow and limited faculties in my best of moments, and I am now still lower in the scale of intelligence. Were you to read that lucid document till we were both grey-headed, it would leave me just as uninformed as to imputed crime as I now am."

"I perceive," said he, gravely. Then, turning to his clerk, he bade him write down, "'And the so-called Harpar, having duly heard and with decorously-lent attention listened to the foregoing act, did thereupon enter his plea of mental incapacity and derangement.'"

"Nay, Herr Procurator, I would simply record that, however open to follow some plain narrative, the forms and subtleties of a legal document only bewilder me."

"What for an ingeniously-worded and with-artifice-cunningly-conceived excuse have we here?" exclaimed he, indignantly. "Is it from England, with her seventeen hundred and odd volumes of an incomplete code, that the imperial and royal government is to learn legislation? You are charged with offences that are known to every state of civilization: highway assault and molestation—attack with arms and deadly implements, stimulated by base and long-heretofore and with-bitterness-imagined plans of vengeance on your countryman and former associate, the so-named Rigges. From him, too, proceeds the information as to your political character, and the ever-to-be-deplored, and only-with-blood-

expiated, error of republicanism by which you are actuated. This brief, but not-the-less-on-that-account lucid
exposition, it is my duty first to read out, and then leave
with you. With all your from-a-wrong-impulse-proceed-
ing and a-spirit-of-opposition-suggested objections, I have
no wish nor duty to meddle. The benign and ever-
paternal rule under which we live, gives even to the
most-with-accusation-surrounded, and with-strong-pre-
sumption-implicated prisoner, every facility of defence.
Having read and matured this indictment, you will, after
a week, make choice of an advocate."

"Am I to be confronted with my accuser?"

"I sincerely hope that the indecent spectacle of insulting attack and offensive rejoinder thus suggested, is
unknown to the administration of our law."

"How, then, can you be certain that I am the man
he accuses of having molested him?"

"You are not here to assail, nor I to defend, the with-
ages-consolidated and by-much-tact-accumulated wisdom
of our imperial and royal code."

"Might he not say, when he saw me, 'I never set eyes
on this man before?'"

He turned again to his clerk, and dictated something
of which I could but catch the concluding words—"And
thereby imputing perjury to the so-called Rigges."

It was all I could do to repress an outburst of anger
at this unjustifiable system of inference, but I did restrain

myself, and merely said, " I impute nothing Herr Procurator; I simply suggest a possible case, that everything
suffered by Rigges was inflicted by some other than I."

" If you had accomplices, name them," said he,
solemnly.

This overcame all my prudent resolves. I was nowise
prepared for such a perversity of misconception, and,
losing all patience, and all respect for his authority, I
burst out into a most intemperate attack on Austria, her
code, her system, her ignorant indifference to all European
enlightenment, her bigoted adherence to forms either
unmeaning or pernicious, winding up all with a pleasant
prediction that in a few short years the world would
have seen the last of this stolid and unteachable empire.

Instead of deigning a reply, he merely bent down to
the table, and I saw by the movement of his lips, and
the rapid course of the clerk's pen, that my statement
was being reduced to writing.

" When you have completed that," said I, gravely, " I
have some further observations to record."

" In a moment—in a moment," patiently responded
the procurator; "we have only got to 'the besotted
stupidity of her pretentious officials.' "

The calm quietude of his manner as he said this threw
me into a fit of laughter, which lasted several minutes.

" There, there," said I, " that will do; I will keep the
remainder of my remarks for another time and place."

" ' Reserving to himself,' " dictated he, " ' the right of uttering still more bitter and untruthful comments on a future occasion.' "   And the clerk wrote the words as he spoke them.

" You will sign this here," said he, presenting me with the pen.

" Nothing of the kind, Herr Procurator. I will not lend myself to any, even the most ordinary, form of your stupid system."

" ' And refuses to sign the foregoing,' " dictated he, in the same unmoved voice. This done, he arose and proceeded to draw on his gloves.   " The act of allegation I now commit to your hands," said he, calmly, " and you will have a week to reflect upon the course you desire to adopt."

" One question before you go: Is the person called Rigges here at this moment, and can I see him ? "

He consulted for a few seconds with his subordinate, and then replied: " These questions we are of opinion are irrelevant to the defence, and need not be answered."

" I only ask you, as a favour, Herr Procurator," said I.

" The law recognises no favours, nor accepts courtesies."

" Does it also reject common sense ?—is it deaf to all intelligence ?—is it indifferent to every appeal to reason ? —is it dead to —— "

But he would not wait for more, and having saluted

me thrice profoundly, retired from the gallery, and left
me alone with my indignation.

The great pile of paper still lay on the table next me,
and in my anger I hurled it from me to the middle of
the room, venting I know not what passionate wrath at
the same time on everything German: "This the land of
primitive simplicity and patriarchal virtues, forsooth!
This the country of elevated tastes and generous instincts! Why, it is all Bureau and Barrack!" I went
on for a long time in this strain, and I felt the better for
it. The operative surgeons tell us that no men recover
so certainly or so speedily after great operations as the
fellows who scream out and make a terrible uproar. It
is your patient, self-controlling creature who sinks under
the suffering he will not confess; and I am confident that
it is a wise practice to blow off the steam of one's indignation, and say all the most bitter things one can think
of in moments of disappointment, and, so to say, prepare
the chambers of your mind for the reception of better
company.

After a while I got up, gathered the papers together,
and prepared to read them. Legal amplifications and
circumlocutions are of all lands and peoples; but for the
triumph of this diffusiveness commend me to the Germans. To such an extent was this the case, that I
reached the eigth page of the precious paper before I got
finally out of the titular description of the vice-governor

in whose district the event was laid. Armed, however, with heroic resolution, I persevered, and read on through the entire night—I will not say without occasional refreshers in the shape of short snaps—but the day was already breaking when I turned over the last page, and read the concluding little blessing on the Emperor under whose benign reign all the good was encouraged, all evil punished, and the Hoch-gelehrter—Hoch wohl-geborner Herr der Hofrath, Ober Procurators-fiscal-Secretär, charged with the due execution of the present decree.

In the language of *précis* writing the event might be stated thus: "A certain Englishman named Rigges, travelling by post, arrived at the torrent of Dornbirn a short time before noon, and while waiting there for the arrival of some peasants to accompany his carriage through the stream, was joined by a foot-traveller, by whom he was speedily recognised. Whatever the nature of the relations previously subsisting between them—and it may be presumed they were not of the most amiable —no sooner had they exchanged glances than they engaged in deadly conflict. Rigges was well armed; the stranger had no weapon whatever, but was a man of surpassing strength, for he tore the door of the carriage from its hinges, and dragged Rigges out upon the road before the other could offer any resistance. The postilion, who had gone to summon the peasants, was speedily recalled by the report of fire-arms; three shots were fired in rapid succession, and when he reached the spot it was to see two men struggling violently in the torrent, the stranger dragging Rigges with all his might towards the middle of the stream, and the other screaming wildly for succour. The conflict was a terrible one, for the foot-traveller seemed determined on self-destruction, if he could only involve the other in his own fate. At last Rigges' strength gave way, and the other threw himself upon him, and they both went down beneath the water.

"The stranger emerged in an instant, but one of the peasants on the bank struck him a violent blow with his ash pole, and he fell back into the stream. Meanwhile, the others had rescued Rigges, who lay panting, but unconscious, on the ground. They were yet ministering to his recovery when they heard a wild shout of derisive triumph, and now saw that the other, though carried away by the torrent, had gained a small shingly bank in the middle of the Rhine, and was waving his hat in mockery of them. They were too much occupied with the care of the wounded man, however, to bestow more attention on him. One of Rigges' arms was badly fractured, and his jaw also broken, while he complained still more of the pain of some internal injuries: so severe, indeed, were his sufferings, that he had to be carried on a litter to Feldkirch. His first care on arriving was to denounce the assailant, whose name he gave as Harpar, declaring him to be a most notorious member of a

242   A DAY'S RIDE:

"Rouge" society, and one whose capture was an object of European interest. In fact, Rigges went so far as to pretend that he had himself perilled life in the attempt to secure him.

" Detachments of mounted gendarmes were imme-diately sent off in pursuit, the order being to arrest any foot-traveller whose suspicious appearance might chal-lenge scrutiny."

It is needless to say how much I appeared to fulfil the signs they sought for, not to add that the intemperance of my language, when captured, was in itself sufficient to establish a grave charge against me. It is true, there was in the act of allegation a lengthened description of me, with which my own appearance but ill corresponded. I was described as of middle age, of a strong frame and muscular habit, and with an expression that denoted energy and fierceness. How much of that vigour must they imagine had been washed away by the torrent, to leave me the poor helpless-looking thing I now appeared!

I know it is a very weak confession, I feel as I make it how damaging to my character is the acknowledgment, and how seriously I compromise myself in my reader's estimation; but I cannot help owning that I felt very proud to be thought so wicked, to be classed with those Brutuses of modern history, who were scattering explo-sive shells like bonbons, and throwing grenades broadcast like "confetti" in a carnival. I fancied how that miserable Staats Procurator must have trembled in his inmost heart as he sat there in close proximity with such an infuriate desperado as I was. I hoped that every look, every gesture, every word of mine, struck terror into his abject soul. It must also unquestionably do them good, these besotted, self-satisfied, narrow-minded Germans, to learn how an Englishman, a born Briton, regards their miserable system of government, and that poor and meagre phantasm they call their "civilisation." Well, they have had their opportunity now, and I hope they will make much of it.

As I pondered over the late incident as recorded in the allegation, I remembered the name of Rigges as that of the man Harpar mentioned as having "run" or escaped with their joint finances, and had very little difficulty in filling up the probable circumstances of their rencontre. It was easy to see how Rigges, travelling "extra-post," with all the appearance of wealth and station, could impute to the poor wayfarer any criminality he pleased. Cunningly enough, too, he had hit upon the precise imputation which was sure to enlist Austrian sympathies in the pursuit, and calling him a " Socialist and a Rogue" was almost sealing his fate at once. How glad I felt that the poor fellow had escaped, even though it cost me all the penalty of personating him; yes, I really was generous enough for that sentiment, though I perceive that my reader smiles incredulously as I declare it. "No, no," mutters he, "the arrant snob must not try to impose upon us in that fashion. He was trembling to the very marrow of his bones, and nothing was further from his thoughts than self-sacrifice or devotion." I know your opinion of me takes this lively shape, I feel it, and I shrink under it; but I know, besides, that I owe all this depreciating estimate of me to nothing so much as my own frankness and candour. If my reader, therefore, scruples to accord me the merit of the generosity that I lay claim to, let him revel in the depreciating confession that I am about to make. I knew that when it was discovered I was not Harpar, I must instantly be set at liberty. I felt this, and could therefore be at any moment the arbiter of my own freedom. To do this, of course, would set in motion a search after the real delinquent, and I determined I would keep my secret till he had ample time to get away. When I had satisfied myself that all pursuit of him must be hopeless, I would declare myself to be Potts, and proudly demand my liberation.

My convalescence made now such progress that I was able to walk about the gallery, and indeed occasionally to stroll out upon a long terrace which flanked the entire building, and gaze upon a garden, beyond which again I could see the town of Feldkirch and the open Platz in which the weekly market was held. By the recurrence of these—they always fell upon a Saturday—was I enabled to mark time, and I now reckoned that three weeks had gone over since the day of the Herr Procurator's visit, and yet I had heard nothing more of him, nor of the accusation against me. I was seriously thinking whether my wisest plan might not be to take French leave and walk off, when my gaoler came one morning to announce that I was to be transferred to Innspruck, where, in due course, my trial would take place.

"What if I refuse to go?" said I; "what if I demand my liberation here on the spot?"

"I don't imagine that you'd delay your journey much by that, my good friend," said he; "the Imperial and Royal Government takes little heed of foolish remonstrances."

"What if the Imperial and Royal Government, in the plenitude of its sagacity, should be in the wrong? What if I be not the person who is accused of this crime? What if the real man be now at liberty? What if the accuser himself will declare, when he sees me, that he never met me before, nor so much as heard of me?"

"Well, all that may happen; I won't say it is impossible, but it cannot occur here, for the Herr Von Rigges has already set off for Innspruck, and you are to follow him to-morrow."

CHAPTER XIX.

IF there be anything in our English habits upon which
no difference of opinion can exist, it is our proneness to
extend to a foreigner a degree of sympathy and an amount
of interest that we obstinately deny to our own people.
The English artist struggling all but hopelessly against
the town's indifference has but to displace the consonants
or multiply the vowels of his name to be a fashion and a
success.   Strange and incomprehensible tendency in a
nation so overwhelmingly impressed with a sense of its
own vast superiority! But so it is. Mr. Brady may sing
to empty benches, while il Signor Bradini would "bring
down the house." What set me thinking over this was,
that, though Silvio Pellico was a stock theme for English
pity and compassion, I very much doubted if a single tear
would fall for the misfortunes of a Potts. And yet there
was a marvellous similarity in our sufferings. In each
case was the Austrian the gaoler; in each case was the
victim a creature of tender mould and gentle nature.

I travelled in a sort of covered cart, with a mounted

gendarme at either side of me. Indeed the one faintly
alleviating circumstance of my captivity was the sight of
those two heavily equipped giants, armed to the teeth,
who were supposed to be essential to my safe conduct. It
was such an acknowledgment of what they had to apprehend from my well-known prowess and daring, so palpable a confession that every precaution was necessary
against the bold intrepidity of a man of my stamp! At
times, I almost wished they had put chains upon me. I
thought how well it would read in my Memoirs; how I
was heavily "manacled"—a great word that—"orders
being given to the escort to shoot me if I showed the
slightest intention to escape." It was an intense pleasure
to me to imagine myself a sort of Nana Sahib, and whenever we halted at some way-side public, and the idle
loungers would draw aside the canvass covering and stare
in at me, I did my utmost to call up an expression of ogre-
like ferocity and wildness, and it was with a thrill of
ecstasy I saw a little child clasp its mother by the neck,
and scream out to come away as it beheld me.

On the second night of our journey we halted at a little
village at the foot of the Arlberg, called Steuben, where,
in default of a regular prison, they lodged me in an old
tower, the lower part of which was used for a stable. It
stood in the very centre of the town, and from its narrow
and barred windows I could catch glimpses of the little
world that moved about in happy freedom beneath me. I

could see the Marktplatz, from which the booths were
now being taken down, and could mark that preparations
for some approaching ceremony were going on, but of
what nature I could not guess. A large place was neatly
swept out, and at last strewn with sawdust—signs unerring of some exhibition of legerdemain or conjuring, of
which the Tyrolese are warm admirers. The arrange-
ments were somewhat more portentious than are usually.
observed in open air representations, for I saw seats prepared for the dignitaries of the village, and an evident
design to mark the entertainment as under the most distinguished protection. The crowd—now considerable—
observed all the decorous bearing of citizens in presence
of their authorities.

I nestled myself snugly in the deep recess of the window
to watch the proceedings, nor had I long to wait; some
half-dozen gaily-dressed individuals having now pierced
their way through the throng, and commenced those peculiar gambols which bespeak backbones of gristle and legs
of pasteboard. It is a class of performance I enjoy
vastly. The two fellows who lap over each other like
the links of a chain, and the creature who rolls himself
about like a ball, and the licensed freed ms of that man
of the world—the clown—never weary m , and I believe
I laugh at them with all the more zest that I have so
often laughed at them before. It was plain, after a while,
that a more brilliant part of the spectacle was yet to

come, for a large bluff-looking man, in cocked-hat and
jack-boots, now entered the ring and indignantly ejected
the clowns by sundry admonitions with a lash-whip, which
I perceived were not merely make-believes.

"Ah, here he comes! here he is!" was now uttered in
accents of eager interest, and an avenue was quickly made
through the crowd for the new performer. There was
delay after this, and though doubtless the crowd below
could satisfy their curiosity, I was so highly perched and
so straitened in my embrasure that I had to wait, with
what patience I might, the new arrival. I was deep in
my guesses what sort of "artist" he might prove, when I
saw the head of a horse peering over the shoulders of the
audience, and then the entire figure of the quadruped as he
emerged into the circle, all sheeted and shrouded from
gaze. With one dexterous sweep the groom removed all
the clothing, and there stood before me my own lost treasure—Blondel himself! I would have known him among
ten thousand. He was thinner, perhaps, certainly thinner,
but in all other respects the same; his silky mane and
his long tassel of a tail hung just as gracefully as of yore,
and, as he ambled round, he moved his head with a courteous inclination, as though to acknowledge the plaudits
he met with.

There was in his air the dignity that said, "I am one
who has seen better days. It was not always thus with
me. Applaud if you must, and if you will; but re-

member that I accept your plaudits with reserve, perhaps even with reluctance." Poor fellow, my heart bled for him! I felt as though I saw a cathedral canon cutting somersaults, and all this while, by some strange inconsistency, I had not a sympathy to bestow on the human actors in the scene. "As for them," thought I, "they have accepted this degradation of their own free will. If they had not shirked honest labour they need never have been clowns or pantaloons; but Blondel—Blondel, whom fate had stamped as the palfrey of some high-born maiden, or, at least, as the favourite steed of one who would know how to lavish care on an object of such perfection—Blondel, who had borne himself so proudly in high places, and who, even in his declining fortunes, had been the friend and fellow-traveller of —— Yes, why should I shame to say it? Posterity will speak of Potts without the detracting malice and envious rancour of contemporaries; and when, in some future age, a great philanthropist or statesman should claim the credit of some marvellous discovery, some wondrous secret by which humanity may be bettered, a learned critic will tell the world how this great invention was evidently known to Potts, how at such a line, or such a page, we shall find that Potts knew it all."

The wild cheering of the crowd beneath cut short these speculations, and now I saw Blondel cantering gaily round the circle, with a handkerchief in his mouth. If in sportive levity it chanced to fall, he would instantly wheel about, and seize it, and then, whisking his tail and shaking his long forelock, resume his course again. It was fine, too, to mark the haughty indifference he manifested towards that whip-cracking monster who stood in the centre, and affected to direct his motions. Not alone did he reject his suggestions, but in a spirit of round defiance did he canter up behind him, and alight with his fore-legs on the fellow's shoulders.. I am not sure whether the spectators regarded the tableau as I did, but to *me* it seemed an allegorical representation of man and his master.

The hard breathing of a person close behind me now made me turn my head, and I saw the gaoler, who had come with my supper. A thought flashed suddenly across me. "Go down to those mountebanks, and ask if they will sell that cream-coloured pony," said I. "Bargain as though you wanted him for yourself—he is old and of little value, and you may perhaps secure him for eighty or ninety florins, and if so, you shall have ten more for your pains. It is a caprice of mine, nothing more, but help me to gratify it."

He heard me out with evident astonishment, and then gravely asked if I had forgotten the circumstance that I was a prisoner, and likely to remain so for some time.

"Do as I bade you," said I, "and leave the result to

me. There, lose no more time about it, for I see the performance is drawing to a close."

"Nay, nay," said he; "the best of all is yet to come. The pretty Moorish girl has not yet appeared. Ha! here she is."

As he spoke he crept up into the window beside me, not less eager for the spectacle than myself. A vigorous cheer, and a loud clapping of hands below, announced that the favourite was in sight long before she was visible to our eyes.

"What can she do?" asked I, peevishly perhaps, for I was provoked how completely she had eclipsed poor Blondel in public favour. "What can she do? Is she a rope-dancer, or does she ride in the games of the ring?"

"There, there! Look at her—yonder she goes! and there's the young prince—they call him a prince, at least —who follows her everywhere."

I could not but smile at the poor gaoler's simplicity, and would willingly have explained to him that we have outlived the age of Cinderellas. Indeed, I had half turned towards him with this object, when a perfect roar of the crowd beneath me drew off my attention from him to what was going on below. I soon saw what it was that entranced the public: it was the young girl, who now, standing on Blondel's back, was careering round the circle at full speed. It is an exercise in which neither the horse nor the rider are seen to advantage;

the heavy monotonous tramp of the beast, cramped by
the narrow limits, becomes a stilty, wooden gallop. The
rider, too, more careful of her balance than intent upon
graceful action, restricts herself to a few, and by no
means picturesque, attitudes. With all this, the girl now
before me seemed herself so intensely to enter into the
enjoyment of the scene, that all her gestures sprang out
of a sort of irrepressible delight. Far from unsteadying
her foot, or limiting her action, the speed of the horse
appeared to assist the changeful bendings of her graceful
figure, as now, dropping on one knee, she would lean over
to caress him, or now, standing erect, with folded arms
and leg advanced, appear to dare him to displace her.
Faultlessly graceful as she was, there was that in her
own evident enjoyment that imparted a strange delight
to the beholder, and gave to the spectacle the sort of
magnetism by which pleasure finds its way from heart to
heart throughout a multitude. At least, I suppose this
must have been so, for in the joyous cheering of that
crowd there was a ring of wild delight far different from
mere applause.

At last, poor Blondel, blown and wearied, turned
abruptly into the middle of the ring, and with panting
sides and shaking tail came to a dead halt. The girl,
with a graceful slide, seated herself on his back and
patted him playfully. And to me this was by far the
most graceful movement of the whole.

It was really a picture! and so natural and so easy
withal, that one forgot all about her spangles and tinsel,
the golden fillet of her hair, and the tawdry fringe of her
sandals; and, what was even harder still, heard not the
hoarse-mouthed enthusiasm that greeted her. At length,
a tall man, well dressed and of striking appearance,
pushed his way into the ring, and politely presented her
with a bouquet, at which piece of courtesy the audience,
noways jealous, again redoubled their applause. She
now looked round her with an air of triumphant pleasure,
and while, with a playful gesture, she flung back the
ringlets on her neck, she lifted her face full to my view,
and it was Tintefleck! With all my might I cried out,
"Catinka! Catinka!" I know not why, but the impulse
never waited to argue the question. Though I screamed
my loudest, the great height at which I was placed, and
the humming din of the crowd, totally drowned my
words. Again and again I tried it, but to no purpose.
There she sat, slowly making the round of the circus,
while the stranger walked at her side, to all seeming
conversing as though no busy and prying multitude stood
watching and observing them. Wearied with my failure
to attract notice, I turned to address the gaoler, but he
had already gone, and I was alone. I next endeavoured
by a signal to call attention to me, and, at last, saw how
two or three of the crowd had observed my waving
handkerchief, and were pointing it out to others.

Doubtless they wondered how a poor captive could care for the pleasant follies of a life of whose commonest joys he was to be no sharer, and still greater was their astonishment as I flung forth a piece of money—a gold Napoleon it was—which they speedily caught up and gave to Catinka. How I watched her as she took it and showed it to the stranger. He, by his gesture, seemed angry, and made a motion as though asking her to throw it away; and then there seemed some discussion between them, and his petulence increased; and she, too, grew passionate, and, leaping from the horse, strode haughtily across the circus and disappeared. And then arose a tumult and confusion, the mob shouting madly for the Moorish girl to come back, and many much disposed to avenge her absence on the stranger. As for him, he pushed the mob haughtily aside and went his way, and though for a while the crowd continued to vent its expressions of displeasure and disappointment, the performance soon concluded, and all went their several roads homeward; and when I looked out upon the empty Platz, over which the dusky shadows of the old houses were now stealing to mingle together, and instead of the scene of bustle and excitement saw a few lingering townsfolk moody and purposeless, I asked myself if the whole incidents were not a vision mind-drawn and invented. There was not one single clue by which I could trace it to reality.

More than once in my life had my dreamy temperament played me such pranks, and, strangely too, even when I had assured myself of the deception, there would yet linger in my mind thoughts and impressions strong enough to influence my actions, just as we often see that our disbelief in a scandalous story is not sufficient to disabuse us of a certain power it wields over us.

Oh, what a long and dreary night was that, harassed with doubts, and worn out with speculations. My mind had been much weakened by my fever, and whenever I followed a train of thought too long, confusion was sure to ensue. The terror of this chaotic condition, where all people, and lands, and ideas, and incidents, jostle against each other in mad turmoil, can only be estimated by one who has felt it. Like the awful rush of sensations of him who is sliding down some steep descent to a tremendous precipice, one feels the gradual approach of that dreamy condition where reason is lost, and the mind a mere waif upon the waters.

" Here's your breakfast," said the gaoler, as he stopped the course of my reverie. " And the brigadier hopes you'll be speedy with it, for you must reach Maltz by nightfall."

" Tell me," said I, eagerly, " was there a circus company here yesterday evening? Did they exhibit on the Platz there?"

" You are a deep one, you are!" muttered he, sulkily to himself, and left the cell.

CHAPTER XX.

I CORE up admirably on my journey. I felt I was doing a very heroic thing. By my personation of Harpor, I was securing that poor fellow's escape, and giving him ample time to get over the Austrian frontier, and many a mile away from the beaks of the Double Eagle. I had read of such things in history, and I resolved I would not derogate from the proudest records of such self-devotion. Had I but remembered how long my illness had lasted, I might have easily seen that Harpar could by this time have arrived at Calcutta; but, unfortunately for me, I had no gauge of time whatever, and completely forgot the long interval of my fever.

On reaching Innspruck, I was sent on to an old château some ten miles away, called the Ambras Schloss, and being consigned to the charge of a retired artillery officer there, they seemed to have totally forgotten all about me. I lived with my old gaoler just as if I were his friend: we worked together in the garden, pruned, and raked, and hoed, and weeded; we smoked and fished,

and mended our nets on wet days, and read, living
exactly as might any two people in a remote out-of-the-
world spot.

There is a sort of armoury at the Ambras, chiefly of
old Tyrolese weapons of an early period—maces and
halberds, and double-handed swords, and such like—and
one of our pastimes was arranging, and settling, and
cataloguing them, for which, in the ancient records of
the Schloss, there was ample material. This was an
occupation that amused me vastly, and I took to it with
great zeal, and with such success that old Hirsch, the
gaoler, at last consigned the whole to my charge, along
with the task of exhibiting the collection to strangers—
a source from which the honest veteran derived the
better part of his means of life.

At first, I scarcely liked my function as showman, but
like all my other experiences in life, habit sufficed to
reconcile me, and 1 took to the occupation as though I
had been born to it. If now and then some rude or
vulgar traveller would ruffle my temper by some illiterate
remark or stupid question, I was well repaid by intercourse with a different stamp. They were to me such
peeps at the world as a monk might have from the
windows of his cloister, tempting perhaps, but always
blended with the sense of the security that encompassed
him, and defended him from the cares of existence.

Perhaps the consciousness that I could assert my

innocence and procure my freedom at any moment, for the first few months reconciled me to this strange life; but certainly after a while I ceased to care for any other existence, and never troubled my head either about past or future. I had, in fact, arrived at the great monastic elevation, in which a man, ceasing to be human, reaches the dignity of a vegetable.

I had begun, as I have said, by an act of heroism, in accepting all the penalties of another, and, long after I ceased to revert to this sacrifice, the impulse it had once given still continued to move me. If Hirsch never alluded to my imputed crime to me, I was equally reserved towards him.

CHAPTER XXI.

FROM time to time, a couple of grave, judicial-looking men would arrive and pass the forenoon at the Ambras Schloss, in reading out certain documents to me. I never paid much attention to them, but my ear at moments would catch the strangest possible allegations as to my exalted political opinions, the dangerous associates I was bound up with, and the secret societies I belonged to. I heard once, too, and by mere accident, how, at Steuben, I had asked the gaoler to procure me a horse, and thrown gold in handfuls from the windows of my prison to bribe the townsfolk to my rescue, and I laughed to myself to think what a deal of pleading and proof it would take to rebut all these allegations, and how little likely it was I would ever engage in such a conflict.

By long dwelling on the thought of my noble devotion, and how it would read when I was dead and gone, I had extinguished within my heart all desire for other distinction, speculating only on what strange and ingenious theories men would spin for the secret clue to my motives.

"True," they would say, "Potts never cared for Harpar. He was not a man to whom Potts would have attached himself under any circumstances; they were, as individuals, totally unlike and unsympathetic. How, then, explain this extraordinary act of self-sacrifice? Was he prompted by the hope that the iniquities of the Austrian police system would receive their death-blow from his story, and that the mound that covered him in the churchyard would be the altar of Liberty to thousands? or was Potts one of those enthusiastic creatures only too eager to carry the load of some other pilgrim in life?"

While I used thus to reason and speculate, I little knew that I had become a sort of European notoriety. Some English woman, however, some vagrant tourist, had put me in her book as the half-witted creature who showed the coins and curiosities at Ambras, and mentioned how for I know not how many years I was never heard to utter a syllable except on questions of old armour and antiquities. In consequence I was always asked for by my travelling countrymen, and my peculiarities treated with all that playful good taste for which tourists are famous. I remember one day having refused to perform the showman to a British family. I had a headache, or was sulky, or a fit of rebellion had got hold of me, but I sauntered out into the grounds and would not see them. In my walk through a close alley of laurels, I chanced to overhear the stranger conversing

with Hirsch, and making myself the subject of his
inquiries; and as I listened, I heard Hirsch say that one
entire room of the château was devoted to the papers
and documents in my case, and that probably it would
occupy a quick reader about twelve months to peruse
them. He added, that as I made no application for a
trial myself, nor any of my friends showed an inclination
to bestir themselves about me, the government would
very probably leave me to live and die where I was.
Thereupon, the Briton broke out into a worthy fit of
indignant eloquence. He denounced the Hapsburgs and
praised the Habeas Corpus; he raved of the power of
England, our press, our public opinion, our new frigates.
He said he would make Europe ring with the case.   It
was as bad, it was worse than Caspar Hauser's, for he
was an idiot outright, and *I* appeared to have the enjoyment of certain faculties. He said it should appear in
the *Times* and be mentioned in the House; and as I
listened, the strangest glow ran through me, a mild and
pleasurable enthusiasm, to think that all the right,
majesty, and power of Great Britain was about to
interest itself in behalf of Potts!

The Briton kept his word; the time, too, favoured him.
It was a moment when wandering Englishmen were
exhuming grievances throughout every land of Europe;
and while one had discovered some case of religious
intolerance in Norway, another beat him out of the field

with the cold-blooded atrocities of Naples. My Englishman chanced to be an M.P., and therefore he asked,
" in his place," if the Foreign Secretary had any information to afford the House with respect to the case of the
man called Harper, or Harpar, he was not certain which
and who had been confined for upwards of ten months in
a dungeon in Austria, on allegations of which the accused
knew nothing whatever, and attested by witnesses with
whom he had never been confronted.

In the absence of his chief, the under-secretary rose to
assure the right honourable gentleman that the case was
one which had for a considerable time engaged thè attention of the department he belonged to, and that the most
unremitting exertions of her Majesty's envoy at Vienna
were now being devoted to obtain the fullest information
as to the charges imputed to Harpar, and he hoped in a
few days to be able to lay the result of his inquiry on the
table of the House.

It was in about a week after this that Hirsch came to
tell me that a member of her Majesty's legation at
Vienna had arrived to investigate my case, and
interrogate me in person. I am half-ashamed to say
how vaingloriously I thought of the importance thus lent
me. I felt somehow as though the nation missed me.
Waiting patiently, as it might be, for my return, and yet
no tidings coming, they said, "What has become of
Potts?" It was clearly a case upon which they would

not admit of any mystification or deceit. "No secret
tribunals, no hole-and-corner commitments with us!
Where is he? Produce him. Say, with what is he
charged?" I was going to be the man of the day. I
knew it, I felt it; I saw a great tableau of my life
unrolling itself before me. Potts, the young enthusiast
after virtue—hopeful, affectionate, confiding, giving his
young heart to that fair-haired girl as freely as he would
have bestowed a moss-rose; and she, making light of the
gift, and with a woman's coquetry, torturing him by
a jealous levity till he resented the wrong, and tore
himself away. And then Catinka—how I tried the gold
of my nature in that crucible, and would not fall in love
with her before I had made her worthy of my love; and
when I failed in that, how I had turned from love to
friendship, and offered myself the victim for a man I
never cared about. No matter; the world will know me
at last. Men will recognise the grand stuff that I am
made of. If commentators spend years in exploring the
recondite passages of great writers, and making out
beauties where there were only obscurities, why should
not all the dark parts of my nature come out as
favourably, and some flattering interpreter say, "Potts
was for a long time misconceived; few men were more
wrongfully judged by their contemporaries. It was to a
mere accident, after all, we owe it that we are now
enabled to render him the justice so long denied him.

His was one of those remarkable natures in which it is difficult to say whether humility or self-confidence predominated?"

Then I thought of the national excitement to discover the missing Potts; just as if I had been a lost Arctic voyager. Expeditions sent out to track me—all the thousand speculations as to whether I had gone this way or that—where and from whom the latest tidings of me could be traced—the heroic offers of new discoverers to seek me living, or, sad alternative, restore to the country that mourned me the *reliquia Pottsi.* I always grew tender in my moods of self-compassion, and I felt my eyes swimming now in pity for my fate; and let me add in this place my protest against the vulgar error which stigmatises as selfishness the mere fact of a man's susceptibility. How, I would simply ask, can he feel for others who has no sense of sympathy with his own suffering nature? If the well of human kindness be dried up within him, how can he give to the parched throats the refreshing waters of compassion?

Deal with the fact how you may, I was very sorry for myself, and seriously doubted if as sincere a mourner would bewail me when I was gone.

If a little time had been given me, I would have endeavoured to get up my snug little chamber somewhat more like a prison cell: I would have substituted some

straw for my comfortable bed, and gracefully draped a
few chains upon the walls and some stray torture implements out of the Armoury; but the envoy came like
a "thief in the night," and was already on the stairs
when he was announced.

"Oh! this is his den, is it?" cried he from without,
as he slowly ascended the stairs.   "Egad! he hasn't
much to complain of in the matter of a lodging.· I only
wish our fellows were as well off at Vienna."   And with
these words there entered into my room a tall young
fellow, with a light brown moustache, dressed in a loose
travelling suit, and with the lounging air of a man
sauntering into a *café*.   He did not remove his hat as
he came in, or take the cigar from his mouth; the
latter circumstance imparting a ̄certain confusion to his
speech that made him occasionally scarce intelligible.
Only deigning to bestow a passing look on me, he moved
towards the window, and looked out on the grand
panorama of the Tyrol Alps, as they enclose the valley
of Innspruck.

"Well," said he to himself, "all this ain't so bad for
a dungeon."

The tone startled me.   I looked again at him, I
rallied myself to an effort of memory, and at once
recalled the young fellow I had met on the South-
Western line and from whom I had accidentally carried
away the despatch-bag.   To my beard, and my long

imprisonment, I trusted for not being recognised, and I sat patiently awaiting my examination.

"An Englishman, I suppose?" asked he, turning hastily round. "And of English parents?"

"Yes," was my reply, for I determined on brevity wherever possible.

"What brought you into this scrape?—I mean, why did you come here at all?"

"I was travelling."

"Travelling? Stuff and nonsense! Why should fellows like you travel? What's your rank in life?"

"A gentleman."

"Ah! but whose gentleman, my worthy friend? Ain't you a flunkey? There, it's out! I say, have you got a match to light my cigar? Thanks—all right. Look here, now—don't let us be beating about the bush all the day—I believe this government is just as sick of you as you are of them. You've been here two months, ain't it so?"

"Ten months and upwards."

"Well, ten months. And you want to get away?"

I made no answer; indeed, his free-and-easy manner so disconcerted me that I could not speak, and he went on:

"I suspect they haven't got much against you, or that they don't care about it; and, besides, they are civil to us just now. At all events, it can be done—you understand? —it can be done."

"Indeed," said I, half superciliously.

"Yes," resumed he, "I think so; not but you'd have managed better in leaving the thing to *us*. That stupid notion you all have of writing letters to newspapers and getting some troublesome fellow to ask questions in the House, that's what spoils everything! How can *we* negotiate when the whole story is in the *Times* or the *Daily News?*"

"I opine, sir, that you are ascribing to me an activity and energy I have no claim to."

"Well, if you didn't write those letters, somebody else did. I don't care a rush for the difference. You see, here's how the matter stands. This Mr. Brigges, or Rigges, has gone off, and doesn't care to prosecute, and all his allegations against you fall to the ground. Well, these people fancy they could carry on the thing themselves, you understand; we think not. They say they have got a strong case; perhaps they have; but we ask, 'What's the use of it? Sending the poor beggar to Spielberg won't save you, will it?' And so we put it to them this way: 'Draw stakes, let him off, and both can cry quits.' There, give me another light. Isn't that the common-sense view of it?"

"I scarcely dare to say that I understand you aright."

"Oh, I can guess why. I have had dealings with fellows of your sort before. You don't fancy my not alluding to compensation, eh? You want to hear about the money part of the matter?"

And he laughed aloud, but whether at *my* mercenary spirit or *his own* shrewdness in detecting it, I do not really know.

"Well, I'm afraid," continued he, "you'll be disappointed there. These Austrians are hard up; besides, they never do pay. It's against their system, and so we never ask them."

"Would it be too much, sir, to ask why I have been imprisoned?"

"Perhaps not; but a great deal too much for me to tell you. The confounded papers would fill a cart, and that's the reason I say, cut your stick, my man, and get away." Again he turned to the window, and looking out, asked, "Any shooting about here? There ought to be cocks in that wood yonder?" and without caring for reply, went on: "After all, you know what Bosh it is to talk about chains and dungeons and bread-and-water and the rest of it. You've been living in clover here. That old fellow below tells me that you dine with him every day; that you might have gone into Innspruck, to the theatre if you liked it.—I'll swear there are snipes in that lowland next the river.—Think it over Rigges, think it over."

"I am not Rigges."

"Oh, I forgot! you're the other fellow. Well, think it over, Harpar."

"My name is not Harpar, sir."

"What do I care for a stray vowel or two? Maybe you call yourself Harpar or Harpér? It's all the same to *us*."

"It is not the question of a vowel or two, sir; and I desire you to remark it is the graver one of a mistaken identity!' I said this with a high-sounding importance that I thought must astound him, but his light and frivolous nature was impervious to rebuke.

"*We* have nothing to say to that," replied he, carelessly. "You may be Noakes or Styles. I believe they are the names of any fellows who are supposed by courtesy to have no name at all, and it's all alike to *us*. What I have to observe to you is this: nobody cares very much whether you are detained here or not; nobody wants to detain you. Just reflect, therefore, if it's not the best thing you can do to slope off, and make no more fuss about it?"

"Once for all, sir," said I, still more impressively, "I am not the person against whom this charge is made. The authorities have all along mistaken me for another."

"Well, what if they have? Does it signify one kreutzer? We have had trouble enough about the matter already, and do not embroil us any further."

"May I ask, sir, just for information, who are the 'we you have so frequently alluded to?"

Had I asked him in what division of the globe he

understood us then to be conversing, he would not have regarded me with a look of more blank astonishment.

"Who are we?" repeated he. "Did you ask who are we?"

"Yes, sir, that was what I made bold to ask."

"Cool, certainly; what might be called uncommon cool. To what line of life were you brought up to, my worthy gent? I have rather a curiosity about your antecedents."

"That same curiosity cost you a trifle once before," said I, no longer able to control myself, and dying to repay his impertinence. "I remember, once upon a time, meeting you on a railroad, and you were so eager to exhibit the skill with which you could read a man's calling, that you bet me a sovereign you would guess mine. You did so, and lost."

"You can't be—no, it's impossible. Are you really the goggle-eyed fellow that walked off with the bag for Kalbbratenstadt?"

"I did, by mistake, carry away a bag on that occasion, and so punctiliously did I repay my error, that I travelled the whole journey to convey those despatches to their destination."

"I know all about it," said he, in a frank, gay manner. "Doubleton told me the whole story. You dined with him and pretended you were I don't remember whom, and then you took old Mamma Keats off to Como and

made her believe you were Louis Philippe, and you made
fierce love to your pretty companion, who was fool
enough to like you. By Jove! what a rig you must have
run. We have all laughed over it a score of times."

"If I knew who 'we' were, I am certain I should feel
flattered by any amusement I afforded them, notwithstanding how much more they are indebted to fiction than
fact regarding me. I never assumed to be Louis Philippe,
nor affected to be any person of distinction. A flighty
old lady was foolish enough to imagine me a prince of
the Orleans family ——"

"You—a prince! Oh, this is too absurd!"

"I confess, sir, I cannot see the matter in this light.
I presume the mistake to be one by no means difficult to
have occurred. Mrs. Keats had seen a deal of life and
the world ——"

"Not so much as you fancy," broke he in. "She was
a long time in that private asylum up at Brompton, and
then down in Staffordshire; altogether she must have
passed five-and-twenty or thirty years in a rather
restricted circle."

"Mad! Was she mad?"

"Not what one would call mad, but queer. They were
all queer. Hargrave, the second brother, was the fellow
that made that shindy in the Mauritius, and our friend
Shalley isn't a conjuror. And we thought you were
larking the old lady, I assure you we did."

"'We' were once more mistaken, then," said I, sneeringly.

"We all said, too, at the time, that Doubleton had been 'let in.' He gave you a good round sum for expenses on the road, didn't he, and you sent it all back to him?"

"Every shilling of it."

"So he told us, and that was what puzzled us more than all the rest. Why did you give up the money?"

"Simply, sir, because it was not mine."

"Yes, yes, to be sure, I know that; but I mean, what suggested the restitution?"

"Really, sir, your question leads me to suppose that the 'we' so often referred to are not eminently remarkable for integrity."

"Like their neighbours, I take it—neither better nor worse. But won't you tell why you gave up the tin?"

"I should be hopeless of any attempt to explain my motives, sir; so pray excuse me."

"You were right, at all events," said he, not heeding the sarcasm of my manner. "There's no chance for the knaves now, with the telegraph system. As it was, there were orders flying through Europe to arrest Pottinger—I can't forget the name. We used to have it every day in the Chancellerie: Pottinger, five feet nine, weak-looking and vulgar, low forehead, light hair and eyes, slight lisp, talks German fluently, but ill. I have copied that portrait of you twenty, ay, thirty times."

"And yet, sir, neither the name nor the description apply. I am no more Pottinger than I am ignoble-looking and vulgar."

"What's the name, then?—not Harpar, not Pottinger? But who cares a rush for the name of fellows like you? You change them just as you do the colour of your coat."

"May I take the liberty of asking, sir, just for information, as you said a while ago, how you would take it were I to make as free with you as you have been pleased to do with *me?* To give a mock inventory of your external characteristics, and a false name to yourself?"

"Laugh, probably, if I were amused—throw you out of the window, if you offended me."

"The very thing I'd do with you this moment if I was strong enough," said I, resolutely. And he flung himself into a chair, and laughed as I did not believe he could laugh.

"Well," cried he, at last, "as this room is about fifty feet or so from the ground, it's as well as it is. But now let us wind up this affair. You want to get away from this, I suppose; and as nobody wants to detain you, the thing is easy enough. You needn't make a fuss about compensation, for they'll not give a kreutzer, and

you'd better not write a book about it, because 'we' don't
stand fellows who write books; so just take a friend's
advice, and go off without military honours of any
kind."

"I neither acknowledge the friendship nor accept the
advice, sir. The motives which induced me to suffer
imprisonment for another are quite sufficient to raise me
above any desire to make a profit of it."

"I think I understand *you*," said he, with a cunning
expression in his half-closed eyes. "You go in for being
a 'character.' Haven't I hit it? You want to be
thought a strange, eccentric sort of fellow. Now, there
was a time the world had a taste for that kind of thing.
Romeo Coates, and Brummel, and that Irish fellow that
walked to Jerusalem, and half a dozen others, used to
amuse the town in those days, but it's all as much bygone now as starched neckcloths and Hessian boots.
Ours is an age of paletots and easy manners, and you
are trying to revive what our grandfathers discarded
and got rid of. It won't do, Pottinger; it will not."

"I am not Pottinger; my name is Algernon Sydney
Potts."

"Ah! there's the mischief all out at last. What
could come of such a collocation of names but a life of
incongruity and absurdity! You owe all your griefs to
your godfathers, Potts. If they'd have called you Peter,
you'd have been a well-conducted poor creature. Well,

I'm to give you a passport. Where do you wish to go?"

"I wish, first of all, to go to Como."

"I think I know why. But you're on a wrong cast there. They have left that long since."

"Indeed, and for what place?"

"They've gone to pass the winter at Malta. Mamma Keats required a dry, warm climate, and you'll find them at a little country-house about a mile from Valetta: the Jasmines, I think it's called. I have a brother quartered in the island, and he tells me he has seen them, but they won't receive visits, nor go out anywhere. But, of course, a royal highness is always sure of a welcome. Prince Potts is an Open, sesame! wherever he goes."

"What atrocious tobacco this is of yours, Buller," said I, taking a cigar from his case as it lay on the table. "I suppose that you small fry of diplomacy cannot get things in duty free, eh?"

"Try this cheroot; you'll find it better," said he, opening a secret pocket in the case.

"Nothing to boast of," said I, puffing away, while he continued to fill up the blanks in my passport. "Would you like an introduction to my brother? He's on the government staff there, and knows every one. He's a jolly sort of fellow, besides, and you'll get on well together."

"I don't care if I do," said I, carelessly, "though, as a rule, your red-coat is very bad style—flippant without smartness, and familiar without ease."

"Severe, Potts, but not altogether unjust; but you'll find George above the average of his class, and I think you'll like him."

"Don't let him ask me to his mess," said I, with an insolent drawl. "That's an amount of boredom I could not submit to. Caution him to make no blunder of that kind."

He looked up at me with a strange twinkle in his eyes, which I could not interpret. He was either in intense enjoyment of my smartness, or Heaven knows what other sentiment then moved him. At all events, I was in ecstasy at the success of my newly discovered vein, and walked the room, humming a tune, as he wrote the letter that was to present me to his brother.

"Why had I never hit upon this plan before?" thought I. "How was it that it had not occured that the maxim of homœopathy is equally true in morals as in medicine, and that '*similia similibus curantur!*' So long as I was meek, humble, and submissive, Buller's impertinent presumption only increased at every moment. With every fresh concession of mine he continued to encroach, and now that I had adopted his own strategy, and attacked, he fell back at once." I was proud, very proud of my discovery. It is a new contribution to that knowledge of life which, notwithstanding all my disasters, I believed to be essentially my gift.

At last he finished his note, folded, sealed, and directed it—"The Hon. George Buller, A.D.C., Government House, Malta, favoured by Algernon Sydney Potts, Esq."

"Isn't that all right?" asked he, pointing to my name. "I was within an ace of writing Hampden-Russell, too." And he laughed at his own very meagre jest.

"I hope you have merely made this an introduction?" said I.

"Nothing more; but why so?"

"Because it's just as likely that I never present it! I am the slave of the humour I find myself in, and I rarely do anything that costs me the slightest effort." I said this with a close and, indeed, a servile imitation of Charles Mathews in Used Up; but it was a grand success, and Buller was palpably vanquished.

"Well, for George's sake, I hope your mood may be the favourable one. Is there anything more I can do for you? Can you think of nothing wherein I may be serviceable?"

"Nothing. Stay, I rather think our people at home might with propriety show my old friend Hirsch here some mark of attention for his conduct towards me. I don't know whether they give a C.B. for that sort of thing, but a sum—a handsome sum—something to mark the service, and the man to whom it was rendered. Don't you think 'we' could manage that?"

"I'll see what can be done. I don't despair of success."

"As for your share in the affair, Buller, I'll take care that it shall be mentioned in the proper quarter. If I *have* a characteristic—my friends say I have many—but if I have one, it is that I never forget the most trifling service of the humblest of those who have aided me. You are young, and have your way to make in life. Go back, therefore, and carry with you the reflection that Potts is your friend."

I saw he was affected at this, for he covered his face with his handkerchief and turned away, and for some seconds his shoulders moved convulsively.

"Yes," said I, with a struggle to become humble, "there are richer men, there are men more influential by family ties and connections, there are men who occupy a more conspicuous position before the public eye, there are men who exercise a wider sway in the world of politics and party; but this I will say, that there is not one—no, not one—individual in the British dominions who, when you come to consider either the difficulties he has overcome, the strength of the prejudices he has conquered, the totally unassisted and unaided struggle he has had to maintain against not alone the errors, for errors are human, but still worse, the ungenerous misconceptions, the—I will go further, and call them the wilful misrepresentations of those who, from education and rank and condition, might be naturally supposed—indeed confidently affirmed to be—to be ——"

"I am certain of it!" cried he, grasping my hand, and rescuing me from a situation very like smothering—"I am certain of it!" And with a hurried salutation, for his feelings were evidently overcoming him, he burst away, and descended the stairs five steps at a time, and although I was sorry he had not waited till I finished my peroration, I was really glad that the act had ended and the curtain fallen.

"What a deal of bad money passes current in this world," said I, as I was alone; "and what a damper it is upon honest industry to think how easy it is to eke out life with a forgery."

"What do you say to a dinner with me at the Swan in Innspruck, Potts?" cried out Buller, from the court-yard.

"Excuse me, I mean to eat my last cutlet here, with my old gaoler. It will be an event for the poor fellow as long as he lives. Good-by, and a safe journey to you."

CHAPTER XXII.

I WAS now bound for the first port in the Mediterranean from which I could take ship for Malta; and the better to carry out my purpose, I resolved never to make acquaintance with any one, or be seduced by any companionship, till I had seen Miss Herbert, and given her the message I was charged with. This time, at least, I would be a faithful envoy, at least as faithful as a man might be who had gone to sleep over his credentials for a twelvemonth. And so I reached Maltz, and took my place by diligence over the Stelvio down to Lecco, never trusting myself with even the very briefest intercourse with my fellow-travellers, and suffering them to indulge in the humblest estimate of me, morally and intellectually—all that I might be true to my object and firm to my fixed purpose. For the first time in my life I tried to present myself in an unfavourable aspect, and I was astonished to find the experiment by no means unpleasing, the reason being, probably, that it was an eminent success. I began to see how the surly people are such acute philosophers in

life, and what a deal of selfish gratification they must
derive from their uncurbed ill humour. I reached Genoa
in time to catch a steamer for Malta. It was crowded,
and with what, in another mood, I might have called
pleasant people; but I held myself estranged and aloof
from all. I could mark many an impertinent allusion to
my cold and distant manner, and could see that a young
sub on his way to join was even witty at the expense of
my retiring disposition. The creature, Groves he was
called, used to try to " trot me out," as he phrased it; but
I maintained both my resolve and my temper, and gave
him no triumph.

I was almost sorry on the morning we dropped anchor
in the harbour. The sense of doing something, anything,
with a firm persistence had given me cheerfulness and
courage. However, I had now a task of some nicety
before me, and addressed myself at once to its discharge.
At the hotel I learned that the cottage inhabited by Mrs.
Keats was in a small nook of one of the bays, and only an
easy walk from the town; and so I despatched a messenger at once with Miss Crofton's note to Miss Herbert,
enclosed in a short one from myself, to know if she would
permit me to wait upon her, with reference to the matter
in the letter. I spoke of myself in the third person and
as the bearer of the letter.

While I was turning over the letters and papers in my
writing-desk, awaiting her reply, I came upon Buller's

note to his brother, and, without any precise idea why, I sent it by a servant to the Government House, with my card. It was completely without a purpose that I did so, and if my reader has not experienced moments of the like "inconsequence," I should totally break down in attempting to account for their meaning.

Miss Herbert's reply came back promptly. She requested that the writer of the note she had just read would favour her with a visit at his earliest convenience.

I set forth immediately. What a strange and thrilling sensation it is when we take up some long-dropped link in life, go back to some broken thread of our existence, and try to attach it to the present! We feel young again in the bygone, and yet far older even than our real age in the thought of the changes time has wrought upon us in the mean while. A week or so before I had looked with impatience for this meeting, and now I grew very faint-hearted as the moment drew nigh. The only way I could summon courage for the occasion was by thinking that in the mission entrusted to me *I* was actually nothing. There were incidents and events not one of which touched me, and I should pass away off the scene when our interview was over, and be no more remembered by her.

It was evident that the communication had engaged her attention to some extent by the promptitude of her message to me; and with this thought I crossed the little lawn, and rang the bell at the door.

" The gentleman expected by Miss Herbert, sir," asked
a smart English maid. "Come this way, sir. She will
see you in a few minutes."

I had fully ten minutes to inspect the details of a pretty
little drawing-room, one of those little female temples
where scattered drawings and books and music, and, above
all, the delicious odour of fresh flowers, all harmonise
together, and set you a thinking how easily life could
glide by with such appliances were they only set in motion
by the touch of the enchantress herself. The door opened
at last, but it was the maid; she came to say that Mrs.
Keats was very poorly that day, and Miss Herbert could
not leave her at that moment; and if it were not perfectly convenient to the gentleman to wait, she begged to
know when it would suit him to call again?

" As for me," said I, "I have come to Malta solely on
this matter; pray say that I will wait as long as she
wishes. I am completely at her orders."

I strolled out after this through one of the windows
that opened on the lawn, and gaining the sea-side, I sat
down upon a rock to bide her coming. I might have sat
about half-an-hour thus, when I heard a rapid step
approaching, and I had just time to arise when Miss
Herbert stood before me. She started back, and grew
pale, very pale, as she recognised me, and for fully a
minute there we both stood, unable to speak a word.

" Am I to understand, sir," said she, at last, "that you

are the bearer of this letter?" And she held it open towards me.

"Yes," said I, with a great effort at collectedness. " I have much to ask your forgiveness for. It is fully a year since I was charged to place that in your hands, but one mischance after another has befallen me; not to own that in my own purposeless mode of life I have had no enemy worse than my fate."

"I have heard something of your fondness for adventure," said she, with a strange smile that blended a sort of pity with a gentle irony. "After we parted company at Shaffhausen, I believe you travelled for some time on foot? We heard, at least, that you took a fancy to explore a mode of life few persons have penetrated, or, at least, few of your rank and condition."

"May I ask, what do you believe that rank and condition to be, Miss Herbert?" asked I, firmly.

She blushed deeply at this; perhaps I was too abrupt in the way I spoke, and I hastened to add,

"When I offered to be the bearer of the letter you have just read, I was moved by another wish than merely to render you some service. I wanted to tell you, once for all, that if I lived for a while in a fiction land of my own invention, with day-dreams and fancies, and hopes and ambitions all unreal, I have come to pay the due penalty of my deceit, and confess that nothing can be more humble than I am in birth, station, or fortune—my

father an apothecary, my name Potts, my means a very
few pounds in the world; and yet, with all that avowal,
I feel prouder now that I have made it, than ever I did
in the false assumption of some condition I had no claim
to."

She held out her hand to me with such a significant
air of approval, and smiled so good-naturedly, that I
could not help pressing it to my lips, and kissing it
rapturously.

Taking a seat at my side, and with a voice meant to
recal me to a quiet and business-like demeanour, she
asked me to read over Miss Crofton's letter. I told her
that I knew every line of it by heart, and, more still, I
knew the whole story to which it related. It was a topic
that required the nicest delicacy to touch on, but with a
frankness that charmed me, she said,—

"You have had the candour to tell me freely your
story; let me imitate you, and reveal mine.

"You know who we are, and whence we have sprung;
that my father was a simple labourer on a line of railroad, and by dint of zeal and intelligence, and an energy
that would not be baulked or impeded, that he raised
himself to station and affluence. You have heard of his
connexion with Sir Elkanah Crofton, and how unfortunately it was broken off; but you cannot know the rest
—that is, you cannot know what we alone know, and
what is not so much as suspected by others; and of this

I can scarcely dare to speak, since it is essentially the secret of my family."

I guessed at once to what she alluded; her troubled manner, her swimming eyes, and her quivering voice, all betrayed that she referred to the mystery of her father's fate; while I doubted within myself whether it were right and fitting for me to acknowledge that I knew the secret source of her anxiety. She relieved me from my embarrassment by continuing thus:

"Your kind and generous friends have not suffered themselves to be discouraged by defeat. They have again and again renewed their proposals to my mother, only varying the mode, in the hope that by some stratagem they might overcome her reasons for refusal. Now, though this rejection, so persistent as it is, may seem ungracious, it is not without a fitting and substantial cause."

Again she faltered, and grew confused, and now I saw how she struggled between a natural reserve and an impulse to confide the sorrow that oppressed her to one who might befriend her.

"You may speak freely to me," said I, at last. "I am not ignorant of the mystery you hint at. Crofton has told me what many surmise and some freely believe in."

"But we know it, know it for a certainty," cried she, clasping my hand in her eagerness. "It is no longer a surmise or a suspicion. It is a certainty—a fact! Two

letters in his handwriting have reached my mother; one
from St. Louis, in America, where he had gone first; the
second from an Alpine village, where he was laid up in
sickness.   He had had a terrible encounter with a man
who had done him some gross wrong, and he was
wounded in the shoulder.   After which he had to cross
the Rhine, wading or swimming, and travel many miles
ere he could find shelter.   When he wrote, however, he
was rapidly recovering, and as quickly regaining all his
old courage and daring."

"And from that time forward have you had no tidings
of him?"

"Nothing but a cheque on a Russian banker in London
to pay to my mother's order a sum of money, a considerable one, too; and although she hoped to gain some clue
to him through this, she could not succeed, nor have we
now any trace of him whatever.   I ought to mention,"
said she, as if catching up a forgotten thread in her
narrative, "that in his last letter he enjoined my mother
not to receive any payment from the assurance company,
nor enter into compromise with them; and, above all,
to live in the hope that we should meet again and be
happy."

"And are you still ignorant of where he now is?"

"We only know that a cousin of mine, an officer of
engineers at Aden, heard of an Englishman being engaged
by the Shah of Persia to report on certain silver mines

at Kashan, and from all he could learn, the description would apply to him. My cousin had obtained leave of absence expressly to trace him, and promised in his last letter to bring me himself any tidings he might procure here to Malta. Indeed, when I learned that a stranger had asked to see me, I was full sure it was my cousin Harry."

Was it that her eyes grew darker in colour as this name escaped her—was it that a certain tremor shook her voice—or was it the anxiety of my own jealous humour, that made me wretched as I heard of that cousin Harry, now mentioned for the first time?

"What reparation can I make you for so blank a disappointment?" said I, with a sad, half-bitter tone

"Be the same kind friend that he would have proved himself if it had been his fortune to have come 'first,' said she; and though she spoke calmly, she blushed deeply! "Here," said she, hurriedly, taking a small printed paragraph from a letter, and eagerly, as it seemed, trying to recover her former manner—"here is a slip I have cut out of the *Levant Herald*. I found it about two months since. It ran thus: 'The person who had contracted for the works at Pera, and who now turns out to be an Englishman, is reported to have had a violent altercation yesterday with Musted Pasha, in consequence of which he has thrown up his contract, and demanded his passport for Russia. It is rumoured here that the

Russian ambassador is no stranger to this rupture.'
Vague as this is, I feel persuaded that he is the person
alluded to, and that it is from Constantinople we must
trace him."

"Well," cried I, "I am ready. I will set out at once."

"Oh! can I believe you will do us this great service?"
cried she, with swimming eyes and clasped hands.

"This time you will find me faithful," said I, gravely.
"He who has said and done so many foolish things as I
have, must, by one good action, give bail for his future
character."

"You are a true friend, and you have all my confidence."

"Mrs. Keats's compliments, miss," said the maid at
this moment, "and hopes the gentleman will stay to
dinner with you, though she cannot come down herself."

"She imagines you are my cousin, whom she is aware
I have been expecting," said Miss Herbert, in a whisper,
and evidently appearing uncertain how to act.

"Oh!" said I, with an anguish I could not repress,
"would that I could change my lot with his."

"Very well, Mary," said Miss Herbert; "thank your
mistress from me, and say the gentleman accepts her
invitation with pleasure. Is it too much presumption on
my part, sir, to say so?" said she, with a low whisper,
while a half malicious twinkle lit up her eyes, and I
could not speak with happiness.

Determined, however, to give an earnest of my zeal in her cause, I declared I would at once return to the town, and learn when the first packet sailed for Constantinople. The dinner hour was seven, so that I had fully five hours yet to make my inquiries ere we met at table. I wondered at myself how business-like and practical I had become; but a strong impulse now impelled me, and seemed to add a sort of strength to my whole nature.

"As cousin Harry is the mirror of punctuality, and you now represent him, Mr. Potts," said she, shaking my hand, "pray remember not to be later than seven."

u 2

CHAPTER XXIII

" Constantinople, Odessa, and the Levant.—The *Cyclops*, five hundred horse-power, to sail on Wednesday morning, at eight o'clock. For freight or passage apply to Captain Robert B. Rogers."

This announcement, which I found amidst a great many others in a frame over the fire-place in the coffee-room, struck me forcibly, first of all, because, not belonging to the regular mail packets, it suggested a cheap passage; and, secondly, it promised an early departure, and the vessel was to sail on the very next morning, an amount of promptitude that I felt would gratify Miss Herbert.

Now, although I had been living for a considerable time back at the cost of the Imperial House of Hapsburg, my resources for such an expedition as was opening before me were of the most slender kind. I made a careful examination of all my worldly wealth, and it amounted to the sum of forty-three pounds some odd shillings. On terra firma I could, of course, economise to any extent. With self-denial and resolution I could live on very little. Life in the East, I had often heard, was singularly cheap and inexpensive. All I had read of Oriental habits in the "Arabian Nights" and "Tales of the Genii" assured me that with a few dates and a water-melon a man dined fully as well as need be; and the delicious warmth of the climate rendered shelter a complete superfluity. Before forming anything like a correct budget, I must ascertain what would be the cost of my passage to Constantinople, and so I rang for the waiter to direct me to the address of the advertiser.

"That's the captain yonder, sir," whispered the waiter, and he pointed to a stout, weather-beaten man, who, with his hands in the pockets of his pilot-coat, was standing in front of the fire, smoking a cigar.

Although I had never seen him before, the features reminded me of some one I had met with, and suddenly I bethought me of the skipper with whom I had sailed from Ireland for Milford, and who had given me a letter for his brother "Bob"—the very Robert Rogers now before me.

"Do you know this handwriting, captain?" said I, drawing the letter from my pocket-book.

"That's my brother Joe's," said he, not offering to take the letter from my hand, or removing the cigar from his mouth, but talking with all the unconcern in life.

"That's Joe's own scrawl, and there ain't a worse from this to himself."

"The letter is for you," said I, rather offended at his coolness.

"So I see. Stick it up there, over the chimney; Joe has never anything to say that won't keep."

"It is a letter of introduction, sir," said I, still more haughtily.

"And what if it be? Won't that keep? Who is it to introduce?"

"The humble individual before you, Captain Rogers."

"So, that's it!" said he, slowly. "Well, read it out for me, for, to tell you the truth, there's no harder navigation to me than one of Joe's scrawls."

"I believe I can master it," said I, opening and reading what originally had been composed and drawn up by myself. When I came to "Algernon Sydney Potts, a man so completely after your own heart," he drew his cigar from his mouth, and laying his hand on my shoulder, turned me slowly around till the light fell full upon me.

"No, Joseph," said he, deliberately, "not a bit of it, my boy. This ain't my sort of chap at all!"

I almost choked with anger, but somehow there was such an apparent earnestness in the man, and such a total absence of all wish to offend, that I read on to the end.

"Well," said he, as I concluded, "he usedn't to be so

wordy as that. I wonder what came over him. Mayhap
he wasn't well."

What a comment on a style that might have adorned
the Correct Letter Writer !

"He was, on the contrary, in the enjoyment of perfect
health, sir," said I, tartly.

"All I can pick out of it is, I ain't to offer you any
money; and as there isn't any direction easier to follow,
nor pleasanter to obey, here's my hand!" And he wrung
mine with a grip that would have flattened a chain cable.

"What's your line, here? You ain't sodgering, are
you?"

"No; I'm travelling, for pleasure, for information, for
pastime, as one might say."

"In the general do-nothing and careless line of
business? That ain't mine. No, by jingo! I don't eat
my fish without catching, ay, and salting them, too, I
ain't ashamed to say. I'm captain, supercargo, and pilot
of my own craft; take every lunar that is taken aboard;
I've writ every line that ever is writ in the log-book, and
I vaccinated every man and boy aboard for the natural
small-pox with these fingers and this tool that you see
here!" And he produced an old and very rusty instrument of veterinary surgery from his vest-pocket,
where it lay with copper money, tobacco quids, and
lucifer matches.

I quickly remembered the character for inordinate

boastfulness his brother had given me, and of which he
thus, without any provocation on my part, afforded me a
slight specimen. Now, perhaps at this stage of my
narrative, I might never have alluded to him at all, if it
were not for the opportunity it gives me of recording
how nobly and how resolutely I resisted what may be
called the most trying temptation of human nature. An
inveterate dram-drinker has been known to turn away
from the proffered glass; an incurable gambler has been
seen to decline the invitation to "cut in;" dignitaries of
the church have begged off being made bishops; but is
there any mention in history of an anecdote-monger
suffering himself to be patiently vanquished, and retiring
from the field without firing off at least an "incident that
occurred to himself?" If ever a man was sorely tried,
· I was. Here was this coarsely-minded vulgar dog, with
nothing pictorial nor imaginative in his nature, heaping
story upon story of his own feats and achievements, in
which not one solitary situation ever suggested an
interest or awakened an anxiety; and I, who could have
shot my tigers, crippled my leopards, hamstrung my
lionesses, rescued men from drowning, and women
from fire—with little life touches to thrill the heart and
force tears from the eyes of a stockbroker—I, I say, had
to stand there and listen in silence! Watching a creature
banging away at a target that he never hit, with an old
flint musket, while you held in your hand a short Enfield

that would have driven the ball through the bull's-eye is
nothing to this; and to tell the truth, it nearly choked
me. Twice I had to cough down the words, "Now let
me mention a personal fact." But I did succeed, and I
am proud to say I only grew very red in the face, and
felt that singing in the ears and general state of muddle
that forebodes a fit. But I rallied, and said in a voice
slow, from the dignity of a self-conquest,

"Can you take me as a passenger to Constantinople?"

"To Constantinople? Ay, to the Persian Gulf, to
Point de Galle, to Cochin China, to Ross River; don't
think to puzzle me with navigation, my lad."

"Are there many other passengers?"

"I could have five hundred, if I'd take 'em! Put Bob
Rogers on a placard, and see what'll happen. If I said,
'I'm agoing to sea on a plank to-morrow,' there's men
would rather come along with me than go in the *Queen*,
or the *Hannibal*. I don't say they're right, mind ye;
but I won't say they're wrong, neither."

"Oh, why didn't I meet this wretch when I was a
child? Why didn't my father find a Helot like this, to
tell lies before me, and frighten me with their horrid
ugliness?" This was the thought that flashed through
me as I listened. I felt, besides, that such stupid, purposeless inventions, corrupted and blunted the taste for
graceful narrative, just in the same way that an un-

deserving recipient of charity offends the pleasure of real benevolence.

"May I ask, Captain Rogers, what is the fare?" said I, with a bland courtesy.

"That depends upon the man, sir. If you was Ram-sam Can-tanker-abad, I'd say five hundred gold pagodas. If you was a Cockney stripling, with a fresh-water face, and a spunyarn whisker, I'd call it a matter of seven or eight pound."

"And you sail at eight?"

"To the minute. When Bob Rogers says eight o'clock, the first turn of the paddles will be the first stroke of the hour."

"Then book me, pray, for a berth; and, for surety's sake, I'll go aboard to night."

"Meet me, then, here at ten o'clock, and I'll take you off in my gig, an honour to be proud on, my lad; but as Joe's friend, I'll do it."

I bowed my acknowledgments and went off, neither delighted with my new acquaintance, nor myself for the patience I had shown him. After all, I had secured an early passage, and was thus able to show Kate Herbert that I was not going to let the grass grow under my feet this time, and that she might reckon on my zeal to serve her in future. As I retraced my road to the cottage, I forgot all about Captain Rogers, and only thought of Kate, and the interests that were hers. It

was next to a certainty that her father was yet alive;
but how to find him in a strange land, with a feigned
name, and most probably with every aid and appliance
to complete his disguisement! It was, doubtless, a
noble enterprise to devote oneself for such as she was,
but not very hopeful withal; and then I went over
various plans for my future guidance: what I should do
if I fell sick? what if my money failed me? what if I
were waylaid by Arabs, or carried away to some fearful
region in the mountains, and made to feed a pet alligator,
or a domestic boa-constrictor? I hoped sincerely that I
was over-estimating my possible perils, but it was wise
to give a large margin to the unknown; and so I did
not curb myself in the least.

As I entered the grounds, the night was falling, and I
could see that the lamps were already lighted in the
drawing-room. What surprised me, however, was to
see a very smart groom, well mounted, and leading
another horse up and down before the door. There was
evidently a visitor within, and I felt indisposed to enter
till he had gone away. My curiosity, however, prompted
me to ask the groom the name of his master, and he
replied, "The Honourable Captain Buller."

The very essence of all jealousy is, that it is unreason-
ing. It is well known that husbands—that much-
believing and much-belied class—always suspect every
one but the right man; and now, without the

faintest clue to a suspicion, I grew actually sick with jealousy!

Nor was it altogether blamable in me, for as I looked through the uncurtained window, I could see the captain, a fine-looking, rather tigerish sort of fellow, standing with his back to the fireplace, while he talked to Miss Herbert, who sat some distance off at a work-table. There was in his air that amount of jaunty ease and self-possession that said, "I'm at home here; in this fortress I hold the chief command." There was about him, too, the tone of an assumed superiority, which, when displayed by a man towards a woman, takes the most offensive of all possible aspects.

As he talked, he moved at last towards a window, and, opening it, held out his hand to feel if it were raining.

"I hope," cried he, "you'll not send me back with a refusal; her ladyship counts upon you as the chief ornament of her ball."

"We never do go to balls, sir," was the dry response.

"But make this occasion the exception. If you only knew how lamentably we are off for pretty people, you'd pity us. Such garrison wives and daughters are unknown to the oldest inhabitant of the island. Surely Mrs. Keats will be quite well by Wednesday, and she'll not be so cruel as to deny you to us for this once."

"I can but repeat my excuses—I never go out."

"If you say so, I think I'll abandon all share in the

enterprise. It was a point of honour with me to persuade you; in fact, I pledged myself to succeed, and if you really persist in a refusal, I'll just pitch all these notes in the fire, and go off yachting till the whole thing is over." And with this he drew forth a mass of notes from his sabretasche, and proceeded to con over the addresses: "'Mrs. Hilyard,' 'Mr. Barnes,' 'Mr. Clintosh,' 'Lady Blagden.' Oh, Lady Blagden! Why it would be worth while coming only to see her and Sir John; and here are the Crosbys, too; and what have we here? Oh! this is a note from Grey. You don't know my brother Grey—he'd amuse you immensely. Just listen to this, by way of a letter of introduction:

" 'DEAR GEORGE,—Cherish the cove that will hand you this note as the most sublime Snob I have ever met in all my home and foreign experiences. In a large garrison like yours, you can have no difficulty in finding fellows to give him a field-day. I commit him, therefore, to your worthy keeping, to dine him, draw him forth, and pitch him out of the window when you've done with him. No harm if it is from the topmost story of the highest barrack in Malta. His name is Potts—seriously and truthfully, Potts. Birth, parentage, and belongings all unknown to, " 'Yours ever,

" 'GREY BULLER.' "

"You are unfortunate, sir, in confiding your correspondence to me," said Kate, rising from her seat, "for that gentleman is a friend, a sincere and valued friend, of my own, and you could scarcely have found a more certain way to offend me than to speak of him slightingly."

"You can't mean that you know him—ever met him?"

"I know him and respect him, and I will not listen to one word to his disparagement. Nay, more, sir, I will feel myself at liberty, if I think it fitting, to tell Mr. Potts the honourable mode in which your brother has discharged the task of an introduction, its good faith, and gentlemanlike feeling."

"Pray let us have him at the mess first. Don't spoil our sport till we have at least one-evening out of him."

But she did not wait for him to finish his speech, and left the room.

It is but fair to own he took his reverses with great coolness: he tightened his sword-belt, set his cap on his head before the glass, stroked down his moustache, and then lighting a cigar, swaggered off to the door with the lounging swing of his order.

As for myself, I hastened back to the town, and with such speed that I traversed the mile in something like thirteen minutes. I had no very clear or collected plan of action, but I resolved to ask Captain Rogers to be my friend, and see me through this conjuncture. He had just dined as I entered the coffee-room, and consented to have his brandy-and-water removed to my bedroom while I opened my business with him.

I will not, at this eleventh hour of revelations, inflict upon my reader the details, but simply be satisfied to state that I found the skipper far more practical than I looked for. He evidently, besides, had a taste for these sort of adventures, and prided himself on his conduct of them. "Go back now, and eat your dinner comfortably with your friends; leave everything to me, and I promise you one thing—the Cyclops shall not get full steam up till we have settled this small transaction."

CHAPTER XXIV.

THOUGH I was a few minutes late for dinner, Miss Herbert did not chide me for delay. She was charming in her reception of me; nor was the fascination diminished to me by feeling with what generous warmth she had defended and upheld me.

There is a marvellous charm in the being defended by one you love, and of whose kind feeling towards you, you had never dared to assure yourself till the very moment that confirmed it. I don't know if I ever felt in such spirits in my life. Not that I was gay or light-hearted so much as happy—happy in the sense of a self-esteem I had not known till then. And what a spirit of cordial familiarity was there now between us! She spoke to me of her daily life, its habits and even of its trials; not complainingly nor fretfully, far from it, but in a way to imply that these were the burdens meted out to all, and that none should arrogantly imagine he was to escape the lot of his fellows. And then we talked of the Croftons, of whom she was curious to hear details—their ages, appearance, manner, and so on—lastly, how I came to know them, and thus imperceptibly led me to tell of myself and of my story. I am sure that we each of us had enough of care upon our hearts, and yet none would have ever guessed it to have seen how joyously and merrily we laughed over some of the incidents of my chequered career. She bantered me, too, on the feeble and wayward impulses by which I had suffered myself to be moved, and gravely asked me, had I accomplished any single one of all objects I had set before my mind in starting.

Far more earnestly, however, did we discuss the future. She heard with joy that I had already secured a passage for Constantinople, and declared that she could not dismiss from her mind the impression that I was destined to aid their return to happiness and prosperity. I liked the notion, too, of there being a fate in our first meeting; a fate in that acquaintanceship with the Croftons, which gave the occasion to seek her out again; and last of all, if it might be so, a fate in the influence I was to exercise over their fortunes. I was so absorbed in these pleasant themes, that I, with as little of the lion in my heart as any man breathing, never once thought of the quarrel and its impending consequences. How my heart beat as her soft breath fanned me while she spoke! As she was telling when and from whence I was to write to her, the servant came to say that a

gentleman outside begged to see Mr. Potts.   I hurried to
the hall.

"Not come to disturb you, Potts," said the skipper, in
a brisk tone; "only thought it best to make your mind
easy.   It's all right."

"A thousand thanks, captain," said I, warmly.   "I
knew when the negotiation was in your hands, it would
be so."

"Yes; his friend, a Major Colesby, boggled a bit at
first.   Couldn't see the thing in the light I put it.
Asked very often 'who were you?' asked, too, 'who *I*
was?'   Good that! it made me laugh.   Rather late
in the day, I take it, to ask who Bob Rogers is!
But in the end, as I said, it all comes right, quite
right."

"And his apology was full, ample, and explicit?   Was
it in writing, Rogers?   I'd like it in writing."

"Like what in writing?"

"His apology, or explanation, or whatever you like to
call it."

"Who ever spoke of such a thing?   Who so much as
dreamed of it?   Haven't I told you the affair is all
right? and what does all right mean, eh?—what does it
mean?"

"I know what it ought to mean," said I, angrily.

"So do I, and so do most men in this island, sir.   It
means twelve paces under the Battery wall, fire together,

and as many shots as the aggrieved asks for. That's all right, isn't it?"

"In one sense it is so," said I, with a mock composure.

"Well, that's the only sense I ever meant to consider it by. Go back now to your tea, or your sugar-and-water, or whatever it is, and when you come home to-night, step into my room, and we'll have a cozy chat and a cigar. There's one or two trifling things that I don't understand in this affair, and I put my own explanation on them, and maybe it ain't the right one. Not that it signifies *now*, you perceive, because you are here to the fore, and can set them right. But as by this time to-morrow you might be where—I won't mention—we may as well put them straight this evening."

"I'll beat you up, depend upon it," said I, affecting a slap-dash style. "I can't tell you how glad I am to have fallen into your hands, Rogers. You suit me exactly."

"Well it's more than I expected when I saw you first, and I kept saying to myself, 'Whatever could have persuaded Joe to send me a creature like that?' To tell you the truth, I thought you were in the cheap funeral line."

"Droll dog!" said I, while my fingers were writhing and twisting with passion.

"Not that it's fair to take a fellow by his looks. I'm aware of that, Potts. But go back to the parlour—

x 2

that's the second time the maid has come out to see what keeps you. Go back, and enjoy yourself; maybe you won't have so pleasant an opportunity soon again."

This was the parting speech of the wretch as he buttoned the collar of his coat, and with a short nod bade me good-by, and left me.

"Why did you not ask your friend to take a cup of tea with us?" said Kate, as I re-entered the drawing-room.

"Oh! it was the skipper, a rough sort of creature, not exactly made for drawing-room life; besides, he only came to ask me a question."

"I hope it was not a very unpleasant one, for you look pale and anxious."

"Nothing of the kind—a mere formal matter about my baggage."

It was no use; from that moment, I was the most miserable of mankind. What availed it to speculate any longer on the future? How could I interest myself in what years might bring forth? Hours, and a very few of them, were all that were left to me. Poor girl! how tenderly she tried to divert my sorrow; she, most probably, ascribed it to the prospect of our speedy separation; and with delicacy and tact, she tried to trace out some faint outlines of what painters call "extreme distance"—a sort of future, where all the skies would be rose-coloured and all the mountains blue. I am sure, if a choice had been given me at that instant, I would rather have been a courageous man than the greatest genius in the universe. *I* knew better what was before me. At last it came to ten o'clock, and I arose to say good-by. I found it very hard not to fall upon her neck, and say, "Don't be angry with poor Potts; this is his last as it is his first embrace."

"Wear that ring for me and for my sake," said she, giving me one from her finger; "don't refuse me—it has no value save what you may attach to it from having been mine."

Oh dear! what a gulp it cost me not to say, "I'll never take it off while I live," and then add, "which will be about eight hours and a half more."

When I got into the open air, I ran as if a pack of wolves were in pursuit of me. I cannot say why; but the rapid motion served to warm my blood, so that when I reached the hotel, I felt more assured and more resolute.

Rogers was asleep, and so soundly, that I had to pull the pillow from beneath his head before I could awaken him; and when I had accomplished the feat, either the remote effect of his last brandy-and-water, or his drowsiness, had so obscured his faculties, that all he could mumble out was, "Hit him where he can't be spliced—hit him where they can't splice him!" I tried for a long time to recal him to sense and intelligence, but I got nothing from him save the one inestimable precept;

and so I went to my room, and throwing myself on my
bed in my cloak, prepared for a night of gloomy retro-
spect and gloomier anticipation; but, odd enough, I was
asleep the moment I lay down.

"Get up, old fellow," cried Rogers, "shaking me violently, just as the dawn was breaking; "we're lucky if
we can get aboard before they catch us."

"What do you mean?" said I. "What's happened?".

"The governor has got wind of our shindy, and put
all the red-coats in arrest, and ordered the police to nab
us too."

"Bless him! bless him!" muttered I.

"Ay, so say I. He be blessed!" cried he, catching
up my words; "but let us make off through the garden;
my gig is down in the offing, and they'll pull in when
they hear my whistle. Ain't it provoking—ain't it
enough to make a man swear?"

"I have no words for what I feel, Rogers," said I,
bustling about to collect my stray articles through the
room. "If I ever chance upon that governor—he has
only five years of it—I believe ——"

"Come along! I see the boat coming round the point
yonder." And with this we slipped noiselessly down
the stairs, down the street, and gained the jetty.

"Steam up?" asked the skipper, as he jumped into
the gig.

"Ay, ay, sir; and we're short on the anchor, too."

In less than half an hour we were under weigh, and I don't thir⁀ I ever admired a land prospect receding from view with more intense delight than I did that, my last glimpse of Malta.

CHAPTER XXV.

OUR voyage had nothing remarkable to record: we
reached Constantinople in due course, and during the
few days the *Cyclops* remained I had abundant time to
discover that there was no trace of any one resembling
him I sought for. By the advice of Rogers, I accompanied him to Odessa. There, too, I was not more
fortunate; and though I instituted the most persevering
inquiries, all I could learn was that some Americans were
employed by the Russian Government in raising the
frigates sunk at Sebastopol, and that it was not impossible an Englishman, such as I described, might have
met an engagement amongst them. At all events, one of
the coasting craft was already at Odessa, and I went on
board of her to make my inquiry. I learned from the
mate, who was a German, that they had come over on
rather a strange errand, which was to convey a corps of
circus people to Balaclava. The American contractor at
that place being in want of some amusement, had
arranged with these people to give some weeks' per-

formances there, but that, from an incident that had just occurred, the project had failed. This was no less than the elopement of the chief dancer, a young girl of great beauty, with a young Prince of Bavaria. It was rumoured that he had married her, but my informant gave little credence to this version, and averred that he had bought, not only herself, but a favourite old Arab horse she rode, for thirty thousand piastres. I asked eagerly where the others of the corps were to be found, and heard they had crossed over to Simoom, all broken up and disjointed, the chief clown having died of grief after the girl's flight.

If I heard this tale rudely narrated, and not always with the sort of comment that went with my sympathies, I sorrowed sincerely over it, for I guessed upon whom these events had fallen, and recognised poor old Vaterchen and the dark-eyed Tintefleck.

"You've fallen into the black melancholies these some days back," said Rogers to me. "Rouse up, and take a cruise with me. I'm going over to Balaclava with these steam-boilers, and then to Sinope, and so back to the Bosphorus. Come aboard to-night, it will do you good."

I took his counsel, and at noon next day we dropped anchor at Balaclava. We had scarcely passed our "health papers," when a boat came out with a message to inquire if we had a doctor on board who could speak English, for

the American contractor had fallen from one of the
scaffolds that morning, and was lying dreadfully injured
up at Sebastopol, but unable to explain himself to the
Russian surgeons. I was not without some small skill in
medicine; and, besides, out of common humanity, I felt
it my duty to set out, and at about sunset I reached
Sebastopol.

Being supposed to be a physician of great skill and
eminence, I was treated by all the persons about with
much deference, and, after very few minutes' delay,
introduced into the room where the sick man lay. He
had ordered that when an English doctor could be found,
they were to leave them perfectly alone together; so that
as I entered, the door was closed immediately, and I
found myself alone by the bedside of the sufferer. The
curtain was closely drawn across the windows, and it was
already dusk, so that all I could discover was the figure
of a man, who lay breathing very heavily, and with the
irregular action that implies great pain.

"Are you English?" said he, in a strong, full voice.
"Well, feel that pulse, and tell me if it means sinking—
I suspect it does."

I took his hand and laid my finger on the artery. It
was beating furiously—far too fast to count, but not
weakly nor faintly.

"No," said I; "this is fever, but not debility."

"I don't want subtleties," rejoined he, roughly. "I

want to know am I dying? Draw the curtain there, open the window full, and have a look at me."

I did as he bade me, and returned to the bedside. It was all I could do not to cry out with astonishment; for, though terribly disfigured by his wounds, his eyes actually covered by the torn scalp that hung over them, I saw that it was Harpar lay before me, his large reddish beard now matted and clotted with blood.

"Well, what's the verdict?" cried he, sternly; "don't keep me in suspense."

"I do not perceive any grave symptoms so far ——"

"No cant, my good friend, no cant! It's out of place just now. Be honest, and say what is it to be—live or die?"

"So far as I can judge, I say, live."

"Well, then, set about the repairs at once. Ask for what you want—they'll bring it."

Deeming it better not to occasion any shock whatever to a man in his state, I forbore declaring who I was, and set about my office with what skill I could."

With the aid of a Russian surgeon, who spoke German well, I managed to dress the wounds and bandage the fractured arm, during which the patient never spoke once, nor, indeed, seemed to be at all concerned in what was going on.

"You can stay here, I hope," said he to me, when all was finished. "At least, you'll see me through the worst of it. I can afford to pay, and pay well."

"I'll stay," said I, imitating his own laconic way; and no more was said.

Now, though it was not my intention to pass myself off for a physician, or derive any, even the smallest advantage from the assumption of such a character, I saw that, remote as the poor sufferer was from his friends and country, and totally destitute of even companionship, it would have been cruel to desert him until he was sufficiently recovered to be left with servants.

From his calm composure, and the self-control he was able to exercise, I had formed a far too favourable opinion of his case. When I saw him first, the inflammatory symptoms had not yet set in; so that, at my next visit, I found him in a high fever, raving wildly. In his wanderings he imagined himself ever directing some gigantic enterprise, with hundreds of men at his command, whose efforts he was cheering or chiding alternately. The indomitable will of a most resolute nature was displayed in all he said; and though his bodily sufferings must have been intense, he only alluded to them to show how little power they had to arrest his activity. His ever-recurring cry was, "It can be done, men! It can be done! See that we do it!"

I own that, even though stretched on a sick-bed, and raving madly, this man's unquenchable energy impressed me greatly; and I often fancied to myself what must have been the resources of such a bold spirit in sad contrast to a nature pliant and yielding like mine. To the violence of the first access, there soon succeeded the far more dangerous state of low fever, through which I never left him. Care and incessant watching could alone save him, and I devoted myself to the last with the resolve to make this effort the first of a new and changed existence.

Day and night in the sick room, I lost appetite and strength, while an unceasing care preyed upon me and deprived me even of rest. The very vacillations of the sick man's malady had affected my nerves, rendering me over-anxious, so that just as he had passed the great crisis of the malady, I was stricken down with it myself.

My first day of convalescence, after seven weeks of fever, found me sitting at a little window that looked upon the sea, or rather the harbour of Sebastopol, where two frigates and some smaller vessels were at anchor. A group of lighters and such unpicturesque craft occupied another part of the scene, engaged as it seemed in operations for raising other vessels. It was in gazing for a long while at these, and guessing their occupation, that I learned to trace out the past, and why and how I had come to be sitting there. Every morning the German servant who tended me through my illness, used to bring

me the "Herr Baron's" compliments to know how I was,
and now he came to say, that as the "Herr Baron" was
able to walk so far, he begged that he might be
permitted to come and pay me a visit. I was aware of
the Russian custom of giving titles to all who served the
government in positions of high trust, and was therefore
not astonished when the announcement of the Herr
Baron was followed by the entrance of Harpar, who,
sadly reduced, and leaning on a crutch, made his way
slowly to where I sat. I attempted to rise to receive him,
but he cried out, half sternly:

"Sit still! we are neither of us in good trim for
ceremony."

He motioned to the servants to leave us alone; then,
laying his wasted hand in mine, for we were each too
weak to grasp the other, he said:

"I know all about it. It was you saved my life, and
risked your own to do it."

I muttered out some unmeaning words—I know not
well what—about duty and the like.

"I don't care a brass button for the motive. You stood
to me like a man." As he said this, he looked hard at
me, and shading the light with his hand, peered into my
face. "Haven't we met before this? Is not your name
Potts?"

"Yes, and you're Harpar."

He reddened, but so slightly, that but for the previous

paleness of his sickly cheek it would not have been noticeable.

"I have often thought about *you*," said he, musingly. "This is not the only service you have done me; the first was at Lindau; mayhap you have forgotten it. You lent me two hundred florins, and, if I'm not much mistaken, when you were far from being rich yourself."

He leaned his head on his hand, and seemed to have fallen into a musing fit.

"And after all," said I, "of the best turn I ever did you, you have never heard in your life, and what is more, might never hear, if not from myself. Do you remember an altercation on the road to Feldkirch, with a man called Rigges?"

"To be sure I do; he smashed the small-bone of this arm for me; but I gave worse than I got. They never could find that bullet I sent into his side, and he died of it at Palermo. But what share in this did you bear?"

"Not the worst nor the best; but I was imprisoned for a twelvemonth in your place."

"Imprisoned for *me*?"

"Yes; they assumed that I was Harpar, and as I took no steps to undeceive them, there I remained till they seemed to have forgotten all about me."

Harpar questioned me closely and keenly as to the reasons that prompted this act of mine—an act all the more remarkable, as, to use his own words, "We were men who had no friendship for each other, actually strangers;" and, added he, significantly, "the sort of fellows who, somehow, do not usually 'hit it off' together. You a man of leisure, with your own dreamy mode of life; I, a hard worker, who could not enjoy idleness; and in this sense, far more likely to hold each other cheaply than otherwise."

I attempted to account for this piece of devotion as best I might, but not very successfully, since I was only endeavouring to explain what I really did not well understand myself. Nor could a vague desire to do something generous, merely because it *was* generous, satisfy the practical intelligence of him who heard me.

"Well," said he, at last, "all that machinery you have described is so new and strange to me, I can tell nothing as to how it ought to work; but I'm as grateful to you as a man can be for a service which he could not have rendered *himself*, nor has the slightest notion of what could have prompted *you* to do. Now, let me hear by what chance you came here?"

"You must listen to a long story to learn that," said I; and as he declared that he had nothing more pressing to do with his time, I began, almost as I have begun with my reader. On my first mention of Crofton, he asked me to repeat the name; and when I spoke of meeting Miss Herbert at the Milford station, he slightly moved his chair, as if to avoid the strong light from the window; but from that moment till I finished, he never interrupted me by a word, nor interposed a question.

"And it was she gave you that old seal-ring I see on your finger?" said he, at last.

"Yes," said I. "How came you to guess that?"

"Because *I* gave it to her the day she was sixteen! I am her father."

I drew a long breath, and could only clutch his arm with astonishment, without being able to speak.

"It's all well known in England, now. Everybody has been paid in full, my creditors have met in a body, and signed a request to me to come back and recommence business. They have done more; they have bought up the lease of the Foundry, and sent it out to me. Ay, and old Elkanah's mortgage, too, is redeemed, and I don't owe a shilling."

"You must have worked hard to accomplish all this?"

"Pretty hard, no doubt. You remember those little boats with the holes in 'em at Lindau. *They* did the business for me. I was fool enough at that time to imagine that you had got a clue to my discovery, and were after me to pick up all the details. I ought to have known better! It was easy enough to see that *you* could have no head for anything with a 'tough bone' in it!

Light, thoughtless creatures of *your* kind are never dangerous anywhere! "

I was not quite sure whether I was expected to return thanks for this speech in my favour, and therefore only made some very unintelligible mutterings.

"There's only one liner now to be raised, and all the guns are already out of her, but I can return to-morrow. I am free; my contract is completed; and the *Ignatief* sloop-of-war is at my orders at Balaclava to convey me to any port I please in Europe."

He said this so boastfully and so vaingloriously, that I really felt Potts in his humility was not the smaller man of the two. Nor, perhaps, was my irritation the less at seeing how little surprise our singular meeting had caused him, and how much he regarded all I had done in his behalf as being ordinary and commonplace services. But, perhaps, the *coup de grace* of my misery came as he said:

"Though I forwarded that ten-pound note you lent me to Rome, perhaps you'll like to have it now. If you need any more, say so."

My heart was in my mouth, and I felt that I'd have died of starvation rather than accept the humblest benefit at his hands.

"Very well," said he to my refusal; "all the better that you've no need of cash, for, to tell the truth, Potts, you're not much of a doctor, nor are you very remarkable

as a man of genius; and it is a kind thing of Providence
when such fellows as you are born with even a 'pewter
spoon' in their mouths."

I nearly choked, but I said nothing.

"If you'd like me to land you anywhere in the Levant,
or down towards the Spanish coast, only tell me."

"No, nothing of the kind. I'm going north; I'm
going to Moscow, to Tobolsk: I'm going to Persia and
Astracan," said I, in wildest confusion.

"Well, I can give you a capital travelling cloak—
it's one of those buntas they make in the Banat, and
you'll need it, for they have fearfully severe cold in those
countries."

With this, and not waiting my resolute refusal, he
rose, hobbled out of the room, and I—ay, there's no concealing it—burst out a crying!

Weak and sick as I was, I procured an "araba" that
night, and, without one word of adieu, set out for
Krim.

It was about two years after this—my father had died
in the interval, leaving me a small but sufficient fortune
to live on, and I had just arrived in Paris, after a long
desultory ramble through the east of Europe—I was
standing one morning early in one of the small alleys of
the Champs Elysées, watching with half listless curiosity

the various grooms as they passed to exercise their
horses in the Bois de Boulogne. Group after group
passed me of those magnificent animals in which Paris
is now more than the rival of London, and at length I
was struck by the appearance of a very smartly-dressed
groom, who led along beside him a small-sized horse,
completely sheeted and shrouded from view. Believing
that this must prove some creature of rare beauty, an
Arab of purest descent, I followed them as they went,
and at last overtook them.

The groom was English, and by my offer of a cigar,
somewhat better than the one he was smoking, he was
very willing to satisfy my curiosity.

"I suppose he has Arab blood in him," said he, half
contemptuously; "but he's forty years old now if he's a
day. What they keep him for I don't know, but they
make as much work about him as if he was a Christian;
and, as for myself, I have nothing else to do than walk
him twice a day to his exercise, and take care that his
oats are well bruised and mixed with linseed, for he
hasn't a tooth left."

"I suppose his master is some very rich man, who can
afford himself a caprice like this."

"For the matter of money, he has enough of it. He
is the Prince Ernest Maximilian of Würtemberg, and,
except the Emperor, has the best stable in all Paris.
But I don't think that *he* cares much for the old horse;

it's the *Princess* likes him, and she constantly drives out to the wood here, and when we come to a quiet spot, where there are no strangers, she makes me take off all the body-clothes and the hoods, and she'll get out of the carriage and pat him. And he knows her, that he does! and lifts up that old leg of his when she comes towards him, and tries to whinny, too. But here she comes now, and it won't do if I'm seen talking to you, so just drop behind, sir, and never notice me."

I crossed the road, and had but reached the opposite pathway, when a carriage stopped, and the old horse drew up beside it. After a word or two, the groom took off the hood, and there was Blondel! But my amazement was lost in the greater shock, that the Princess, whose jewelled hand held out the sugar to him, was no other than Catinka!

I cannot say with what motive I was impelled—perhaps the action was too quick for either—but I drew nigh to the carriage, and raising my hat respectfully, asked if her highness would deign to remember an old acquaintance.

"I am unfortunate enough, sir, not to be able to recal you," said she, in the most perfect Parisian French.

"My name you may have forgotten, madame, but scarcely so either our first meeting at Schaffhausen, or our last at Bregenz."

"These are all riddles to me, sir; and I am sure you
are too well bred to persist in an error after you have
recognised it to be such."   With a cold smile and a
haughty bow, she motioned the coachman to drive on,
and I saw her no more.

Stung to the very quick, but yet not without a mis-
giving that I might be possibly mistaken, I hurried to
the police department, where the list of strangers was
preserved.   By sending in my card I was admitted to
see one of the chiefs of the department, who politely
informed me that the princess was totally unknown
as to family, and not included in the Gotha Alma-
nack.

"May I ask," said he, as I prepared to retire, "if this
letter here—it has been with us for more than a year—is
for your address?   It came with an enclosure covering
any possible expense in reaching your address, and has
lain here ever since."

"Yes," said I, "my name is Algernon Sydney Potts."

Strange are the changes and vicissitudes of life!   Just
as I stood there, shocked and overwhelmed with one trait
of cold ingratitude, I found a letter from Kate (she who
was once Kate Herbert), telling me how they had sent
messengers after me through Europe, and begging, if
these lines should ever reach me, to come to them in
Wales.   "My father loves you, my mother longs to

know you, and none can be more eager to thank you than your friend Kate Whalley."

I set off for England that night—I left for Wales the next morning—and I have never quitted it since that day.

THE END.

ꙅ

W. H. SMITH & SON, PRINTERS, 186, STRAND, LONDON.